The House Party

The House Party

Fenella-Jane Miller

ROBERT HALE · LONDON

ISBN 978-0-7090-8536-2

Robert Hale Limited
Clerkenwell House
Clerkenwell Green
London EC1R 0HT

www.halebooks.com

2 4 6 8 10 9 7 5 3 1

Typeset in 11/14pt Palatino
Printed and bound in Great Britain by
Biddles Limited, King's Lynn

For Patricia, my cousin in Geneva.

Chapter One

England 1814

'GOD DAMN IT! Am I to have no peace?' Edward Weston, the Earl of Rushford swore without raising his eyes from the paper he was studying.

'Stow it, Weston, I'm not one of your unfortunate servants. I am here on official business.'

'Carstairs, what the devil are you doing here? Last time I heard you were in Paris with Wellington.'

The man in faded regimentals folded himself on to the nearby chair and smiled. 'It's on his command that I'm here. Don't shoot the messenger, my friend.'

Lord Weston pushed his chair back and strode to the bell-strap. He was glad of the excuse to take a break; estate business had never been a favourite pastime. 'I must apologize for my rudeness; I have been trapped at my desk for the past three days trying to catch up with things.'

'Well, your estate will have to wait. I have an urgent commission for you.' Major Richard Carstairs stood up and joined his friend at the window. 'This is not your usual mission, Ned. It does not involve travelling far.'

A timid knock on the door prevented Carstairs from saying anything further.

'Enter.' Weston turned to greet the footman who had answered his summons. 'Have coffee brought here and some of that plum cake I had yesterday. Tell Mrs Brown to make up a room for the major.' The footman bowed and nervously backed out of the room.

'He obviously drew the short straw,' Major Carstairs said. 'I'm amazed you retain your staff, you treat them so badly.'

'But I pay them far more than they could get elsewhere. And don't forget over the past few years I have been absent more than I have been in residence.' The earl towered over his friend, his flaming red hair a warning to all that he was not a man to trifle with. 'Shall we be seated? I'm eager to hear what my next task shall be.'

'There's a chance that the smugglers who work around this coastline are carrying more than contraband in their holds. The Duke believes that gold's leaving these shores destined for Bonaparte's supporters. We don't want the French to raise another army and release their Emperor from imprisonment.'

Lord Weston shook his head. 'In Suffolk? Surely not. I have yet to meet a man who supports the French. I doubt that anyone local could be involved.'

'Have you heard of the Suffolk Aeronautical Society?'

'Indeed I have. In fact I gave them permission to use my name and have donated far more than I'm prepared to admit. However, I have had nothing to do with them since the outbreak of war.'

'I'm relieved to hear you say so. We believe that Bonaparte's supporters could be using balloon ascents all over the county as a cover for something nefarious. No one is surprised to find the pilots are Frenchmen and what better way for a spy to travel the country?'

They were interrupted by the arrival of the refreshments. Lord Weston waved the footman away impatiently. He wanted to hear exactly what Wellington wished him to do. The coffee was cold before either of them thought to drink it.

'Let me get this straight. I'm to invite this particular bunch of aeronauts to a local event and by mingling with them, discover if your suspicions are correct?'

'Yes, that's exactly what we wish you to do. You have long had an interest in this association so why should anyone suspect you're more than a wealthy aristocrat with more money than sense?'

'I never attend public functions and to do so now would be totally out of character.'

'We've considered that possibility and have the perfect answer. I've been reliably informed that a year ago you danced attendance on a certain young lady by the name of Miss Penelope Coombs but were called abroad before you made the arrangement official. Did you know Miss Coombs resides not five miles from Ipswich? No one would think it odd of you to attend a balloon ascent in order to renew your acquaintance, especially as you're known to favour brunettes with green eyes.'

'I hardly think the comparison to my latest flirt is appropriate.' Lord Weston's eyes were hard. The major did not look away. Finally Weston spoke again. 'So, you wish me to break the heart of a lovely young woman twice in as many years? I shall not do it. You must find someone else.'

'There's no one else and it's an order. You've no choice. All you have to do is ensure that Miss Coombs and her aunt attend the event. A man of your ingenuity should have no difficulty with that.'

'What did you say, Aunt Lucy?' Penelope Coombs stared at her aged aunt with undisguised amazement. 'Attend a balloon ascent?'

'My dear, have I not told you how enthralled I have become of late with all things aeronautical?'

'No, Aunt, you have not. Indeed, I can say without fear of contradiction that this is the very first time you have ever expressed so much as a passing interest in the matter.'

Lady Dalrymple patted the *chaise-longue* making the feather on her maroon turban flutter. 'Do come and sit down, my dear, your pacing is making me dizzy.'

Penelope paused at the far side of the drawing-room, the hem of her pale-green muslin skirt swirling around her ankles. 'I cannot sit still. I'm certain that the letter from London will come today.'

Lady Dalrymple snorted. 'In my opinion the whole thing is fustian. Your poor father would turn in his grave if he knew how you intend to spend his money.'

'That's doing it too brown, Aunt Lucy. I only intend to invest half my funds in shipping – and there will be more than enough left over to keep us both in luxury for the rest of our lives.' Penelope walked over to join her aunt. 'What is all this about balloons, Aunt? Tell me more?'

'If you stop perambulating around the room for five minutes I shall be happy to do so.'

'Very well. I suppose your tale will pass the time.'

'I came by a poster advertising the ascent a week ago and quite made up my mind to attend. There are to be rides for the public and I am determined that I shall be first in the line.'

Penny gazed at her elderly aunt with affection. 'You're almost eighty years old, Aunt Lucy. Ballooning is for the young and agile.'

'Stuff and nonsense! I am fitter now than some people half my age. It is because of my approaching name day that I wish to do it. The good Lord might call me back at any moment. Can you think of a better way to go than when one is already halfway to Heaven?'

Penny chuckled. 'Now I know you've run mad. Are you trying to tell me in a roundabout fashion that you hope to perish in the basket of the balloon?'

'What a ridiculous notion. Of course not. I have a list here of ten things I wish to experience before I depart this world and a ride in a balloon is but third on it. I am determined that I shall accomplish them all before I turn up my toes.'

Penny held out her hand. 'Please show me, Aunt. My heart quails at the prospect of discovering the two items that precede the ascent.'

Lady Dalrymple placed the paper in the outstretched hand, her eyes lowered, not wishing her astute great-niece to see her expression. She considered that her imaginary list was a masterstroke. When Penny had been obliged to return to the family home, on the sudden demise of Sir John Coombs just over a year ago, it had been in the happy expectation of receiving an offer from Edward Weston. Lady Dalrymple smiled as she recalled the exact words on the bill advertising the forthcoming balloon ascent.

This event has been fully funded by the Earl of Rushford. Lord Weston is a founder member of the Suffolk Aeronautical Association.

With any luck his lordship would attend the event bringing several of his gentlemen friends. Whatever her personal feelings on the matter, Lady Dalrymple was of the firm opinion that any earl was better than none.

Penny scanned the neatly penned list with growing consternation. Number one was a visit to Paris, number two a trip along the canals of Venice and number three, an ascent in a balloon. 'Aunt Lucy, I know Bonaparte is imprisoned on Elba but I don't believe it to be safe to travel abroad at the moment.'

'Which is why, my dear, I intend to start with number three. It is fortuitous that such an event is to take place in our neighbourhood. It is high time you were seen in public again. What is the point of having a new wardrobe in the first stare of fashion if you do not intend to be seen wearing it?'

'Very well, I concede. Tomorrow we shall drive into Ipswich. However reluctant an aeronaut I am, I cannot allow you to take a flight unaccompanied. If you insist on this folly then we shall suffer the experience together.' Penny grinned. 'Don't look so smug, Aunt Lucy, I promise you might well regret your determination to cheat the laws of nature. From what I have read on the subject many people experience nausea and all return frozen to the marrow.'

Saturday, the day of the expedition, dawned fair and cloud free. According to Tom, the coachman, it was the perfect weather for a balloon ascent. The barouche selected for the journey was waiting outside the house when Penny and her Aunt Lucy emerged, dressed in their finest.

'It is a perfect May day, my dear,' Lady Dalrymple said, pushing up her parasol. 'Let us hope it does not become too hot.'

The carriage eventually joined the throng of like-minded vehicles on the main road into the bustling market town of Ipswich. As usual the streets were packed with vendors, pedestrians, carts, wagons and coaches, making progress slow.

Eventually they arrived at their destination and looked

around the already crowded field with interest. Penny climbed down from the carriage glad they had chosen one that did not require steps.

'Come along, Aunt Lucy; if you seriously intend to travel in the balloon then we must go and put our names down. We're rather later than I would have wished and I can see it is almost ready to fly.' Arm in arm, the two ladies, accompanied by a groom, headed in the direction of the balloon. They stopped to greet various acquaintances as they progressed.

'It is far bigger than I expected. And what is that hideous hissing and gurgling I can hear?'

'I have no idea, Aunt Lucy. I believe it's coming from those barrels placed around the balloon. It must be the noise of the gas they're putting inside that we can hear.' Penny was relieved to see a large notice pinned to a wooden frame. 'Look, there're to be no rides today. It appears it's too dangerous to take passengers aloft.'

Lady Dalrymple schooled her features into the appearance of disappointment. 'How vexing! I was so looking forward to it.'

As they watched, the sphere securely tethered by several cast-iron anchors, strained and pulled like a dog on a leash wishing to be free from restraint. The pilots scrambled into the basket and a dozen men began to release the tethers. As the last one dropped to the ground, the magnificent air balloon shot skywards. It rose at a remarkable rate wafted by a thermal of warm air.

'Well, that was exciting, Aunt Lucy, but hardly worth the effort of coming so far. We've only been here thirty minutes and the spectacle is over. Shall we wander around the field and view the various sideshows?'

Lady Dalrymple was still gazing up following the progress of the balloon. 'I wonder what happens when they wish to descend. I suppose those carts must trundle after them. What did you ask me, my dear?' The elderly woman stopped and exclaimed dramatically, 'Good heavens! Look, Penny. Well I never did!'

Penny glanced over her shoulder to see what it was that had

so excited her aunt. 'If you have arranged this, Aunt Lucy, I shall never forgive you.'

Striding towards them was the very man she had convinced herself she never wished to see again. She was tempted to give him the cut direct, turn her back and walk briskly in the opposite direction, but something compelled her to remain where she was.

Her heart thudded painfully in her chest as Lord Weston approached. She wished that this arrogant man did not still have the power to overwhelm her. She straightened her shoulders and deliberately looked in his direction. His green eyes bored into her. She lowered her head, hiding her face in the deep brim of her poke straw bonnet, hoping to break the connection, give herself time to regain her composure before she was obliged to greet him and the flock of fashionable ladies and gentlemen trailing in his wake.

'Lady Dalrymple, Miss Coombs, what a delightful surprise.'

The voice had not changed. It even now had the power to turn her from a sensible, level-headed young lady into a dizzy debutante. Reluctantly she raised her head.

'Lord Weston, I had not expected to see *you* here today.' She did not offer a hand, merely dipped her head in greeting. It was as if no one else stood near them. They might as well have been alone, not standing in an open field surrounded by milling crowds.

He stepped nearer; too close. The smell of leather and lemon soap washed over her, a painful reminder of his callous rejection last year. He was a monster. He had all but proposed to her, then abandoned her to grieve for her beloved father alone. There would not be a second chance. She had learned her lesson. Only fools put their hands back in the fire for a second time.

'Miss Coombs, I owe you a most sincere apology. Last year I was called away on business and when I returned you had vanished. I was bitterly disappointed until I discovered that your father had died and that was the reason you were no longer in town.'

Penny knew this was no excuse. He could have discovered

where she resided and sought her out if he had wished. She had made it her business to find out where his family seat was. The fact that Lord Weston lived but ten miles from her and had never bothered to call and see how she did had almost broken her spirit. She raised her eyebrows a fraction before answering, her words as false as his.

'I must apologize to you, Lord Weston, if I inadvertently misled you. I had no inkling that you were serious in your attentions. I believed that we were of the same mind. That you had as little wish to form a serious attachment last season as I did.' She smiled, the wide brim of her bonnet hiding her expression from all but him. There was a flash of anger in his eyes before his mouth curled in that well-remembered smile.

'And are you still of the same mind, Miss Coombs?' His tone was teasing, his words a challenge.

She swallowed nervously. He was almost impossible to resist when he adopted this playful tone. 'It is my intention to become a woman of business. My agent in London is arranging for me to invest in shipping. I have no interest in matrimony. What possible reason could there be for me to give up my independence and fortune?'

He reached down and took her hands in his. Without breaking eye contact he slowly raised them to his lips. She attempted to remove them but his grip was strong. The all too familiar rush of heat travelled from her toes to her crown. If he kissed her fingers she would be unable to resist.

'Lord Weston, are you in residence at Headingly for the summer?' Lady Dalrymple's question demanded an answer.

Penelope snatched her hands back as his attention turned to her aunt. Surreptitiously stepping away, wanting to put a safe distance between them. She found herself next to a replica of the man she was trying to escape. Her expression of stupefaction made the young man laugh.

He bowed. 'I know, Miss Coombs, we could be brothers, could we not? Allow me to introduce myself. James Weston, at your service.'

'Of course. You are Lord Weston's cousin. He spoke of you

several times but never thought to mention that you could be his twin. Are you of an age?'

'He is two years my senior. Unfortunately we both inherited this hair from our grandfather. It's a family curse.'

Penny found herself relaxing. It had taken only a few moments for her to realize that although externally the two men were identical, James Weston lacked the indefinable charisma and sense of authority that his older relative had in abundance.

'Are you staying at Headingly, Mr Weston?'

'I am, Miss Coombs. It's sometime since the family gathered together. Ned has been away on business until recently. We are not a particularly close group, but we do like to re-establish our connections now and again. So my cousin has arranged a house party.'

Penny was aware that Lord Weston had completed his conversation with her aunt and was moving inexorably towards her once more. She smiled radiantly at her companion unaware of the impact she was making.

'Mr Weston, would you be kind enough to escort me to my carriage? I am feeling unwell. It has become unpleasantly warm and I have been standing in the sun too long.'

Immediately the young man offered his arm to her. 'It would be my pleasure, Miss Coombs.' She could feel the animosity pouring from Lord Weston but he didn't intervene, and was relieved to reach the safety of the barouche without further conversation with him.

'Thank you, Mr Weston. It was delightful to meet you.'

Her coachman held open the door and she stepped inside. Mr Weston bowed and with a friendly wave strolled off to join his party. Penelope was obliged to sit and wait a further ten minutes before her aunt was escorted back by Lord Weston.

She leant against the squabs and closed her eyes. She had no wish to speak to him again. The carriage dipped as Aunt Lucy climbed in.

'Good day, Lord Weston. It has been delightful to renew our acquaintance and thank you for your kind invitation.'

'I am honoured that you have accepted it and look forward to seeing you both tomorrow.'

There was a pause and Penny thought it was safe to open her eyes. To her horror he was leaning nonchalantly on the carriage door his eyes alight with amusement. 'Good. I am pleased to see that you are recovered, Miss Coombs.'

She glared at him, but didn't lower herself to respond. The hateful lord moved away and she broke her silence. 'Aunt Lucy, what did Lord Weston mean about seeing him tomorrow?'

Her aunt beamed. 'My dear, I am so excited. When I explained how disappointed I was to miss the opportunity for a balloon ascent, Lord Weston kindly extended an invitation to both of us to join his house party.' Lady Dalrymple beamed. 'His lordship has arranged for the aeronauts to stay on his estate until all his guests, including ourselves, have been able to experience the delights of a flight.'

Chapter Two

PENNY WANTED TO stamp her feet in vexation. Instead she took a deep breath and pinned a cheerful smile to her lips. 'How obliging of him to include us in his house party. I have never visited Headingly but I understand that it's a handsome building. It will be most interesting to see for myself. I shall ride there. It's a long time since Phoenix and I travelled any distance.'

'Ride, Miss Coombs? It is over eight miles from Nettleford to Headingly.' Lord Weston had stepped back closer to the carriage.

Penny smiled sunnily at the man scowling down at her. 'Yes, my mind's quite made up. Which direction do you recommend I take?'

Lord Weston was obliged to instruct her in the shortest cross-county route to his home and the barouche eventually departed with both occupants well pleased with the morning's encounter.

Lady Dalrymple patted Penny's clenched hands. 'Was that not a delightful meeting, my dear? And such a surprise! It will be pleasant to spend a few weeks with Lord Weston and his guests. I declare it is exactly what we both need to lift our spirits.'

'If you say so, Aunt Lucy.'

'Is that all you can say on the matter, my dear? I thought you would be thrilled to renew your acquaintance with his lordship. Did you notice how particular his attentions were today? His cousin, Mr Weston, seemed quite put out. I rather think that young man has developed a *tendre* for you himself.'

'I was astonished at how similar in appearance they are. I was quite taken with Mr Weston. He's an open and sincere young man, quite unlike his cousin.' She smiled at her elderly aunt. 'Indeed, it's only because I wish to get to know Mr Weston that I agreed to this visit.'

The remainder of the journey was spent discussing their imminent removal. As Penny was riding Lady Dalrymple would follow in the carriage with Harvey, her starchy abigail and Mary, Penny's maid. They were expected sometime during the morning.

The next day dawned fine and by eight o'clock both ladies were ready to depart for their extended stay at Headingly. The baggage cart had left at dawn accompanied by Mary and a groom. Harvey was to travel with her mistress. It would not do to arrive before one's luggage!

'Penelope, my dear girl, I am sure that horse is too much for you. He is not a lady's mount. I hope that Lord Weston rides out to meet you.'

Penny frowned and her huge chestnut gelding stamped and shook his head, eager to depart. 'Phoenix is a gentle giant. I promise you I shall come to no harm. And I shall have both Billy and Fred as company, so even if I take a tumble they will be there to pick me up.'

'Please, do not jest about such things. And having two grooms riding with you is no consolation to me. I wish you would change your mind and ride a different horse. Or even better come with me in the carriage. Three hours in the saddle might prove too long in this hot weather.'

'When I hunt, Aunt Lucy, I am out all day in the ice and snow and I cannot remember you telling me it was unsuitable to do so.'

Lady Dalrymple admitted defeat and settled back on the squabs opening her parasol with a decided snap. 'I shall stop for refreshments, so do not expect me before noon.'

Phoenix sidled sideways scattering gravel and grooms in all directions. 'Come along, silly boy, let's be on our way.' Penny gently touched the hunter's flank with her heel and they moved off, closely followed by two grooms mounted on matching bays.

'I intend to travel across country as much as possible this morning. The ground's soft enough after the rain last night to make our journey safe. A good gallop will settle him down.'

They made excellent time and two hours later the three riders approached a bend in the lane they had been travelling along for half a mile. Their passage was blocked by a fallen tree. Penny reined in, puzzled by the obstruction.

'There was no wind last night so why has this tree fallen across our path?' She turned in her saddle to speak to Billy. 'Do you think you and Fred can move this? This lane's the only way unless we retrace our path and find a gate into the field. The hedges either side are far too tall to jump.'

Billy dismounted tossing his reins to the other groom. 'Hold him, whilst I investigate.'

Penny watched him disappear into the undergrowth with a strange feeling of apprehension. It was cold and dark under the overhanging trees and she shivered. Why was Billy taking so long? Surely testing the weight of the obstruction did not take such an age?

She stared back down the tunnel of trees and froze. 'Billy. Get back here quickly. I'm certain this is no accident. It's an ambush. There are footpads approaching. We're trapped here. We cannot go forward and there's no escape into the field.'

The groom scrambled out of the bushes and was in his saddle in seconds. 'We have our cudgels, miss. We'll protect you, never fear.'

The two men edged their horses in front of Phoenix, unstrapping the stout sticks they carried tied to the back of their saddles. Penny knew that these would be no protection against pistols or swords. There had to be another way.

'We must jump out. I know the hedges are high but we've no choice. Quickly, I can hear them getting closer.'

Without waiting to see if they followed she wrenched Phoenix's head around and kicked him into a gallop, thanking God that the grassy path widened enough for her to turn her mount towards the hedge. She had cleared larger obstacles before, but never in such circumstances. She felt her horse gather itself and crouched forward grasping a handful of mane to steady herself.

As she soared into the air she had no time to worry about safe landings. If Phoenix failed to clear the hedge she would certainly crash to her death.

Lord Weston greeted his cousin with a friendly slap on the back. 'James, you're not dressed for riding. I thought you were coming with me to meet Miss Coombs.'

'I have promised Mama that I'll walk with her to the lake this morning. She insists it will be too hot by midday.' The young man shrugged his elegantly clad shoulders. 'You know how she is, Ned.'

'Indeed I do; it's easier to agree than argue once Aunt Elizabeth has made up her mind. I shall see you at dinner.' Lord Weston turned to run down the white marble steps, but paused to call back, 'James, I'm expecting the aeronauts and their entourage to arrive this morning. Could you make sure they're accommodated in the barn behind the stables?'

His cousin raised his hand in acknowledgement. 'Consider it done, old fellow. Consider it done. It will give me an excuse to return to the house in good time.'

Weston vaulted into the saddle of his waiting bay stallion, ramming his boots into the stirrups. With a curt nod to the stable boy he cantered down the drive. However spurious his reasons for inviting Miss Coombs to visit he was looking forward to renewing their acquaintance.

When he had singled her out from the dozens of eager young debutantes to escort to numerous soirées and balls last season it had not been just for her beauty, but also for her ready wit and intelligence. His investigations had obliged him to enter certain houses of the *haut ton* and the only way he could accomplish this without arousing suspicion was to appear to be interested in setting up his nursery.

He frowned as he recalled her trusting *naïveté*, knew that she had expected him to offer for her at the end of the season.

Indeed, society in general held the same opinion. He had achieved his objective and discovered the traitor masquerading as an *émigré* and he had been highly praised in Whitehall for his work. However the whole episode had left a bad taste in his mouth. An innocent girl had been hurt by his pretence and now he had been ordered to repeat the process.

He cursed as his inattention allowed Bruno to grab the bit between his teeth and bolt. By the time he had regained control of his mount he was mud-spattered and flushed. He was also two miles from Headingly in the field that ran parallel to the lane he was supposed be in. He stood in his stirrups and looked up and down the massive hedge trying to remember if there was a gate he could use.

Phoenix stretched out his neck and his front legs cleared the hedge by inches. Penny felt his back arch and instinctively leant forward, encouraging her horse. The ground rushed towards them and she closed her eyes and braced herself, expecting to be catapulted to the ground.

Her magnificent horse scarcely checked. He pricked his ears and continued his headlong gallop away from the narrow lane and possible ambush. Penny transferred her weight to the back of the saddle and pulled steadily on the reins. Crooning softly to the animal, gradually regaining control and was in time to turn and watch her grooms soar over the hedge and land safely. The exhilaration of the jump had temporarily pushed the reason for it from her mind. It was Billy who reminded her.

'They're close behind and they've got rifles, miss. There's three of them and they don't look like any footpads I've ever seen.'

'Rifles? Are you sure? Only soldiers carry rifles.' Without waiting to hear his reply she wrenched the big chestnut's head around and kicked hard with her heel. Phoenix sprang forward and the three raced away from the lane all crouching low, hoping they made too small a target for the marksmen.

The field sloped towards the horizon and they thundered over the brow of the hill sending clods of mud flying out behind.

Penny saw the approaching rider and for a horrified second believed their would-be assassins had a fourth member who was riding towards them. Then she recognized the man and hauled on the reins bringing her mount to a rearing halt beside him.

'Three men, in the lane with rifles, my lord. They almost had us trapped there beyond the hedge.' Her words were forced out between gasps.

He reacted immediately. He swung his horse and shouted. 'Follow me. We shall not be out of range until we are out of this damned field.'

He led them at a gallop downhill and headed straight for the five-barred gate. Bruno cleared it with feet to spare as did the other three. Only then did he slow the pace.

'Tell me what happened back there, Miss Coombs. You're safe here. This track is not overlooked by the lane and even the finest rifleman could not reach you.' This was said as he cantered beside her, guiding her to the safety of his home.

'We were in the lane and discovered a tree blocking the path. At first I was unconcerned, but glimpsed the approach of what I took to be a band of vagrants. We had no alternative but to jump over the hedge.'

'God's teeth! You could have been killed. That hedge is over six feet high.' Lord Weston stared at Penny and she felt herself colour.

'As you can see, my lord, I was not. But if I had remained in the lane I might not have been so lucky.'

She watched him digest this information, could almost hear his formidable intelligence spring into action. On reflection she was surprised he had accepted her garbled explanation without question. It was almost as if he had been expecting an attack to take place. Should she ask him if this was the case? He forestalled her question.

'Miss Coombs, how did you know the men were carrying rifles? Did you see the guns?'

She shook her head, gesturing towards Billy, who was riding with Fred, a polite distance behind them. 'No, but my groom did. It was he who warned me.'

Lord Weston dropped back to question the groom leaving Penny to ride alone. There was something odd about the whole incident. Why would three heavily armed men wish to harm her? She had no enemies. It must be a case of mistaken identity, the men had been expecting someone else.

She glanced over her shoulder. Surely it could not be Lord Weston? He was autocratic and renowned for his cutting set-downs, but this was no reason to kill him. So if it was not him, then who? Perhaps there was someone else expected to arrive today and it was them the ambushers had hoped to catch.

The pad of hoofbeats on the path heralded the return of her host. 'My lord, I cannot believe that anyone would wish to harm either of us. Are you expecting more prestigious visitors this morning?'

'Do the aeronauts count? For they spend a goodly part of their lives above us.'

'You're being ridiculous, sir. This is not a matter for levity.' Penny pressed her lips firmly together determined not to laugh out loud.

His rich, dark chuckle sent an unexpected frisson around her already overheated body. 'You must not disturb yourself over the incident, my dear. There have been reports that a group of ex-soldiers has been congregating in the area. Since Bonaparte is now safely tucked away on Elba, regiments are already cutting their numbers.'

'There has been talk in the village about men rioting. It is the parlous situation these poor men have come back to. It's a great shame that our brave soldiers should come to such a pass.' Penny pushed back a strand of hair that had escaped from under her military style cap. 'But I fail to see why these men should select that lane today. I would imagine it's hardly used. Why did they expect to find rich pickings in such a remote spot?'

'I have no idea, Miss Coombs. Coincidence, no more. No doubt they were *en route* for the toll road and all thieves are opportunists.'

Penny prepared to point out that this had been no spur of the moment attack. It was premeditated. How else could they have had the time to fell the tree that trapped her in the lane? But he prevented her from speaking.

'I shall call out the militia, Miss Coombs. As the magistrate of this area it's my duty to keep the lanes and paths free from all sorts of vermin. Let us speak no more of this.' He smiled, at his most charming. 'Tell me, are you intending to ascend in the balloon?'

'I fear that I am a reluctant aeronaut, my lord. But Lady Dalrymple is determined to go up and I suppose I shall be obliged to accompany her.'

'I am an experienced pilot, my dear. Are you sure I cannot persuade you to accompany me on a flight?'

She shuddered dramatically. 'Absolutely not! I shall only step into the basket if I know the contraption is firmly anchored to the ground. If the good Lord had meant us to fly He would have given us wings like the angels.'

By the time they arrived Penny had all but forgotten her fear. Two grooms ran forward to take the bridles of their mounts. She slid her foot from the iron and was preparing to dismount when Lord Weston appeared at her side.

'Allow me, my dear.' Giving her no time to refuse he encircled her waist and lifted her from the saddle. She had forgotten how strong he was.

Her voice was scarcely more than a whisper and she thanked him politely. Before she could protest he pulled her arm through his. There was to be no escape. The wretched man was determined to escort her all the way to the house; no doubt in full view of all those watching from the drawing-room window.

Mrs Brown, the housekeeper, was waiting in the vast marble-floored hall to escort her to her rooms.

Lord Weston bowed. 'I shall leave you in the capable hands of my housekeeper, Miss Coombs. I look forward to meeting you again at dinner. We do not keep country hours here so I shall see you at seven o'clock in the drawing-room.' Without a backward glance he strode off, his mind obviously elsewhere. Penny turned to speak to the housekeeper.

'If dinner is to be served so late I do hope a nuncheon will be served at midday.'

The devil take it! How could his cover have been blown so easily? For years he had maintained the fiction of being no more than a wealthy aristocrat who enjoyed sailing his yacht around the world. Only a select few, and none of those present today, knew of his work for the government. But he was in no doubt that today the men in the lane had been waiting for Miss Coombs.

A member of the balloon party must have seen them together and decided to organize her abduction believing she would be a useful pawn in their game. This confirmed what Carstairs had told him. He was dealing with ruthless traitors. He would call up the militia and have all of them arrested. Then it would be up to the major to discover what he would.

His long strides led him to his study, a sanctuary where no one who wished to keep their head on their shoulders dared disturb him. He knew he should return to his chambers, remove his soiled riding clothes, but that would have to wait. He needed to think.

Pouring himself a generous measure of brandy from the decanter on his desk he took it to the window. Staring out at the rolling park helped him concentrate. Methodically he reviewed what was fact and what he surmised. Thoughtfully he swallowed the amber liquid. His immediate assumption, that the men were in the employ of the traitors he was searching for, did not make sense. What could they possibly have to gain from the death of either himself or Miss Coombs? If they knew they were discovered all they needed to do was vanish. Why should they wish to risk their lives by drawing attention to themselves? Kidnapping Miss Coombs would bring every available militiaman into the area. How could this help them raise money for that bastard Bonaparte?

God's teeth! He was losing his touch. Under normal circumstances he would have solved this conundrum by now. He scowled into his glass. He must not allow the involvement of

Miss Coombs to interfere with his judgement, but every time he closed his eyes, his head was filled with the image of a girl galloping towards him, crouched low over her horse's withers, her face white with terror.

Chapter Three

WORD OF THE attempted attack on Penny was common knowledge by the time she was ready to descend from her apartments. She was relieved that her aunt had arrived in time to hear the story from her own lips.

'Mary, make sure that all the staff are aware that I was in no danger from the footpads and the incident was no more than an added excitement on my journey.'

The maid pursed her lips. 'If you say so, miss. But you know how they like to gossip downstairs. I reckon Billy and Fred will have told everyone ready to listen that there were a dozen men and you were only saved from the clutches of the monsters by their own bravery.'

'Well, it's up to you to correct their version. I do not wish to make too much of it. Lord Weston is taking care of matters and I would not wish him to think I blamed him in any way for allowing those men to infiltrate his lands.' Penny turned to leave the room. 'I am tardy. I must go down. Did you pull the bell-strap?'

'I did, miss. I'm sure the footman will be here to escort you.' The maid stepped forward and bent to shake out Penny's skirt. 'There! You look pretty as a picture, Miss Coombs, if you don't mind me saying so. Pale green is perfect with your colouring.'

Penny glanced at her reflection in one of the gilt pier glasses that hung either side of the central window. 'I wish I was less tall and more rounded.' She smiled ruefully. 'At least this bodice is well fitted and is giving nature a helping hand.' The loud knock on the door interrupted the conversation.

'Excellent, my guide is here. I intend to explore the gardens after I have eaten so shall need my kid half-boots and bonnet when I return.'

'Will I leave out your matching spencer, miss?'

'No, Mary, thank you. I believe it's too warm to wear a jacket. A light shawl will suffice.'

Outside, the smartly liveried footman bowed. 'Follow me, Miss Coombs, I'll take you to the small dining-room.'

'What's your name? If you're to be my guide for the present I should like to be able to ask for you personally.'

The young man grinned revealing a large gap in his teeth. 'My name's Will, miss.'

'Well, Will, tell me, do you know how many chambers there are here?'

He shook his head. 'Never tried to count them, miss. But there're six apartments on this floor and his lordship's rooms on the ground floor.' He scratched his head, forgetting for a moment that he was wearing his half wig, and it slipped askew. He straightened it, glancing nervously over his shoulder to check his disarray had not been spotted by the eagle-eyed butler, Foster.

Penny followed the footman down several corridors and two flights of stairs before they finally arrived in the impressive entrance hall which she immediately recognized. 'Thank you, Will, I believe I can find my own way from here. I can hear voices along the corridor and one of them is Lady Dalrymple.'

'You'll find the guests are gathered in the morning-room, miss. They haven't gone in to eat so you're not late.'

Penny hurried across the hall, her slippered feet making no sound. She had almost reached her destination when Lord Weston appeared beside her. Startled, she shied sideways knocking her arm painfully on the corner of a heavily carved picture frame.

'Ouch! That hurt. It's inconsiderate of you, my lord, to rush upon a person in this way.'

'Here, let me see.' Before she could protest he peeled away her hand. 'Good grief! My dear girl, you've a nasty gash.'

She glanced down horrified to find blood oozing from between his fingers. 'I had no idea I'd cut myself. I must return to my room to have this dressed.'

Lord Weston removed a crisp white handkerchief from his pocket and pressed it against her injury. 'Hold this firmly in place. It will stem the flow of blood until I can deal with it properly.'

He slid his arm around her waist, as if expecting her to faint away in a fit of the vapours at any moment. She stiffened. 'I have no need of your assistance; the sight of gore does not send me into a faint.'

She tried to move away, but again he was too strong for her. 'Nonsense, Miss Coombs. Allow me to escort you to the library. There's no need for you to return to your chambers. I'm quite capable of dressing your wound.'

She had no choice. Unless she was prepared to struggle in a most unladylike way she was obliged to do as he said. Fortunately the library was nearby and the door ajar.

'Sit down here, my dear. I shall ring for assistance.'

Penny found herself gently placed on a leather-covered chair. Her pulse was racing and her cheeks flushed and she knew it had nothing to do with her arm. From the moment Lord Weston had led her on to the dance floor over a year ago, it had been ever thus. The mere touch of his hand sent inexplicable waves of heat around her body. It was the outside of enough that after so long apart he could still have this effect on her. She kept her head lowered, unwilling to make eye contact.

'Drink this, Miss Coombs, it will restore you.'

She opened her mouth to protest only to have a liberal swallow of brandy tipped carefully down her throat. Penny avoided alcohol of any sort as it made her sick to her stomach. Her hand flew to her mouth as her stomach revolted.

'God's teeth! Hold on. I'll find you something.'

A receptacle was shoved into her hands not a moment too soon as she cast up her accounts. When her retching had finally stopped she felt too unwell to worry about the embarrassment of vomiting in front of her host.

She felt the noxious mess being removed from her lap and gentle hands wipe her face. She leant back in the chair, grateful it was deep enough to allow her to close her eyes and rest for a moment whilst her rebellious digestion recovered. In the distance she heard the murmur of voices and the door opened and closed softly.

'Miss Coombs, I have some boiled water here. Would you care to rinse your mouth?'

Wearily, Penny forced open her eyes to find Mrs Brown, the housekeeper, smiling down at her. Of Lord Weston there was no sign.

'Thank you, but I fear I cannot hold the glass myself for my left arm is hurt.' The housekeeper held it for her. Penny took several mouthfuls, rinsing and spitting into the bowl on her knees before the vile taste had completely gone. 'I feel much better now. Apart from my arm, of course.'

'I'm here to deal with that, Miss Coombs.'

Ten minutes later the cut was cleaned and neatly bandaged. Mrs Brown gathered up the various receptacles she had used and handed them to the waiting parlour maid.

Penny no longer wished to join the other guests. She decided she would return to her room and rest for an hour before taking her walk around the gardens. She thanked the housekeeper and assured her she had no need of further assistance.

She would sit for a few moments longer before attempting to stand. Her eyes were closed and she was resting quietly when she heard the door open again. She didn't bother to look up believing it was her maid sent down to escort her to her chamber.

'I shall be well enough in a moment. Kindly wait for me.'

'I shall be delighted to do so, Miss Coombs. I'm entirely at your disposal.'

Penny shot upright her stomach lurching unpleasantly. 'Lord Weston, I believe I told you earlier that it's not polite to startle people.' She glared at him, her eyes huge in her ashen face.

'Are you still feeling unwell?' He stood up, looking around the room for something suitable.

'I'm not going to be sick again. And I would not have been the first place if you'd not tipped brandy down my throat in that highhanded manner.'

He dropped into a seat opposite her, a slight smile hovering on his lips. 'I must apologize for doing so, my dear. It's not a mistake I care to make again.'

He was laughing at her. How dare he? He had caused her to injure her arm and be horribly ill and now had the temerity to find the situation amusing. She scrambled from the chair forcing him to spring to his feet also.

'I find that I don't like you, Lord Weston. I have no wish to remain under your roof a moment longer. I shall return home immediately.'

His expression changed. She saw anger flicker in his eyes, but his tone was even. 'That's unfortunate, Miss Coombs. However, I cannot allow you to leave today. Might I suggest you return to your chambers until you have…?' He paused, his eyes glacial. 'Until you have recovered. When you are sufficiently restored to hold a conversation I wish to speak to you about this morning's incident.'

Penny stared back, refusing to be cowed. She was no longer the timid girl he had first encountered in London. For the past year she had been managing her own affairs and successfully running the estate. That she was obliged to do this through a third party, her man of business, did not alter the fact that she was fully conversant with matters more normally left to gentlemen.

Slowly she allowed her eyes to travel disdainfully from the toes of his immaculate top boots to the crown of his fashionably cut hair. If he had been angry before now he was incandescent. She would not back down – it was far too late for that.

'I do not believe that you are either my husband or my guardian, Lord Weston. Therefore it is a matter of supreme indifference to me what your wishes are. I intend to leave here today and there is nothing you can do to prevent it.' With a regal nod of her head she turned her back on him and stalked towards the door.

She had taken no more than three steps when she found her passage blocked. 'You're not leaving this room, or my home, until you have heard what I have to say.' She could feel enmity vibrating between them and took an involuntary step backwards. He moved, forcing her to retreat again.

Penny did not stop at the chair she had been seated on, but continued to back away until she had placed the length of the room between them. Only then did she feel safe. She watched him move towards the wall and tug the bell-strap turning his back on her as he did so. The heavy thumping of her heart gradually slowed. She had not realized quite how large he was until he had stood inches from her almost quivering with rage.

A farmyard image of a turkey cock gobbling with anger and visibly swelling as he did so, came unbidden to her mind. She hastily spun to face the window not wishing her amusement to be discovered. She had narrowly avoided a nasty set down and did not wish to antagonize him further.

From her position at the library window it was impossible to hear what instructions Weston gave to the footman. She wished she had not spoken so intemperately. It was unpardonable to tell one's host you held him in dislike, even when it was true. Aunt Lucy had explained to her years ago that in society true feelings were rarely revealed. One must pretend to enjoy the crush and overwhelming smell of barely washed, over-perfumed humanity that you encountered every time you attended a fashionable soirée or ball.

It was the way things were done. If a gentleman wished to find a suitable wife then he was obliged to seek her out at Almack's, or some other event, where the hopeful debutantes were paraded by their doting mamas. She was roused from her reverie a few minutes later by the arrival of Lady Dalrymple who nodded regally to Lord Weston before hurrying to join Penny by the window. They conversed in muted tones, not wishing to be overheard by the glowering man at the far end of the room.

'Penelope, my dear child, I have been searching for you every-where. Why have you not come to join us for luncheon?'

'Aunt Lucy, I'm so glad you are here. I wish to return to Nettleford and Lord Weston has said I cannot leave.'

'He is quite right to say so. Whatever are you thinking of? We have only just arrived and it would be unforgivably rude, and give rise to unpleasant gossip if we were to depart so suddenly.'

'But I do not wish to stay another minute under that man's roof—'

'Enough, Penelope. You are behaving like a child. I thought you had grown out of such temper tantrums.'

Aunt Lucy was quite right to castigate her; she was ashamed of herself. 'I'm sorry, Aunt Lucy. I have no excuse apart from the fact that Lord Weston caused me to injure my arm and then forced brandy down my throat.'

'My goodness! That was unfortunate.' The redoubtable old lady grinned up at her great-niece. 'It is no wonder that you wish to remove yourself. However, I suggest that we hear what Weston has to say before we make a final decision.'

'Very well. I feel more sanguine now that you're here. Shall we join him and discover what it is?'

He bowed politely and gestured towards the *chaise-longue*. 'If you would care to be seated, I have much to say to you.' He waited until they were settled before selecting an upright chair and carrying it to a position opposite them.

Penny wondered why he looked so grave. Surely he was not still annoyed with her? 'I believe that I must apologize, my lord.'

He smiled, his features softening, and she found herself responding. 'It's forgotten, Miss Coombs. Now, could I ask you to listen without interruption?' He raised an eyebrow at her and she grinned.

'I promise to listen without comment, my lord.'

'Excellent. I must first inform you that the militia are already on their way from Ipswich and will search the surrounding neighbourhood for your attackers. However, I believe that they will be long gone.' He stretched out his legs and crossed them at the ankle.

The movement drew Penny's eyes and she could not help but notice the girth of his thighs encased so snugly in his buff inexpressibles. She felt a wave of warmth suffuse her cheeks and hastily removed her gaze to stare at the clenched fingers resting in her lap.

'Go on, sir. I am eager to hear your conclusions on this unfortunate incident.' Lady Dalrymple fixed him with a beady eye. 'I take it you do have conclusions?'

'Indeed I do, my lady. I believe this was a deliberate attempt to abduct Miss Coombs. If you recall, whilst we were at the balloon ascent, you were discussing quite openly your plan to ride across country. There were dozens of gentlemen within earshot and any one of them could have decided you were an easy target.'

Penny had heard enough. 'That's preposterous! It sounds like something from a Gothic romance, my lord, not the explanation I would have expected from a rational man.'

His eyes narrowed but his tone remained bland. 'I believe, Miss Coombs, that you gave your word not to interrupt until I had finished.'

With difficulty she bit back her sharp retort. 'I beg your pardon, Lord Weston. Pray continue your Banbury tale.'

'Miss Coombs, your father was one of the warmest men in the country. Do you think your wealth has gone unnoticed by all the fortune hunters? You've no male relatives to protect you and it would be relatively simple for an unscrupulous man to force you into wedlock.'

Penny felt the colour drain from her face as she understood the full import of his words. He was suggesting that an opportunist rogue had decided to kidnap her and then hold her captive until her good name was gone and she would have no option but to marry him.

It was Lady Dalrymple who broke the silence. 'If you are correct in your assumptions, sir, what are we to do? Every time Penelope leaves the house she will be at risk.'

Penny felt too sick to speak. She could see no way out of the impasse. She raised her head to find herself pinned by the penetrating green gaze of Lord Weston.

'There's a way out of this, Miss Coombs, but you will have to trust me.'

'Tell us at once, Lord Weston, if you please,' Lady Dalrymple demanded.

He nodded. 'You must agree to marry me, Miss Coombs. Then I shall have the right to keep you safe.'

Chapter Four

'HAVE YOU RUN mad? That is an outrageous suggestion.' Penny wished her answer unspoken the moment it had left her lips.

To her astonishment Lord Weston threw back his head and laughed. She exchanged worried glances with her aunt, both convinced the poor man had taken leave of his senses. After several noisy moments he removed his handkerchief from his pocket and mopped his streaming eyes.

'I apologize, Miss Coombs. Obviously I was not suggesting a genuine betrothal. Merely a ruse to allow me to investigate who was behind the attack this morning without anyone questioning my motives.'

Not sure if she was mollified or offended by his explanation, she found herself in a quandary. 'And I beg *your* pardon, my lord. How stupid of me to not to guess that your offer was false.'

'Will you allow me to explain what I have in mind?' Both ladies nodded, but offered no comment. Emboldened by their acquiescence he began to explain the plan he had formulated. 'We shall announce our engagement at dinner tonight. It will hardly come as a surprise to many of the guests. Everyone knows that we spent a deal of time together when you were in town last year. This will enable you to stay here until I have the villains apprehended.'

Penny knew he was waiting for her to speak, to agree that his proposal was not only an excellent idea, but also a kind and thoughtful one. The words would not come. They were stuck somewhere behind her teeth and she was mute. How could he be so heartless? In the long, miserable months following her beloved father's sudden death she had rehearsed the answer she would give when Lord Weston appeared to make his offer.

He had never come. He had not loved her as she had loved him. His particular attention, his appearance to escort her to picnics and parties, had been a hollow sham. At the time she had believed he felt the same way, but with hindsight she had come to realize that a man in love would not have been content to keep his distance. He would have stolen a kiss from her. At no time did he overstep the bounds of propriety and put himself in the position of being compromised by his actions.

'Miss Coombs?' His enquiry was spoken softly and the kindness in his voice released her tongue.

She raised her head. 'I agree, Lord Weston; I'm in no position to do otherwise. I thank you for your offer of protection and gratefully accept. However, I wish it to be clearly understood that this charade ends the moment I'm safe.'

Something she didn't understand flashed in his eyes and was gone. Could it have been triumph? What kind of game was he playing with her? She rose gracefully to her feet and bent to offer her arm to her aunt.

'I believe that I'm hungry again, Aunt Lucy. Shall we repair to the dining-room and see if our fellow guests have left us anything to eat?'

Lord Weston bowed. 'There are still one or two matters we have to settle before this evening, Miss Coombs. I should like to continue this conversation later, if you have no objection.'

She had no intention of being closeted alone with him. 'Lady Dalrymple will be unavailable to chaperon me this afternoon, my lord. Perhaps we could meet here before dinner?'

'I am at your disposal. Shall we say six o'clock?'

It was not until mid-afternoon that Penny was able to find solitude in the rose garden and had time to mull over the extraordinary events of the day. She had been ambushed, injured her arm, cast up her accounts in front of Lord Weston, been inveigled into a false engagement and all before luncheon.

No one could say that life at Headingly was dull. She shuffled back on the warm stone bench so that she was hidden in the arbour of sweetly scented honeysuckle. She tilted her face to the sun, closing her eyes, feeling the tension slowly trickle away. She still found it hard to credit his story, but she could vaguely recall a group of smartly dressed young bucks standing within earshot of her carriage.

It was perfectly possible that one of them had decided to abduct her and force her into marriage in order to gain access to her fortune. Especially as she had reached her majority in March and now had full control of her inheritance.

Why should a fortune hunter believe that the loss of her good name would force her to relinquish control of her wealth? Perhaps a young lady with a more delicate disposition would believe that death was a better option than disgrace? In those circumstances marriage might appear a reasonable option. But she was made of sterner stuff; it would take more than ruin to force her into an unwanted marriage.

Her lips curved as she recalled the conversation in the library. It might be amusing to play the part of besotted fiancée and pretend to hang on his every word knowing that he would have no option but to respond in kind.

She heard the sound of male footsteps approaching and her pulse quickened. Had he come to seek her out so soon? She decided to feign sleep and await events.

'Miss Coombs, how delightful. A picture of loveliness and it's I who have been fortunate enough to see it.'

'Mr Weston, I had thought I was alone here.' Penny's tone reflected her irritation.

'I beg your pardon, Miss Coombs. I had no wish to disturb you. Please forgive me for speaking so …' The young man, his face a study of embarrassment, prepared to back away, realizing he had unwittingly annoyed her.

'No, it's I who must apologize. I spoke too sharply. I'm afraid I was lost in a dream and reluctant to return so suddenly.' She smiled up at him not wishing him to think ill of her. 'Would you care to join me for a stroll around the garden? I'm quite ready to continue my walk.'

His delight at her unexpected invitation was endearing. Gallantly he offered his hand and drew her to her feet. 'Have you visited the maze, Miss Coombs? It's said to be one of the finest in the country.'

'This is my first time here, Mr Weston, so I've seen very little of these magnificent grounds. I should love to see the maze for I've never had the opportunity before.'

He crooked his arm and willingly she slipped hers through it. He was a pleasant young man and it was no hardship to walk at his side.

Lord Weston was in the barn supervising the belated arrival of the motley crew that made up the balloon party. There were three laden carts pulled by sturdy farm horses and one closed carriage in which he expected to find the pilots. He studied the assortment of roughly dressed men scramble down from the carts. Was the man he sought amongst them?

He strode forward waiting impatiently for the carriage door to open. He had spoken to the pilot yesterday and knew him to be no more than he appeared. He had met Monsieur Ducray several times over the past few years and was certain the man was innocent of any wrongdoing. He was a genuine *émigré* and skilled at his trade.

Weston knew the traitor, if there was one, would be masquerading as a helper. Ducray always had a smattering of fellow countrymen working for him and it was amongst these that he must look for clues. It was a damned nuisance to be obliged also to search out and apprehend the man behind the attempted abduction of the delectable Miss Coombs.

He dragged his attention back to the matter in hand. It would not do to let his concentration falter, his very life might depend on his vigilance. 'Welcome, Ducray. I hope you find everything here that you want.' He nodded but did not offer his hand.

The small, neatly garbed Frenchman, bowed deeply. 'My lord, I am so honoured to be 'ere at your so magnificent 'ome.' Monsieur Ducray skipped to one side allowing the second occupant of the coach to descend. 'Allow me to make known to you, the Count of Everex.'

Lord Weston felt a prickle of unease flicker through him as he bowed more formally to the second man. This man was exactly the sort of person one would expect to be involved in treachery. He was of medium height, dark hair swept back and secured by a ribbon at the back of his neck. His aquiline features gave credence to his pedigree. He was every inch an aristocrat. Where had this man sprung from? He had not been in Ipswich yesterday. This man's garments were the height of fashion, no different from his own, hardly what one would expect of a man who made his living flying balloons for the entertainment of the public.

'Lord Weston, I can see that you are surprised by my appearance here. I am, as you have no doubt surmised, an amateur. Ducray has kindly offered to teach me the intricacies of piloting. I hope you do not object to my accompanying him here?' The count's English was accentless, unlike his compatriot who had yet to master it.

'You are welcome, sir. Allow me to take you inside and introduce you to my guests.' Weston smiled, at his most urbane. 'From your faultless English, Count, I would surmise that you have been resident in England for some years.'

The count nodded. 'My mother is English, Lord Weston. My father died when I was a boy and we returned to my mother's ancestral home where I grew up. I have not visited my estates in France since the revolution.'

'Your mother's name? Would I know your family?' He felt the man beside him stiffen and knew he had asked one question too many. 'I only ask, sir, as your face looks familiar. You are the image of Lord Stanhope, a dear friend of my grandfather's; sadly both gentlemen are no longer with us.'

This fabrication appeared to satisfy the count. 'Coincidence, my lord. I am no relation to the Stanhopes.' He did not offer any further information about his ancestry.

'I imagine that you would like to supervise the unloading of your equipment before you come up the house, Ducray?'

'I would, my lord. 'Owever, the count 'as no need to be 'ere with me. I 'ope you 'ave no objection to 'is staying too?'

Weston bowed in the gentleman's direction. 'Of course not, *monsieur*. My guests will be delighted to have another added to their number.'

'It is a large house party you have, my lord?' The count sounded anxious.

'No, not particularly. Your arrival will even up the numbers nicely.'

He turned to lead the way to the front of the house. Immediately he spied his cousin walking arm in arm with Miss Coombs, obviously coming from the direction of the maze. They were talking like old friends, not two people who had only met the previous day. He had no desire to introduce the elegant Frenchman to either of them. He increased his pace allowing his guest no alternative but to hurry after him. The household staff had already been alerted and were waiting to greet the new arrival.

Lord Weston bowed politely. 'I shall hand you over to my staff who will look after your requirements. We dine at seven. I look forward to renewing our acquaintance then.'

He turned smartly and strode off to intercept his cousin and Miss Coombs.

Penny did not see her host heading in her direction but her escort did. 'Come, Miss Coombs, allow me to show you the orangery. It's situated on the far side of the mansion and is well worth a detour.'

'Thank you, Mr Weston, but I believe I'm ready to return to my rooms. Perhaps you could take me tomorrow after breakfast, when it's not so hot?'

'Of course, forgive me. I have had a most enjoyable walk, and shall look forward to escorting you in the morning.' The young man smiled and released his hold. 'If you will excuse me, Miss Coombs, I believe that my mother is trying to attract my attention.' He gestured towards the small group sitting in the shade of an ancient oak tree.

Penny saw a woman of middle years dressed in a sprigged-muslin gown, more suited to someone half her age, waving in their direction. 'Pray don't let me detain you, sir. I'm quite able to find my own way back.'

She watched the young man hurry away his green coat tails flapping behind him. What had upset him? He appeared most agitated.

'Miss Coombs, I wish to speak to you. Do you have a moment?'

Lord Weston! How curious. Why had his appearance driven her escort away in such a flurry? Slowly, she turned to greet the man she had once wished to marry.

'My lord, I'm returning to my chambers. I wish to rest before dinner. Please forgive me.'

Her evasive answer did not please him. 'You have been visiting the maze with my cousin.' It was a statement not, she considered, requiring an answer. He towered above her, using his superior height to dominate.

She stepped backwards catching her heel in hem of her gown. Instantly his arm shot out and saved her from a painful tumble. Flustered by the contact she tried to move away, but for some reason he retained his hold.

'Please, my lord, release me. We're in full view of your guests.'

'Exactly so, my dear. We wish them to believe our announce-ment to be genuine and seeing us like this will help to create the impression that we are romantically involved.' He reached out and casually straightened her bonnet which had slipped side-ways. 'There, Miss Coombs.' His fingers brushed her overheated cheek as he moved back a pace.

Her breathing only returned to normal when she was out of arm's reach. 'Lord Weston, I'm going inside. I don't need your company.' She walked away across the grass knowing she had not acquitted herself well. She got the distinct impression that he was going out of his way to flout convention and cause gossip amongst his family and friends. This was quite out of character and she was at a loss to know how to deal with it.

The sound of horses approaching attracted her attention. She stared down the gravelled drive that led from the front of the house down to the gates which were at least a mile away. The avenue of trees made it impossible to see who was arriving, but was sure there was a glimpse of scarlet and gold between the leaves.

Yes! She was correct, it was the militia. But why did they feel the need to arrive at speed? Could they have apprehended the villains so soon, or were they bringing bad news of another sort?

Chapter Five

LORD WESTON ALSO heard the arrival of the militia and strode across the greensward to arrive at the gravelled turning circle as Captain Smith dismounted. The soldier was a man of around his own age but a good head shorter.

'Good afternoon, my lord. I am glad you're here to greet us. I've pressing news for you.' The captain tossed his reins to his sergeant. 'Is there somewhere private we can talk, Lord Weston?'

'Inside. My study's the best place; nobody would have the temerity to disturb us there.' He led the way across the echoing hall and down the wide, wooden-floored passageway to his sanctuary. Footmen leapt to open doors, but he was so used to the attention he didn't notice. 'In here, Captain Smith.' He gestured to the servant, poised to close the door behind them. 'Have refreshments sent.'

The door closed behind the two men. Weston took the seat behind his polished desk and pointed to a straight-backed wooden chair. 'Bring that closer, Captain. Seated here, we're sufficiently far from the door not to be overheard.'

If Captain Smith was surprised that a member of Weston's own staff might eavesdrop on their conversation, he was wise enough not to comment. When they were both settled, Lord Weston placed his elbows on the desk and rested his chin on his steepled fingers.

'Well, sir, what is it that caused you to arrive at my door in such a hurry?' The captain ran his finger around his close-fitting black stock as if it was unaccountably shrinking.

He cleared his throat noisily. 'It's like this, my lord. We

searched the lane but found no sign of any fallen tree blocking the way. Neither was there any sign of there having been assailants hidden in the hedge. The only hoofprints we could find were those of the three riders who jumped out.'

Whatever he had expected the man to say it had not been this. 'Let me understand you, Captain Smith. You're suggesting, are you not, that Miss Coombs and her two grooms imagined the whole incident?' His voice was even. Years of dissembling meant, when necessary, he was able to disguise his feelings.

'I own I'm puzzled by the whole situation, my lord. Those three riders were so scared they risked breaking their necks by jumping over that hedge. Something spooked them, but I'm not sure it was anything more than a couple of poachers.'

'That doesn't explain the fallen log. I can see no reason why poachers should place it there or wish to remove it after Miss Coombs had gone. Do you have an explanation for this?'

Captain Smith shook his head. 'I don't, sir. Did all three of them see the tree, or was it just the young lady?'

'I have no idea. I can see where your mind is going on this. You think it could have been a trick of the light, no more than a dark shadow across the lane. If the groom heard the poachers and called out a warning it's very possible that Miss Coombs, in her fear, was mistaken.'

The light tap on the door heralded the arrival of the footman bearing a tray laden with coffee, tea and freshly made lemonade. The young man deftly placed it on the desk, bowed, and hurried away.

'Well, thank you for being discreet, Captain Smith. I wouldn't like Miss Coombs to be embarrassed in any way.' Lord Weston raised his eyebrows slightly, waiting for a response.

'Of course not, my lord. I shall mention possible rioters and disaffected labourers in my report.'

'Good man. Now, what can I get you? I've an excellent brandy on the side table, if you would prefer it.'

Ten minutes later Captain Smith departed under the mistaken impression that his host was well satisfied with the outcome of his investigation.

Weston prowled the room deep in thought. He had accepted the explanation without comment. Now was not the time to voice his suspicions. This was something far more sinister than poachers and imaginary logs. If it had been any other young woman of his acquaintance, he might have accepted what Captain Smith had told him, but Miss Coombs was the last person to mistake a shadow for something as substantial as a tree.

God's teeth! He remembered now that one of the grooms had dismounted and attempted to move the obstruction from the path. He had obviously neglected to pass this fact on to the militia. Frowning, he returned to his desk and kicked back his chair. Was there more to all this than he had at first thought? Would a chancer, an opportunist hoping to snatch an heiress, be so meticulous in covering his tracks?

He poured himself a second glass of brandy. He smiled wryly; Miss Coombs had only been back in his life for twenty-four hours and already he was being driven to strong drink. There were now two conundrums to solve: to unmask the traitor, if there was one, masquerading as a labourer with the balloon party, or possibly it was the elegant *émigré*, Count Everex that he should be studying more closely.

Penelope paused long enough to admire the red-coated soldiers as they thundered past but did not stay to watch Lord Weston greet them. No doubt when she met him before dinner he would tell her what the soldiers had discovered. Obviously the fact that they were back so quickly meant that no one had been apprehended.

Shivering as she recalled the shadowy shapes in the darkness of the lane and the very real fear she had experienced. Whoever it was could try again and she was glad to have the protection of Lord Weston, however temporary that might be. She knew that a young lady without a male protector was far more vulnerable to predatory males intent on securing themselves a wealthy wife than a girl with a father or brother to take care of her.

The impressive front door was open to allow a cooling breeze to blow through the house. She was relieved that no vigilant footman leapt out of the gloom to offer to conduct her to her chambers, unused to having so many servants around; at Nettleford House they managed very well with six inside staff and six outside. Goodness knows how many Weston employed – it must be over one hundred.

She ran lightly across the marble hall, her walking boots clicking rhythmically, and up the curving staircase, but was forced to pause to consider her direction when she reached the second floor. Closing her eyes for a moment she tried to recall how many doors down the corridor her own rooms were situated.

No. It is no good she would have to retrace her steps and find a servant to help her. She was about to descend to the hall but the sound of male voices made her instinctively hide herself in the shadows. Lord Weston strode across the empty space followed half a pace behind by a very anxious-looking red-coated captain.

As soon as they had vanished towards the rear of the house she continued her journey. Where was Will when one wanted him? She hesitated, marooned in the centre of the sea of black and white tiles, her rose-pink dimity gown a dramatic contrast to the starkness of the floor.

'Miss Coombs, how delightful, to meet you a second time in one afternoon. Can I be of assistance?'

'You can, Mr Weston. I am afraid that I misremember the exact location of my apartment. And neither can I find a bell-strap to tug, in order to summon someone to take me there.'

Mr Weston smiled and Penelope could not fail to notice that he was an attractive man and so much more obliging than his cousin.

'Your apartment I cannot find, but I know where there is a bell-pull. Allow me to show you where it's hidden.' He walked over to the mantelshelf and reached into an alcove hidden in the wall. 'It's here, Miss Coombs. I've summoned help for you.'

He bowed politely. 'If you'll excuse me, I'm expected elsewhere. I only returned to the house to collect a book from the library that my mother particularly wished to read.'

'Thank you, sir. I'm certain someone will come at any moment to direct me.'

Mary was waiting anxiously when she finally arrived in her apartment. 'There you are, miss, I was that worried you are not going to leave yourself time to change. It's almost four o'clock now.'

'We have plenty of time. I am surprised no one downstairs told you they do not keep country hours here. Dinner isn't served until seven. However, Lord Weston has asked me to come down at six; he has something he wishes to say to me in private.'

Penny knew that her maid would draw her own conclusions about the meeting. It would not hurt for the staff to be half expecting the erroneous announcement that was coming that evening. 'I still have time to rest for an hour, Mary. I shall wear my new evening gown, the one in eau-de-nil silk. I would like the turquoise jewellery set out for me as well.'

Her maid bobbed a curtsy; her narrow features alight with pleasure. 'An excellent choice, Miss Coombs. I'm sure you want to look your very best tonight.'

The bedchamber was pleasantly cool after the heat of the garden. Mary had had the foresight to draw the curtains and close the shutters across the two massive windows. As she disrobed, Penny could sense the excitement in her companion, but Mary was far too well-trained to ask that particular question.

'There, miss, you pop into your bed and rest. I'll call you in an hour. It's a good thing we've been given chambers at the back of the house. It must be like an oven at the front.'

'Being south facing makes Headingly a light house. I think these rooms must be dark and cold in the winter.'

Mary twitched the cotton coverlet across. 'Well, I reckon *you've* been given the best rooms.'

Much as she loved the middle-aged woman who had looked after her since her mother had died ten years ago, Penny sometimes found Mary too quick to spy a possible slight and the maid was overprotective wherever they went. She had been a sore trial during Penny's season in London where every gentleman was scrutinized and any pieces of adverse gossip immediately relayed to her mistress.

Penny settled back amongst the feather pillows a slight smile curving her lips. Her garrulous maid had never a bad word to say about Lord Weston when he had appeared in her drawing-room. She closed her eyes, letting her thoughts drift. Her mind filled with the image of a tall, auburn-haired gentleman, but she was not sure whether her vision was of the charming Mr Weston or his more formidable cousin.

At precisely five minutes to six o'clock Penny was ready to descend. She stood in front of the full-length mirror and stared at herself critically. The *décolletage* of her gown was discreet. The closely fitting, beaded bodice cleverly emphasizing her small breasts.

'The turquoise necklace and ear-bobs are perfect with this dress. And I love the way you have arranged my hair, Mary. It was a stroke of genius to use the spare beads and weave them through.'

'Thank you, miss. That gown is as fine as any you might find in London. You look like a princess tonight. Stand still for a moment longer whilst I check the hang of the overskirt.'

Penny held out her hand obediently and her abigail slipped the loop of ribbon from the demi-train over her wrist. 'When Madame showed me a sample I knew it would be perfect. I couldn't have worn something as sophisticated at my come out, but I'm one and twenty now and can wear whatever I please.'

She turned and the sarcenet overdress sparkled in the evening sunlight revealing her matching silk slippers their toes embroidered with pretty eau-de-nil glass beads. 'Mary, I own I'm feeling a trifle nervous this evening. Do you realize this is the first opportunity I've had to attend a formal dinner since Papa died?'

'He would be proud of you tonight. Both he and your dear mother will be looking out for you. Downstairs there's word there are more guests expected tomorrow. I don't believe you've attended such a grand house party before.'

Penny did not need to be reminded. It was one thing to attend a ball or soirée and then return to the privacy of your own home, but quite another to be on display almost twenty-four hours of the day. She had become unused to company since she had returned from London on the death of her father.

She shivered, inexplicably cold, as if something malignant had brushed her cheek. 'Mary, I shall need the wrap after all. It can turn chilly when it gets dark.'

With the gossamer stole around her shoulders, the ribbons from her reticule and demi-train attached securely to her wrist she was finally ready to descend. She had not rung for assistance. She preferred to make her curtsy to Lord Weston without a circle of curious footmen.

She floated along the carpeted corridors and down the first flight of stairs. She paused to stare out across the park. The wide stone steps that led to the ornamental lake glowed golden as the sun began its nightly journey. It was so beautiful here.

She was about to turn away when a flash of movement caught her eye. Was she mistaken? No, there was someone lurking in the trees that bordered the expanse of green in front of the house. All legitimate guests should now be in their rooms preparing for dinner. So who was it? She pressed closer trying to distinguish the identity of the distant figure.

That he was a gentleman was certain for his garments were not that of a servant or labourer. There was something vaguely familiar about the man, but before she could identify him he vanished beneath the canopy of leaves.

Her brow furrowed to consider the possible implications of her discovery. Had this morning's assailants an accomplice already resident here? She had to discuss her findings with Lord Weston. Immediately. It was fortuitous that she was to meet him before the other guests gathered for sherry wine in the drawing-room.

The library was on the ground floor and it was there that she was due to meet her host. The tall case clock struck six on her arrival in the hall. No less a gentleman than the august butler himself stepped out of the shadows to conduct her to the room she sought.

Her previous nervousness at being closeted alone with Lord Weston had evaporated to be replaced by an anxiety of a different type. She was no longer apprehensive that he would overwhelm her with his masculinity. Now she wished to tell him of the mysterious man hiding in the trees. He could send servants to the chambers of all the male guests to see who was missing. Then they could unmask the villain.

It had not occurred to her that the person she had spotted was on legitimate business and was no more a miscreant than she was. She sailed down the passageway, head up and magnificent green eyes flashing, having no idea how beautiful she looked when she was announced at the entrance to the library.

'Miss Coombs, my lord.' The black-garbed butler stepped aside.

Penny saw him standing in the centre of the room, his hands clasped loosely behind him. Dressed in formal black; his evening trousers emphasized his height, the close fit of his jacket the breadth of his shoulders and the snowy white of his intricate neckcloth drew her eyes to the strong column of his neck.

She dipped in a low curtsy before raising her head and wished she hadn't. It was as if a thread connected her to the man waiting for her to come to him. She must not – it would be disastrous to allow herself to be overwhelmed. But, of their own volition, her slippered feet inched slowly forwards.

She wanted to end the suffocating silence – to speak of mundane things – to break free – to catch her breath, but her voice had vanished like her willpower and she was helpless. Something in his eyes drew her closer until at arm's length from him.

Why didn't he move? Why didn't he say something? Her knees began to tremble and she feared she would collapse in an ignominious heap of silk at his feet.

Chapter Six

LORD WESTON HEARD the clock strike the hour and positioned himself centrally on the closely woven Brussels carpet. He glanced sideways at his reflection in the over-mantel mirror. It was a long time since he had allowed his valet so much time to dress him. He wanted his guests and family to believe this false betrothal was genuine and his immaculate appearance would add credence to their story.

He wondered if Miss Coombs had gone to as much trouble as he to look the part. She had changed since he had escorted her around last year. He gathered from his discreet enquiries that since her majority she had sole charge of Nettleford and her substantial fortune, such responsibilities had given her confidence and an added sparkle to her eyes.

The library door was open so he could hear her approach. The sound of footsteps focused his attention on the doorway. He drew himself up, for some reason wishing to make a good impression. Foster appeared in the entrance blocking his view.

'Miss Coombs, my lord.' The butler stepped to one side and vanished.

Lord Weston was speechless. He had never seen anything so lovely. The young woman who stood so proudly before him was a sea nymph not a mortal. In that moment everything changed.

Swallowing convulsively, knowing he must speak, but could find no words to express his feelings. He was captivated – mesmerized. For the first time in his life no longer in control of events, his razor-sharp brain swamped by an emotion he didn't recognize.

He willed her to walk towards him. It had to be her decision. Even at this pivotal moment managing to restrain his baser passions. Every muscle in his body twitched, but somehow he held himself in check allowing her to make the decision that would irrevocably change their lives.

Like a hound on a leash he tensed, praying for the moment when he could move forward and take this girl into his embrace. She appeared to move unwillingly as if fighting the magnetism between them. His heart pounded. He was burning. He had never felt anything like it before.

Penny could feel his heat pulsing in waves towards her. Knowing little of such matters, but ignorant as she was, she realized after the final step there would be no turning back. She would be totally compromised and they would have no option but to make the engagement genuine.

She hesitated, her knees shaking like a *blancmanger*, trying to find the strength to back away. She could feel his tension. Knew he was fighting the same battle and was leaving the final decision to her. Slowly she raised her hand, not sure if she was warding him off or inviting him to move closer. He swayed towards her, a minimal movement, but enough to cause her fingertips to brush his chest. It was enough. His arms shot out and she toppled into them.

'Miss Coombs, Penny – sweetheart – are you sure about this?' His whispered words brushed her overheated cheek.

'I am. I have never been more certain about anything. I believe that this is where I belong.' She smiled, her face illuminated. 'But I didn't understand it until this moment.'

This was all the encouragement he needed. He drew her closer, so close she could feel the hardness of his chest pressing into the softness of her breasts. She was drowning in exquisite sensations. Her skin was on fire. She wanted something from him but did not understand what it was.

She rested her burning face against the roughness of his coat and could feel his heart pumping beneath her cheek. 'Darling, look at me. Please don't hide your face.'

She raised her head, her lips parted in unconscious invitation and her feet left the floor. When his lips touched hers she shivered and her arm came up to encircle his neck, her questing fingers buried themselves in his thick hair.

He deepened the kiss and she responded by pressing herself closer, wanting to be part of him – to not know where she ended and he began. All the pent-up grief was pouring out of her, she was drowning and didn't know how to save herself.

Weston slipped one hand under her knees to carry her over to the *chaise-longue* to complete what they had started. As he spun she felt his feet become entangled in her demi-train which was held aloft by the ribbon around her wrist.

Unable to release her hold, she clutched tighter as his struggle to retain his balance tightened the constriction round his feet. They landed in a heap of tangled arms and legs. Sanity returned and Penny knew her beautiful gown was about to be ruined.

'Lord Weston, stop struggling this instant. You are breaking my wrist and about to tear my gown.'

Immediately he stilled. 'Bloody hell! What's wrong with me? I'm behaving like a lovesick greenhorn.'

He deftly unhooked the ribbon and the trailing silk fell to the floor and his feet were free. He rolled sideways placing her on the floor. Before she had time to protest he regained his feet taking her with him.

Her elaborate hairstyle had begun to unweave and her right ear-bob was somewhere on the carpet. The whole situation was ridiculous. She felt the irresistible urge to laugh and pressed her lips firmly together hoping to contain her mirth.

'Good God! What was I thinking of? I apologize….'

'Please don't. This was as much my fault as yours. I have no regrets.' She stopped, suddenly unsure, looking up at him, searching for the answer to her unspoken question.

'Darling girl, I'm not apologizing for kissing you, but for losing control and wishing to take matters further. I can't understand it. I managed to keep my behaviour within bounds last year.' He grinned, making him look almost boyish. 'I blame it on that gown. You never wore anything half so alluring before.'

This time she made no attempt to stifle her giggles. 'Thank you, my lord. It's always pleasing for a lady to know she was considered a dowd on her come out.' Spluttering and hiccupping, she raised her hand in order to rummage in her reticule for a handkerchief.

'Devil take it! Did I do that to you?' With gentle fingers Weston lifted her wrist to examine the rent in her flimsy silk evening gloves that revealed a band of dark red where the ribbon had bitten into her flesh.

Penny stared down at the strong fingers encircling her slender arm. A wave of tenderness engulfed her. 'It's nothing. I bruise easily. It hardly hurts at all. Indeed the other elbow, the one I damaged this morning, is far more painful.'

'Show me.'

She twisted her other arm and was shocked to see fresh blood marring the pristine silk of her elbow-length gloves. 'Oh dear! I must have banged it when I fell.'

'My dear, I'm a brute. You've been in my care barely a day and already I've caused you serious harm.' As he spoke he expertly wrapped his handkerchief around her elbow and tied the ends neatly. 'I had intended this evening to be memorable but it's turning out to be a disaster.'

He sounded so despondent, instinctively she reached out to comfort him. The moment her fingertips grazed his face his eyes darkened and he placed his hand on top trapping it there. 'You mustn't do that, darling. Your slightest touch fans the fire inside me that I'm doing my best to bank down.'

'I don't understand what you're telling me. Am I never to feel your arms around me until we're married?'

He shook his head, taking the opportunity to trail hot kisses across her palm. 'No, of course not. However, I'm begging you to keep your distance tonight. I fear I would be unable to prevent matters getting out of hand and I've no wish to cause a scandal so soon in our relationship.'

Reluctantly she pulled her hand away from his cheek. 'Very

well, I shall be a model of propriety.' She smiled down ruefully at her disarray. 'But I can no longer appear in public as I am. I look like a hoyden.'

'You look adorable, my love, but I agree you need the attentions of your maid before you can leave here.' He surged to his feet and yanked the bell-strap. When Foster answered the summons, Weston explained the problem and the butler vanished. At no time had the butler's gaze travelled across the room to stare at Penny.

'We have a few minutes alone before your maid arrives. I've something for you. But first I've something to say.' To her astonishment he dropped to one knee. 'Miss Coombs, would you do me the inestimable honour of becoming my wife?'

'Get up, my lord. There's no need for playacting.' Then she saw his expression and realized the words came from his heart. 'Yes, Lord Weston, I shall be delighted to marry you.'

His wide smile said it all. She watched him spring easily to his feet and reach into his inside pocket to remove a small velvet-covered box.

'I had intended to give you this as a loan, but now, sweetheart it's yours by right. You realize that ours is a true betrothal? Tonight you have consented to be my wife and I have every intention of holding you to that promise. We shall be married in September.'

She held out her left hand and he carefully unbuttoned her glove and removed it. 'You can't wear these anyway, they're both quite ruined.' He flicked open the box and removed the ring nestling inside…. 'It's beautiful. It exactly matches your eyes.'

'And yours, my darling. Any progeny we produce are bound to have green eyes and probably my red hair as well.'

Colour suffused her cheeks. 'My lord! We're only just engaged; it's far too soon to be thinking of such matters.'

'I shall be thinking of nothing else until the night I can share your bed and make you mine. It cannot come soon enough for me.' He slipped the ring over the knuckle of her third finger and smiled triumphantly. 'There; it fits as if made for you. Every countess has worn this and it's never needed to be altered.'

'Like the glass slipper in the fairy-story – only the true bride can wear the ring.' A loud knock on what appeared to be a blank wall startled Penny. 'Whatever's that? Surely you don't have a servant's door in the library?'

'We do. My grandfather had this place constructed with a warren of passageways and staircases running through it. Every room can be reached without a servant ever being seen.'

'Well! I'm surprised that Mary has been able to find her way down here.'

'We had better let her come in and repair the damage to your *ensemble*. It's ten minutes to seven and our guests will be gathering in the drawing-room soon.'

Mary bustled in followed by two chambermaids carrying a variety of bowls and brushes. They all curtsied and waited to be given permission to approach.

'I shall leave you to restore your appearance, Miss Coombs. I shall return in fifteen minutes.'

The room seemed flat and empty after he'd gone. Penny beckoned her maid over to her side. 'I took a tumble and have torn my gloves. Lord Weston trod on my train.' She felt herself blushing under the knowing scrutiny of the two young women. She had to tell someone the news which was bursting to escape.

'Lord Weston and I are betrothed, Mary. We're to be wed in September.'

'Oh! Miss Coombs I'm that pleased for you.' She glared at the two giggling chambermaids. 'That's enough from you two. There'll be no gossiping about this if you wish to keep your position here.'

'Yes, madam. We beg your pardon, Miss Coombs.' The young girls, in smart grey cotton dresses and crisply starched white aprons, eyed Penny nervously.

She realized her announcement had changed everything. She was no longer a house guest but the future mistress of the establishment. It would be her duty to hire and dismiss the indoor staff.

'I hope you brought fresh bandage and the wherewithal to repair my hair?'

'We did, Miss Coombs.' The girls bobbed in unison.

'I have lost one of my ear-bobs. I need you to find it.'

The fifteen minutes allotted for restoring her appearance was almost up and the second ear-bob had still not been found. Mary scrambled up from her knees her face a picture of puzzlement. 'Well, it's a mystery and no mistake. Shall I run upstairs and find you something else to wear?'

'There's no time, Mary. Lord Weston will be returning at any moment. I shall have to remove the other one.' Penny patted her hair. 'This is as good as new, thank you. And I have no need for evening gloves; I wish to be able to show my ring to Lady Dalrymple.'

'It's a pity the dressing on your elbow is so noticeable, miss. A pair of evening gloves would cover it up nicely.'

A soft tap on the door caused the two maids to grab the bowls, bits and pieces, and vanish hastily through the concealed door. Penny smiled. It was becoming painfully obvious that none of her fiancé's staff wished to remain in a room with him any longer than was necessary.

'That will be all, Mary.' She waited until her abigail had also disappeared before inviting Lord Weston to enter.

He strolled in, his eyes alight with laughter. 'I believe, my love, that I've something of yours.' He waved the missing jewel in front of her eyes.

'We've been searching everywhere for that, my lord. Where did you find it?' She had risen on his entrance and walked eagerly towards him tilting her head so that he could replace it.

He chuckled. 'It was snagged on my stock. I wonder how it might have lodged there.'

'I cannot imagine, my lord. It is one of life's great mysteries. Which reminds me, on my way here earlier, I saw a suspicious figure hiding in the woods on the far side of the park. He was too far away to identify, but there was something familiar about his outline.' She had his full attention and he wasn't smiling. 'I had intended to suggest you send footmen to each apartment to see who was missing. However, it's too late to do that now. Whoever it was has had ample time to return to the house undetected.'

He cupped her face in one hand gently brushing his lips across hers, sending spirals of delight down her spine. 'You must not dwell on it, sweetheart. It was probably quite innocent. Smugglers are common in this area. It could have been nothing more sinister than a guest ordering illegal contraband.'

'I hope you're correct, my lord. I heard the clock strike seven. Shall we go up? I don't wish to be late on my first night here.'

He gently restrained her by dropping his hands to her shoulders. 'A moment longer, my love. There is something else we need to discuss. I wish you to call me by my given name, I'm heartily sick of hearing my future wife refer to me as if I was a stranger.'

She giggled. 'I don't know your given name. I rather thought I should call you Weston in future. Is that not the normal practice?'

'My name's Edward, but my intimates sometimes call me Ned.' His smile made her toes curl.

'I shall not use either in public. But when we're private I will endeavour to use Edward, but it will be hard. I've never thought of you as anything but *Lord Weston*.'

'Are you afraid of me, Penny?' His voice was soft, his expression almost anxious as he waited for her reply.

'At this moment, of course not. But you're formidable and I must admit that the thought of angering you does frighten me a little.'

He kissed the corner of her mouth, then whispered in her ear, 'Then you must behave yourself and avoid my wrath.'

She froze, attempting to pull away. His sudden shout of laughter made her look up. 'You're despicable, sir, to tease me in that way. I don't like to be made a figure of fun, even by my fiancé.' She tossed her head, enjoying the playacting. 'I'm to be a countess soon and expect to be treated with respect.'

'Baggage!' He pulled her undamaged arm through his. 'I've asked Foster to have champagne ready. I shall make the announcement now, if you have no objection?'

'Could you give me time to explain to my aunt that matters

have changed between us? I don't wish her to believe that this is still a masquerade.'

Arm in arm they walked back through the house and began to ascend the stairs unaware that they were being watched by someone hidden in the shadows.

Chapter Seven

THE HUM OF voices was clearly audible through the open double doors of the drawing-room. Penny glanced nervously at her escort. 'We're late, Edward. Everyone will stare. I hate being the centre of attention.'

He chuckled, squeezing her arm against his side. 'Then, my angel, you should desist from wearing that gown. All the ladies will be green with jealousy and the men … well, let's say the men will be equally jealous, but of me, not you.'

She was still smiling as they entered the elegant room. Heads turned and several jaws dropped. Penny was thankful Foster had not seen fit to announce them. She could feel herself tingling with embarrassment and wished she had not placed her arm quite so firmly in Edward's.

Mr Weston was the first to move. 'Miss Coombs, Edward, we have been bereft without your company.'

Penny slipped her hand free and curtsied prettily. 'Good evening, Mr Weston. Lord Weston was kind enough to act as my guide. He found me lost in the emptiness below.' Her answer caused a ripple of amusement to travel around the assembled company. She caught the eye of her aunt and moved smoothly in her direction, leaving Edward to charm his way around the group.

'My dear, what has happened to your gloves? You are the only lady present not wearing a pair.'

'It's a long story, Aunt Lucy.' Penny kept her left hand hidden in the folds of her skirt as she ushered Lady Dalrymple to a convenient corner away from prying ears. 'Lord Weston, Edward, has asked me to marry him. It is a true arrangement now. We both realized tonight our feelings are engaged and he proposed. We're to be married in September.'

Lady Dalrymple's expression could only be called smug. 'As I thought, my dear. It is no surprise to me, I can tell you. You are made for each other.' The old lady beamed and stared pointedly at the hidden hand. 'Well, my dear, are you intending to show me your betrothal ring?'

Impulsively, Penny leant down and kissed her aunt's papery cheek. 'So your sudden interest in balloons was a ruse to get us together again? If I'd known I would have refused to come here.' She smiled affectionately. 'However, I shall insist that you ascend when the time comes. It shall be your punishment for deviousness.'

'I shall do no such thing, my girl. I have no need to dissemble about my dislike of such things. If anyone steps into the basket from this family it will have to be you. Now, the ring, if you please.'

Edward had been watching Penny closely, waiting for a sign that Lady Dalrymple knew the truth. He smiled as he saw his fiancée discreetly hold out her left hand with the ring. He smiled politely at Lady Simons, the recently acquired bride of his friend, Sir Richard Simons.

'Pray excuse me I wish to speak to Miss Coombs.'

He nodded to Foster, who was hovering by the concealed entrance at the far side of the room, before strolling casually towards the girl who made his life complete. He did not consider himself a sentimental fellow, had never understood the posturing and soul-searching that appeared to afflict some gentlemen when they viewed the lady of their choice.

From tonight it was all clear to him. It was as if a veil had been drawn aside to reveal Penny as she really was. How could he have not realized she was perfect in every way? To think, if it hadn't been for Wellington he might never have renewed their acquaintance, might never have discovered that he loved her. Shocked to the core by this revelation he almost fell over his feet, much to the amusement of Lady Dalrymple and his fiancée.

'My lord, surely you have not imbibed too much so early in the evening?'

He grinned as he bowed low. 'No, Lady Dalrymple, I have not. I am merely drunk with happiness.' Penny's smile sent coils of heat into his groin. He was going to insist that their nuptials took place at the earliest possible opportunity. He could not wait until September.

'Lord Weston, you look a trifle flushed. Would you care to borrow my fan? I believe I have one somewhere in my reticule.'

He stepped closer in order to whisper in her ear, 'You're impertinent, my darling. I shall expect you to pay penance when we're alone again.' He watched with satisfaction as her face suffused. 'Good, I see we understand each other perfectly.'

'Weston, I think now would be a good time to make your announcement,' Lady Dalrymple commented drily.

Penny felt an inappropriate giggle escape. 'Oh dear, is everybody staring at us? It's your fault, Edward. You've no sense of propriety.'

'None at all, where you're concerned, my love.' He placed a possessive arm around her waist and together they turned to face their audience.

She kept her eyes lowered, not wishing to see the knowing looks, the nods and winks or the lascivious leers from the older gentlemen.

'Lords, ladies and gentlemen it is with great pleasure that I announce my engagement to Miss Coombs.' He waited for the footmen to offer the champagne before continuing, 'I ask you to raise your glasses to the most beautiful lady in England: Miss Penelope Coombs.'

Penny heard her name repeated and nervously raised her head to receive the congratulations. She felt the stem of the crystal glass being pressed into her hand. Instinctively her fingers closed. By the time Foster announced dinner, her mouth was stiff from smiling as she received the felicitations of each member of the house party. If Edward had not kept close by her side she would have fled the room and hidden until dinner was served.

'That was not so bad, was it, sweetheart?' Lord Weston enquired, as he led his future bride into the dining-room.

'It was horrible; you know I hated every minute. If it's going to be like this when we marry I wish to elope.'

His bark of laughter startled Foster who was heading the procession; seeing the dignified butler lose his composure restored Penny's good humour.

It was after midnight when the party finally broke up. It had been a delightful evening after all, Penny decided, as she snuggled down amongst her feather pillows. The French count had been charming. She had also enjoyed the company of Mr Weston, who, as Edward's heir, might have been put out by their announcement. However, he had been as pleased as they were.

Edward had told the assembled company that as soon as the remainder of the house party arrived the next day, Monsieur Ducray was going to inflate his balloon and tether it on the lawn. Flights would then be available for any foolhardy enough to wish to leave the ground.

She stretched contentedly, remembering the few minutes they had spent alone before parting. Edward was insisting they brought forward their wedding day. However, he had been strangely evasive when she had tried to press him to fix the date. He had insisted he had business matters to finalize before he was free to marry.

From the fierceness of his goodnight kiss, the reluctance with which he let her go, it was clear he was as eager as she to tie the knot. Strangely restless, just the thought of Edward making her pulse race, Penny rolled over, enjoying the coolness of the sheets on her overheated skin.

He had persuaded her to agree to be the first to ascend in the wretched balloon. If the weather was still clement then they had a secret dawn assignation for the day after tomorrow. She hoped it would rain.

Edward poured himself a large measure of brandy before collapsing into an armchair in his study. He needed to think – could not retire until he had matters straight. There was something about the French *émigré* that unsettled him. The man was charming and glib, but Edward had spent too long in the clandestine service of his government not to be aware when something was not quite right.

The count's slippers had been soiled when he arrived in the drawing-room, they had obviously been hastily wiped dry with a cloth. Certain that the figure Penny had seen in the park had been this man, he intended to send someone over to look tomorrow morning. It was a matter of urgency that he finished this business for Wellington. Until that was done they were not free to marry.

He felt a tightness in his pantaloons and shifted uncomfortably. Damnit! He was letting his desire to bed his bride overcome his duty. This had *never* happened before. Over the past ten years he had worked assiduously for his government, putting his personal wishes to one side. He grinned – well, to be honest, he did run a ladybird or two when he was at his townhouse in Brook Street.

He shot upright sending a spray of liquid over his jacket. Good God! He would have to sever the connection to the actress stowed away in a small house near Vauxhall Gardens. His man of affairs could see to that; after all he had done it several times before.

Edward knew he would be celibate from now until the night he could make love to Penny. How could he have been so blind last year? If he had only recognized his feelings they could have been married already and he would have been free of his obligations to the Duke.

Thoughtfully he considered the facts. The full moon coincided with high tide at the end of the month – this would be an ideal time for any traitor to transfer gold to a smuggler's ship. The count had joined Ducray recently; was it before he had issued the invitation to fly in Ipswich, or after?

But what about the attempt to abduct Penny? Her decision to ride to Headingly had been overheard by someone and this person was an opportunist who had seen his chance and seized it. It was quite possible, having failed, he wouldn't make a further attempt; especially as his quarry was now under the protection of the local magistrate. He frowned. Perhaps it would be better to let the matter drop: there was no danger now.

No! He would find the bastard and deal with them. No one threatened his beloved and got away with it. The villain must be lured out of hiding, made to show his hand again. He would hold a party for all his tenants and villagers to celebrate his betrothal. Ducray was booked for a month; this event would allow the man he sought access to Headingly, he would do the rest.

His band of trained men, who worked as grooms when he was home, would check every single gentleman that came in. It should not be difficult to ferret out the fortune-hunter. There could not be more than a handful of single gentlemen who were unknown to him in the county.

There was a noise outside in the corridor. Instantly alert, he uncoiled from the chair and, on the balls of his feet, moved silently behind his desk. His right hand slid open a drawer and reached in to remove his pistol. It was already loaded, all he had to do was cock it. He dropped his hand down, hiding the weapon from view. The handle on the heavy door began to turn and his finger closed on the trigger. He held his breath, waiting, watching.

'Good God! James! What the hell are you doing creeping about down here at his time of night?' Edward returned the pistol to the drawer and pushed it closed with his hip.

'Sorry, Ned. I've been outside to blow a cloud and seeing light coming from under your door wanted to come in and congratulate you. I'm delighted you've finally found someone who comes up to your exacting standards.'

'Come in and have a drink. I must apologize for not telling you privately, but I had no idea I was going to propose until I did so.'

James laughed. 'In that case, I forgive you. I never considered you impulsive; how can you be sure you've made the right decision if you've not given it your usual weighty consideration?'

Edward's eyes narrowed and immediately his cousin raised

his hands. 'It's my turn to beg pardon, Ned. My remark was intended as a jest.'

'Pour yourself a brandy and sit down.' He waited until his cousin was seated before continuing, 'I'm intending to hold an open day to celebrate my betrothal. I should dearly like your assistance in the planning.'

'Pleased to help you. Why don't you have a ball in the evening as well? I'm sure Miss Coombs, and the other ladies, would love an excuse to don their finery.'

'An excellent notion. However, I think two events on the same day too much. I rather thought I should hold the public event whilst I have Ducray here, which means sometime in the next three and a half weeks.'

'And the ball? When shall we have that? The following week? That would mean towards the end of June. Why not have it on midsummer's eve and then you already have a theme for the decorations.'

'Perfect. That gives us ample time to send out invitations. I want Venetia and Elizabeth to attend – you know how long it takes my sisters to prepare for any journey.' Edward yawned hugely. 'Sorry, James. You're not boring me, but I think it's time we both retired. Can we continue this tomorrow, when Miss Coombs is present? I wish her to be involved in the planning too.'

The following day sped past. Penny was introduced to the new arrivals but knew she would never remember all their names. The Remingtons were a large family with two gangly sons, who seemed in awe of their surroundings, and three giggling daughters. They were friendly and good-humoured and as they were Headingly's nearest neighbours she knew she would be seeing more of them.

The other two couples were aristocratic friends from London, very high in the instep, and not at all impressed by Edward's choice of bride. Penny decided she much preferred the down-to-earth Remingtons. She was pleased that her future husband counted a local squire as a friend for she was certain that neither of the London couples would deign to include such folk in their circle.

She was changing out of her riding habit into an afternoon dress of buttercup-yellow, spotted muslin when she heard Edward's voice in her parlour. 'Quickly, Mary, Lord Weston is waiting.'

'Stand still, miss, and it will only take a second to tie the sash. There – all done.'

Penny flew from the room her skirts swirling around her feet revealing her embroidered stockings and matching yellow pumps.

'Edward, is something wrong? I thought we were to meet in the library with Mr Weston at four o'clock?'

'We are, my darling. But I could not wait.' He was standing with his back to the window and the sun made his russet hair appear like a circle of fire around his head.

'You're lucky that I'm ready early. I believe that I'm unique in this respect.' She ran across to greet him and he picked her up and spun her round like a child, laughing down at her.

'Put me down, Edward. You're making me giddy.'

In answer he allowed her to slide down his chest, the contact making them both breathless. 'Look out of the window, Penny. I have a surprise for you.'

Obediently she turned her head. 'The balloon! They are setting it up on the lawn. Are there to be flights today?'

'Not today, Penny. It will not be inflated until this evening.' He pulled her close to his side, his arm firmly around her waist. 'You remember your promise? I want us to be the first to go up. Will you agree to meet me at dawn tomorrow? It is the best time to ascend as the air is still.'

She was about to refuse, but seeing the look of boyish enthusiasm on his face decided she would do as he asked. 'Very well, but don't ask me to make a habit of it. This will be the one and only ascent that I make.'

After dinner the guests assembled on the terrace to watch Ducray and his men finishing their preparations. The balloon was winched down, inflated a little more, then returned to the end of its rope about 300 feet above the ground, where it danced and swayed like an oversized ballerina.

The wind dropped and the aerostat hung in the navy sky, a huge gaudy sphere, through which the last rays of the sun shone, giving it a ghostly luminescence. Penny thought it looked quite magical, like something from another realm. She was almost looking forward to her ascent at dawn the next day.

Chapter Eight

'I**S IT DAWN** already, Mary? I seem to have only just closed my eyes.'

'It is, miss. And a fine clear one too. The weather is set fair, not a breath of wind out this morning.' Her maid dressed her hair simply, half piled on top of her head, the rest tumbling loose down her back, cream and yellow ribbons threaded through. The scooped neckline of her long-sleeved gown was edged with tiny yellow satin roses, and larger versions of the rose encircled the hem. Even the slippers were similarly decorated. The outfit was perfectly complemented by a pretty chip-straw bonnet lined with yellow silk and tied with a matching ribbon. She wondered if it was going to prove too flimsy for her excursion skywards.

'I must take my cloak. Lord Weston says it's always chilly aloft.'

'I shall bring it down for you, miss. Carrying it will spoil the line of your gown.'

'Thank you. And you can stay and watch if you wish. Lady Dalrymple will be there as well, if she has woken up in time.'

Penny nodded at her reflection, satisfied she had done the best. She was not exactly an antidote but neither, in her opinion, was she a diamond of the first water. However dressed as she was, she knew she could not fail to please him.

She floated down the stairs and sped through the strangely hushed house. The side door was open; Edward was obviously here before her. She paused to twitch her skirt into place, check that her sash was tied correctly, her bonnet straight and then stepped out into the silvery-grey light. Were those voices she could hear? Lady Dalrymple was waiting on the terrace to greet her.

'Good morning, my dear. Is it not a perfect day to celebrate your engagement properly?'

'Indeed it is; thank you for taking the trouble to come down and watch.' Penny hurried over and hugged her, shocked at how insubstantial the old lady had become.

From the terrace she scanned the rolling parkland. She could see the balloon was two-thirds inflated and secured at ground level by four stout ropes attached to iron anchors. A small flight of steps led up to the woven gondola. Edward was standing beside it, talking to the Frenchman and three others. He was draped in his heavy driving cape. She waited whilst Mary put hers over her shoulders.

As the balloon swayed and strained at its moorings her enthusiasm for this venture began to fade, her courage seeping away with each step she took towards it. Edward strode to greet her.

'Good morning, sweetheart. You look enchanting. It's a glorious morning, perfect ballooning weather.'

'I'm sorry, but I find I've changed my mind. I'm not setting foot in that contraption, Edward.'

He chafed her cold hands and drew her close, planting a hard kiss on her open mouth before she could protest again. 'There's not a breath of wind. It's ideal weather. I really want to share a sunrise with you. We'll never have a better opportunity to see it than today. I promise you, it's completely safe. We're firmly anchored and the balloon's not fully inflated.'

She was unconvinced, but allowed him to lead her to the steps. He picked her up and placed her where she could see into the gondola. She gasped.

'Oh Edward! Did you arrange all this? It looks like a Sultan's palace. Where did you obtain the beautiful silk cushions and Kashmir rugs?'

'I have an attic full of such paraphernalia. Do you like it? There's also a hamper stuffed full of all delicacies, and cold champagne and lemonade to wash it down. We shall eat breakfast watching the sunrise over the sea. It will be unique. No other couple will have had such an experience.'

She hesitated, her old antipathy to balloons holding her back. But it looked so inviting – so exotic – and he had gone to such trouble to make this morning memorable. She held up a finger to test the breeze; there was none. It was, as Edward had said, as still as a millpond.

'Very well, if you're quite certain it's safe, I'll come up with you, but only this once, as it's a special occasion.'

The smile he gave her convinced her she had made the correct decision. He lifted her into the basket, then stepped in himself. As soon as they were comfortably settled he waved a small flag over the side, obviously provided for that very purpose.

The men took hold of the handles. They obviously had strict instructions to raise the balloon gradually in order not to alarm her before they were aloft. She lay back on the colourful cushions finding she was actually enjoying the novelty. She rested her head on Edward's shoulder and he reciprocated by slipping his arm around her waist.

'This is really quite enjoyable. I never thought I could feel contented in a balloon.'

He bent his head and nibbled at her ear. 'Is it possible that I could have something to do with your change of heart, my love?' His words, whispered into her hair, sent frissons of excitement coursing down her spine to pool in a most surprising place.

'My lord! I thought we were in this basket to watch the sunrise?'

'Then you were sadly mistaken, sweetheart. I have a far more interesting pastime in mind.'

For a few blissful minutes he demonstrated his intentions until common sense restrained him. He propped himself up on one elbow and studied Penny's flushed cheeks, her swollen lips and the dazed expression in her eyes. Enough was definitely enough!

He sat up, allowing her time to adjust her clothing and recover her composure. The balloon was perfectly positioned for his purposes. Its movement was minimal, the tethers holding it steady. He stood up and pulled a spyglass from a pocket in his cape. Flicking it open, he put it to his eye and rotated carefully, scanning the horizon in all directions. Excellent, no clouds, no wind, the weather remained perfect.

Penny joined him, commenting on how stable the gondola was. He pulled her tight to his side and she went willingly. 'I hadn't realized it would be possible to move about up here. I had imagined it more like a small boat, only safe if its occupants remain seated.'

'Not so, my dear. I believe that in France, some years ago, eight people ascended and actually danced a quadrille, several hundred feet above the ground.'

'How extraordinary!' She breathed in deeply, filling her lungs with fresh morning air. 'It even smells different up here. Can you hear the birds? I have never heard the dawn chorus sound so clear.' She risked a peek over the side and shivered 'We're so high up, how far is it to the ground?'

'About three hundred feet, no more. There are trees as tall as this in the New World.'

Holding tight to his arm she ventured closer to the edge of the basket. Its sides reached to just below her shoulders, giving her an illusion of safety. As the wicker beneath her feet did not rock alarmingly she transferred her hands to the rim. Feeling braver she risked another peep.

'Where are the men? Why have they left us up here?' Her voice rose a little, believing she was stranded in midair at the mercy of the elements.

'I expect they've gone back to break their fast. They'll return long before we wish to descend. Don't look so worried, sweetheart, you're perfectly safe.' He grinned wolfishly. 'Well, safe from the elements, anyway. I cannot promise you're not in any danger from me.'

'Don't be ridiculous, Edward. It's far too cold to indulge in the things you have in mind. And you promised to restrain yourself until we're married.'

'That's a pity, but I will abide by your wishes. We have the rest of our lives ahead of us; there's no need to rush into something that, in my opinion, is best done slowly.'

'You're impossible, Lord Weston!' She inched her way gingerly round the edge of the basket, beginning to enjoy the experience. 'Look, Edward, the sun's starting to rise over the sea. The water's turning orange and gold; it's as though God's pouring celestial paint upon the earth for our delight.'

They stood, enthralled, watching until the spectacle was completed and the world bathed in early morning sunshine. The basket rocked a little, as though pushed by an unseen hand. Penny laughed, clutching at Edward to steady herself.

'Thank you, that was a magical experience. One I shall treasure for the rest of my life.' She pulled her cloak together. 'It's cold standing up, shall we sit down and open the hamper? All this fresh air has restored my appetite.'

Edward served her with lobster patties, chicken legs, cheese dainties, apple turnovers and plum cake, all washed down with freshly made lemonade.

She became so engrossed that she didn't notice the increased movement of the basket or the sudden drop in temperature. Suddenly the balloon lurched violently to one side, tipping her into Edward's lap. Laughing as they unentangled themselves, then Edward swore.

Penny shocked by his outburst, remonstrated, 'Please don't use such language. I don't like to hear it.' He ignored her lady-like protest. He was on his feet, the basket still askew, the flag for attracting attention in his hand.

'God damn it, where is everyone? We need to come down. It's going to get unpleasant up here very soon.' The park was deserted apart from two small figures sitting, watching, on the terrace.

'What is it? Why are we rocking so violently? I don't like it, Edward.'

'Neither do I, sweetheart. Everything will be fine; don't worry. The men will be back to lower us at any minute now. The balloon is so securely tethered it will not pull free even in a storm. I checked the anchors were sufficient last night.' He waved his flag vigorously over the side of the basket and Mary ran from the terrace in the direction of the barn.

'Sit down, Penny. It's safer in the bottom of the basket. I'm sorry our morning has been spoilt. It's uncomfortable, but I promise it's not dangerous.'

She was only too happy to do as she was bid but she could see Edward was concerned by the brutal rocking. Crouching, terrified, under the rugs, she watched as he balanced under the neck of the sphere fighting to release the valve that prevented the hydrogen from escaping. The noise of the wind made speech impossible, but she could see that he had finally been successful by the expression on his face. It lurched again and he lost his footing and fell heavily on top of her. He rolled away.

'I'm sorry, did I hurt you?' He was obliged to shout directly into her ear to make himself heard above the terrifying roar of the wind. She shook her head, not attempting to answer. 'The gas is being released, the balloon will deflate and we'll descend, but it's going to take a little while,' he bellowed. 'You mustn't worry, it's merely uncomfortable, not dangerous.'

The basket rocked violently and Penny watched a look of horror spread across Edward's face. He struggled upright and, clinging to the basket, peered over.

He was thrown to the floor again as two of the anchors tore out of the ground, the aerostat now held by only two ropes and the weight of the winch. There was nothing he could do except hold her in his arms and pray that the men arrived before the final anchors ripped free and the balloon carried them out to sea. He knew this was no accident. Someone had deliberately loosened the restraints hoping they would tear free and be taken to their deaths.

Chapter Nine

PENNY HUDDLED IN the bottom of the basket and even Edward's warmth could not prevent her shivering. He knew what she was thinking – should not have listened to him – should have remained safely on the ground. The sun was rudely obliterated by towering black clouds and the skies opened.

In seconds they were both drenched, their cloaks and blankets no protection from the downpour. Edward staggered to his feet and saw the men racing desperately across the grass hoping to reach the winch before it was torn from its moorings. There was nothing he could do apart from offer comfort and reassurance to his petrified fiancée.

He realized, even if she did not, that their time was running out. The balloon was not deflating quickly enough and with only the one remaining anchor they could tear free at any moment. The ferocity of the wind increased and the final anchor lifted. Then the cast-iron winch was wrenched from the ground, even its enormous weight not sufficient to hold them down.

Edward sensed the instant they were airborne, unrestrained, racing towards the open sea. A balloon usually travelled at the speed of the prevailing wind, but as theirs was trailing several iron objects it would, he prayed, move more slowly. He gathered Penny closer in order to shout into her ear. It was imperative she knew what to expect.

'Penny, we're heading out towards the sea. The weight of the anchors will prevent us from ascending any further. Do you understand? Nod if you do.' She nodded, her face paper white, hair plastered to her head, bonnet long gone, ripped away by the wind. 'I anticipate we'll land on the sea not far from shore. When we do you must hang on to the net.' He pointed to the intricate mesh that enveloped the balloon and to which the basket was attached.

She was too scared to question his instructions and her teeth were chattering too much for her to do more than nod again.

'Good girl.' He smiled, hoping his confidence would reassure her. 'We're going to scramble up on to the balloon – there will be enough hydrogen in it to keep us afloat.'

His next words were lost in the wind but she heard enough. The word, *afloat*, lodged in her subconscious and was sufficient to keep her from hysteria.

Next she saw him remove his boots and stockings and throw them to one side. The rain was falling horizontally and copious amounts of icy water were whipping through the sides of the basket adding to the deluge pouring on them from above. The balloon was noticeably lower, barely above the tree tops and Penny prayed that it would land before they reached the coast. Edward removed his cape and stuck a long- bladed knife into his waistband. Was he going to try and puncture the balloon in order to speed the release of the hydrogen?

He intercepted her stare and dropped down to his knees beside her cupping his hands round her ear. 'If we land out to sea I must cut the gondola from the net or the weight of the anchors and the winch will pull us under.'

She followed his example and placed her hands against his head and screamed into his ear. 'Why not do it now? You might not be able to cut all the ropes quickly enough once we're in the sea.'

He shook his head, abandoning any attempt to speak. He mimed the effect such a premature action would have. She sank back, understanding what his demonstration meant. If he released the weights too soon then the balloon could rise and carry them further out.

The howl of the wind seemed to change pitch, become deeper

somehow. One look at his horrified expression told her what it was. It was the noise of the waves underneath she could hear. He leant down and pointed to her feet, indicating she should remove her cloak, petticoats, slippers and stockings. He pointed to his bare feet and mimed climbing up the net. She nodded; he was telling her it would be safer to scramble up with bare feet. Frantically she pulled off her sodden petticoats and stockings, realizing that there was very little time.

He bent forward and, seizing her round the waist, threw her on to the net. She began to climb, fear giving her the strength to grip the slippery rope. The gondola was bumping along the waves and he was slashing like a madman at the pieces of rope that held the basket to the balloon itself.

Within seconds of their landing the basket was submerging – there were huge waves breaking over him. Still he sawed away – their lives depended on his success. The icy North Sea slapped her ankles, promoting a frenzy of climbing. The balloon, although now almost empty, had more than enough buoyancy to hold her.

She fell into a hollow on its surface and the balloon appeared to flatten under her, easily supporting her weight. The rain continued to lash her face but she was safe from the waves. Gulping in a lungful of air, her heart pumping painfully in her chest, she began to believe she was going to survive, that she wasn't going to drown.

Held safely in the dip one could not see the waves below, couldn't see what he was doing. Why wasn't he climbing up to join her? Gingerly she rolled to the edge and, using it to support her, peered over the top. She was surrounded by heaving, slate-grey water; there was no sign of the gondola or Edward. Her throat constricted. Where was he?

'Edward, Edward.' Her cries were carried away by the howling wind. The makeshift boat rocked violently almost pitching her into the waves. Terrified, she slid backwards, her mind refusing to accept the awful truth. He was dead. Her beloved had drowned.

Numb with misery, she prayed that God would take her too;

she didn't want to be on this earth without him. The balloon rocked violently a second time and she was tumbled, end over end, to the centre where the rainwater that had collected submerged her completely. She lay winded, face down, believing her prayers were being answered. Drowning would not be so bad; she opened her mouth to let the water do its work.

Edward saw Penny disappear over the edge of the floating balloon and, confident she was safe, turned his attention back to slicing the ropes. All but two were severed when the waves swallowed the basket taking him with it. Desperately sawing, knowing that when the ropes were fully stretched it would, inexorably, follow.

His fingers felt the last fibres split and the combined weight of the anchors and winch tore the rope end from his hand. His lungs were bursting; he needed air. He kicked violently and shot up but his head did not break the surface of the water, it bumped against something solid.

He had come up under the balloon. He knew he was almost done, had seconds left to live – his reserves were exhausted. He had failed. Then, floating before him, he saw Penny's image; she was smiling at him; he had to survive for without him she, too, would surely perish. With savage kicks he swam parallel to the sphere, praying to reach the end of it before his lungs gave out.

Suddenly there was nothing under his groping hand – he was free. With the last of his energy, he swam up and this time his head broke the surface of the water. Instinctively he clutched out and rammed his fingers in the netting. The tide was strong, the waves powerful, and he could be swept away in a second.

For several minutes he hung, gasping, drawing air into his chest. The water was freezing and his life ebbing away. He had to climb up the netting; join Penny on top where they would both be safe.

He rested his forehead on the slippery side, gathering the remnants of his strength for one final push. He felt the balloon rock sideways as a large wave surged under it, and, seizing his opportunity, began his frantic scramble. His weight tipped the balloon, and for a horrible moment thought it would capsize. Then it righted and using that motion to assist him flung himself over the rim and fell inside.

The water slopping about in the hollow was almost bath like in comparison to the sea and it revived him. He rolled upright, but couldn't see her. Then, in the centre of the dip, where the water was deepest, he saw her, lying face down.

With a roar of anguish he hurtled forward dragging her out of the pool. Not now, not after all this! How could he bear it? Finally he had found his perfect partner, a woman to love for the rest of his life, and had lost her.

His face contorted with grief as he dragged the limp form to the edge where he cradled her, his tears adding to the rain that streamed down his face. So lost in his sorrow was he, for a moment he didn't recognize the signs: this was not her corpse, at least not yet; she had a pulse.

He would not lose her, they had been given a second chance. He flipped her over, draping her across his raised knees, and began to systematically pummel her back, starting at the base of her spine and ending between her shoulders. He repeated this twice, then rolling her back, he placed his mouth over her icy lips, attempting to breathe life into her.

From a deep darkness Penny heard a voice – his voice. 'Sweetheart, darling, don't leave me. I love you, I need you. Please don't die.' The words were being repeated over and over, like a refrain. And then she understood. Edward was alive, he was calling her back. They were to be given another chance.

She convulsed, the water spewing from her mouth, emptying her lungs and allowing life-giving air to flood in. She felt herself being cradled in strong arms, and drawing a shuddering breath, opened her eyes.

'Thank the sweet Lord, thank God, my darling you're safe now. I thought I'd lost you.' He pulled her up, supporting her against his chest. 'Rest, sweetheart, I have you now. You'll be safe. I'll not let anything else take you from me.'

She tried to raise her arm, to reach up to touch his dear face;

the face she had never thought to see again in this world, but inertia held her fast. Instead she smiled into his eyes and mouthed, 'I love you.' Then her lids drooped and blessed sleep took her.

'Wake up, darling. You mustn't sleep, you're too cold. You'll die if you don't stay awake.' Rough hands were shaking her, forcing her to return to the nightmare that surrounded them. 'Good girl – now I'm going to start rotating your arms, try to restore your circulation.'

It was impossible to remain comatose with a maniac shaking her about like a rag doll. 'Stop it, Edward, you're hurting me. You're pulling my arms out of their sockets.'

She realized there was no need to shout; her words were audible. The wind had dropped and the rain slackened to a drizzle. 'I feel as I've swallowed a bucket of water and it's slopping about inside me.'

'Stick your fingers down your throat and bring it up. You'll feel much better, I promise you.' Even in her weakened state such a suggestion appalled her. She forced herself out of his grasp, intending to protest, but the sudden movement had the desired effect. He held her head as she retched helplessly, regurgitating the last of the water that had almost drowned her.

'You will feel much better now, my darling.'

She flopped back into his arms. 'Well, I could hardly feel any worse. I seem to be making a habit of this.' Tempted to close her eyes, to sleep, but knew that if she did the wretched man would start his shaking and pummelling again. She prised her salt-sticky eyes apart and stared upwards.

'Look, the clouds are breaking. I can see a patch of blue sky.'

'It will start to get warmer soon, sweetheart, and we'll both feel better.' He propped her, unresisting, against the springy edge, and pulled himself upright. 'Thank God! Penny, darling, look, we're drifting into the shore. The tide is strong here and it's carrying us in with it.'

Penny found energy from somewhere, and with his assistance gained the edge and peered into the drizzle. Her heart lifted. 'That's the beach; I can see it. I'm not imagining it, am I?'

'No, darling, you're not. We should be beached in about fifteen minutes. We're saved, somehow we've both been spared.'

She slipped back down into the hollow of their odd boat and he joined her, reaching out and pulling her on to his lap. A feeling of joy swept over her. They had nearly perished, but now they were safe.

Chapter Ten

A WATERY SUN emerged from behind the remaining clouds and they basked in its welcome heat. Too exhausted to speak, they rested, waiting for the bump that would indicate they had arrived on the sand. The balloon bottomed, tipping them forward.

'We're there, sweetheart. Come along, let me help you.'

Getting out was considerably easier. Allowing gravity to do the work they rolled one after the other over the edge and down to the wet sand. Penny had difficulty regaining her feet, the weight of her sodden skirts holding her down.

'Up you come.' He heaved her upright. 'We must walk about, try and restore some blood to our limbs and allow our garments to dry.'

She stared at him, an unexpected smile splitting her wan face. 'You look like a buccaneer, my love. And you have lost your lovely Hessians. What a shame!'

'Good God, do you think I care about that?' He grinned, holding her at arm's length. 'We do indeed make a sorry pair.' He stepped closer and hugged her hard. 'But we're alive and well. Do you know, I have never felt happier than I do at this moment?'

'In spite of being half drowned and scared to death.' She sighed. 'Oh, Edward, I do love you so much, and I feared I would never be in a position to say those words again.'

'My darling, I'm the luckiest man alive.' They gazed into each other's eyes, lost in love and happiness. The sun shone, warming them, drying their clothes and sending a different sort of heat surging through their veins.

'Lord Weston! Lord Weston!' A shout from the dunes startled them apart.

'It's Ducray and my men from Headingly.' He waved one arm, reluctant to remove the other from his fiancée. They began to walk towards the rescue party, unwilling to rejoin the bustle of reality.

Soon Penny was warmly wrapped in rugs, sitting in the back of the carriage that had come to find them. They had no need to talk; they were content to enjoy the warmth of their shared affection. Even the discomfort of sticky, damp clothes did not intrude in their oasis of happiness.

'What will happen to the balloon? Will they bother to collect it?'

'The wagon will be there already. It's odd how close to home we are, I felt as though we were in a foreign land.'

'The last two people on earth, I know exactly what you mean.' She stretched up and pushed a strand of hair from his forehead. 'It's remarkable that they found us so quickly, but I'm glad they did. I cannot wait to bathe and change into something dry.'

His eyes teased her. 'I was rather hoping we would have no need of clothes, dry or otherwise.'

She giggled. 'Edward, you're impossible. Our narrow escape does not give you leave to take advantage. Such things must wait until we're man and wife. Can you imagine what Aunt Lucy would have to say on the subject?'

'Shame! But I'm having the banns called today. We shall tie the knot in three weeks.'

She slipped off his lap, attempting to arrange herself demurely on the squabs.

'You look like a sea nymph, or a mermaid, with your hair loose like that.' His eyes darkened and he prepared to join her. She shook her head as the carriage began to slow. 'I'm relieved that your guests are still safely in their beds. I have no wish to be seen looking like this. I shall return to my room for a hot bath and intend to rest until noon.'

The carriage rattled to a halt and two footmen opened the door and lowered the steps. Penny noticed they kept their eyes firmly to the ground; they had obviously been warned not to stare. Edward climbed out first and she saw that his expression was no longer that of someone whose life had been miraculously saved. He looked fierce, and something she didn't recognize flickered in his eyes.

'Edward?' She had been about to ask him what was wrong, but when he raised his head she saw only his love reflected there. Perhaps she had imagined it.

'Yes, sweetheart? Is something wrong?' He reached in and, gripping her firmly around the waist, lifted her to the gravel.

'No, everything is splendid. I can hardly believe it's still so early and yet so much has happened to us. I shall never take anything for granted again.'

His smile made her wish she was prepared to throw convention to one side and agree to share his bed tonight.

'Lady Dalrymple already knows that we are safe. No doubt she will wish to visit you in your chambers as soon as you're ready.'

Edward watched her hurry inside trailing rugs and water behind her. He stood, unable to take his eyes from her until she vanished. She was his life and the bastard who had almost taken her from him was going to regret it.

'My lord, I have a bath ready.'

The quiet reminder from his valet refocused his attention on the present. 'Yes, I'm coming presently. First I have some urgent business to attend to.'

His intention was to find his men and start investigating how the anchors had been loosened. The near tragedy would be referred to as an accident; Penny had been frightened enough by the experience. He did not wish her to know that someone had deliberately tried to kill them. He would deal with it – his way. He found Reynolds, one of the four men he sought, examining the holes in the lawn. 'God damn it! Where are the others?' He did not enjoy traipsing round the place in search of his minions.

'They're already investigating what took place here, my lord.' His face was grave. 'This is a nasty business. Someone came out here last night and loosened the ground. How many of your guests knew that you were intending to take Miss Coombs for a flight this morning, my lord?'

'None of them. Lady Dalrymple knew, of course and Ducray and that *émigré*. I suspect it was the count. Somehow he's got wind of the investigation and hoped to divert attention from himself by murdering myself and Miss Coombs.'

'Are you suggesting that he knows it's you who's leading the search, my lord?'

'No, I'm certain he does not. His manner towards me is that of a fellow aristocrat. His behaviour, his expression would have revealed his suspicions.'

He kicked a lump of turf and swore. He had forgotten he was still in his stockings. 'I must remove these sodden garments and put on some boots. If anyone sees me prancing about out here dressed as I am, they'll think I'm ready for Bedlam.' He turned to go. 'Reynolds, where have you sent the other men? Walk with me and explain.'

'Perkins and Jones accompanied the wagon that has gone to collect the balloon. If any of the labourers are not what they say those two will soon discover it.' The young man grinned. 'I sent Jed to scout around the grounds. It's possible intruders came in from outside during the night. If they left any evidence, he's the man to find it.'

'Excellent! My information is that the traitor we seek has close links with the free traders. Have you had a chance to search the barn for gold?'

'No, my lord; there's always someone in there. However, we have a chance to poke about whilst they're all down the beach salvaging the balloon.'

'Give me ten minutes to change and I shall be back down – if the gold's already in the barn this is the perfect opportunity to discover it.'

The barn was, as expected, deserted. Edward glanced round. 'Reynolds, take the far side where the men have their belongings and I'll examine the boxes and barrels.' After twenty minutes' methodical searching neither men had found anything suspicious.

'If they have the gold it's certainly not in here, my lord.'

'It must be arriving separately; the highest tide is not for another two weeks. Plenty of time for them to have it delivered. The count obviously has several accomplices working for him; it's those we have to apprehend before they succeed in harming Miss Coombs.'

Reynolds scratched his head. 'It's a rum do, sir. It don't seem sensible to draw attention to themselves like, by these attacks on your young lady. If it was me, I'd keep me head down until the gold actually arrives.'

'I believe they wish to keep the militia and myself occupied. Whilst we're chasing possible abductors and potential killers we're not watching the coast for smugglers and the lanes for a diligence filled with gold.' He brushed the dust from his coat, and removing a kerchief from his pocket, bent down to clean his top boots.

'I reckon as you could be right, my lord. Seeing as you're the magistrate it don't mean they know you're a government agent as well, do it?'

'I sincerely hope they do not. I have successfully maintained my cover for the past ten years and cannot conceive that I have revealed myself this time. I shall continue my enquiries inside.' He prepared to leave the gloom of the barn. 'Remember, no one must suspect that the narrow escape Miss Coombs and I had this morning was anything more than an accident – I have no wish to alert the perpetrators. Let them believe they're safe from discovery.'

He returned to the house not wishing to remain visible for any longer than was necessary. He glanced up at the thirty or so windows that faced southwards and was relieved to see that not one of them had open shutters. It was a little after eight o'clock – far too early for most of his guests to be up.

'Reynolds, I shall be in my study. Let me know what Perkins discovers.'

'Please, Aunt Lucy, don't fuss so. I'm perfectly well. A hot bath was sufficient to restore me. It was an accident that would have been a tragedy, but for Lord Weston's quick thinking and courage.'

'I cannot understand how such a thing could have happened. What was he thinking of to take you up when the weather was so blustery?'

'My dear Aunt Lucy, I have explained at great length about all aspects of this morning's misadventure. I should prefer to speak of something else.' Penny smiled to take the sting from her words. 'In fact I have momentous news for you. Lord Weston and I have decided to arrange our wedding for the middle of June – not September.'

'Good heavens! That gives us less than a month to organize your trousseau and invite the guests.'

'It is quite long enough. Instead of having a betrothal ball and garden party for Lord Weston's tenants and villagers, we shall now make it a celebration of our wedding. I don't believe I shall have ballooning as a feature, not after today.'

'I should think not. Do you have a list of guests already drawn up?'

'No. Perhaps both you and Mrs Weston could help me with this? I fear if you left it to me I should forget to invite someone important.'

Penny had intended to rest on her day-bed until noon but was feeling so invigorated at the thought of her forthcoming nuptials she sat up, swinging her legs to the floor. 'I shall need to get dressed. My *demi-toilette* is not suitable for appearing in public.'

Her great-aunt pushed herself to her feet. 'In that case, my dear, I shall leave you. Where shall we meet to discuss our plans?'

'In the library; it's a pleasant room and the French doors open on to the terrace. So if we wish we can remove ourselves outside.'

It was hard to credit that scarcely four hours ago she had been hurrying downstairs for her dawn assignation. Indeed, so much had happened since they had renewed their acquaintance she was almost tempted to believe the two things connected. She heard Mary enter from the dressing-room in answer to her summons.

'I should like to wear my new walking dress of jaconet muslin. The rose pink is exactly right for a warm summer's day.'

'Very well, miss. Will you be wanting the jacket?'

Penny thought for a moment. This dress had long sleeves which should be sufficient for conversing in the library. 'If I decide to walk in the garden after my meeting then I shall come up for my bonnet, gloves and parasol.'

Downstairs the house was alive with guests and all had heard about her adventure and all wanted to commiserate, congratulate, or speculate. It took Penny more than thirty minutes to reach the library and both Lady Dalrymple and Mrs Weston were already there.

'I do apologize; I must have been waylaid by a dozen people all wishing to know the details of this morning's accident.'

Mrs Weston had risen on her entrance. 'What a dreadful thing to happen, Miss Coombs. I, for one shall not be queuing up for a ride in that contraption.'

Penny was embarrassed that a lady who was her senior had felt obliged to stand. 'Please, Mrs Weston, do be seated. I have no wish to stand on ceremony; after all we're to be related very soon, are we not?'

'How kind! Edward has always been a favourite of mine. James and he are as close as brothers. When dear Edward's parents were taken in an epidemic of the fever he was up at Oxford with James. It was a difficult time for the family, but both James and I were here to give our support.' She arranged the skirt of her smart maroon walking dress around her feet.

'Shall I ring for refreshments to be served here? It's almost noon and I believe nuncheon will be served in the small dining-room soon.'

Lady Dalrymple smiled at her niece. 'We took the liberty of asking for coffee and pastries to be brought here. We have much to discuss and very little time in which to do it.'

'Then I can relax and join you at the table.' Penny pulled out a chair, carefully smoothing the back of her dress before she sat. 'Now, I see you have paper, pens and ink ready. Who shall be our scribe this morning?'

It wasn't until mid-afternoon that Penny was released from the library. She was heartily sick of hearing about people she had never met, who simply must be included on the guest list. In the end she had agreed to leave this to her aunt and Mrs Weston. She had insisted, however, that the list should be submitted to Edward before the invitations were written.

She had no interest in the details of floral decorations for the ball that was to precede her wedding. Neither had she any desire to be involved with the menu for the wedding breakfast. Both Aunt Lucy and Mrs Weston were more than delighted to take joint charge of everything.

The mantua-maker from Ipswich who made all her clothes had been sent for and was expected to arrive the next morning with up-to-date fashion plates from *La Belle Assemblée* and *Ackermann's Repository* from which she could select her trousseau.

She already had a prodigious amount of new garments which had been made up for her when she came out of mourning for her father. But both ladies had assured her that as a countess she would require even more. With a sigh, Penny hurried upstairs to her chamber determined to escape from the house for an hour or so. She would take her horse for a gallop around the park. This should blow the cobwebs and restore her equanimity. She was descending the second flight of stairs, whip in one hand, the skirt of her riding habit in the other, when she was waylaid.

'Miss Coombs, how are you? I have been hearing from Edward about your exciting excursion this morning.'

'Mr Weston, good afternoon. I am fully recovered and have no wish to dwell on it.' Penny grinned. 'I can assure you anything aeronautical is now very low on my list of enthusiasms.'

'You're wise to avoid them. I have never understood Ned's fascination. If I wish to fly, I jump a hedge.'

'Exactly my sentiments. Pray excuse me, Mr Weston, I'm intending to ride out and do not wish to keep my mount waiting.'

'You must allow me to accompany you. I'm certain that Edward does not wish you to ride alone. Although the militia searched the area one cannot be too careful.'

'If Edward cannot come with me then you would be my second choice.'

The young man bowed and, smiling, offered his arm and they strolled down the stairs and out of the house.

Phoenix was saddled and waiting for his mistress at the foot of the steps. He was plunging and stamping almost lifting the unfortunate stable boy from his feet. There were two grooms standing by their own mounts, obviously intending to escort her.

On her appearance one of the men handed his reins to the other and stepped forward to toss Penny aboard. She turned, smiling ruefully at James. 'There, Edward has already thought of it. You're free of obligation, sir. Thank you for your kind offer, but as you can see I have no need to ruin your afternoon.'

'In that case, Miss Coombs, I shall bid you farewell until this evening.'

Penny watched him disappear back into the house her brow creased. She had offended him; he was obviously displeased at her dismissal. But his mount was not ready – he had not been intending to ride even though he was dressed appropriately. She would have been obliged to wait whilst his horse had been fetched and Phoenix was in no mood to stand.

She shrugged, dismissing the incident. She ran her hand along the gleaming chestnut neck of her horse. 'Shall we go, Phoenix? I wish to go down to the sea? Is that possible?'

Perkins replied cheerfully, 'Yes, miss. If we cut through the park there's a path that leads to the beach. It'll take about half an hour.'

'Then I shall follow you. I don't know my way about.' She gathered up her reins and forced her excited horse to drop in between the two grooms. She thought she caught a glimpse of a pistol tucked into the pocket of the leading man, but dismissed her idea as fanciful.

She did not see the two shadowy figures vanish into the wood and, moments later, gallop away, heading for the bridge that crossed the turbulent river that led down into the creek.

Chapter Eleven

L ORD WESTON SWORE causing a nearby gardener to snigger. He glared and the man instantly lowered his head, tugging his forelock and muttering as he scurried off. Edward had been trying to speak to his beloved the past three hours, but each time he had ventured in it was to be told, 'Miss Coombs is still in the library with the ladies, my lord.'

He didn't hesitate. 'Saddle Bruno,' he shouted as he raced round to the stable yard. Tom coachman had heard his call and the huge bay stallion was already outside the loose box being tacked up by two nervous under grooms.

With a cursory nod of thanks he vaulted into the saddle and was cantering after his errant fiancée scarcely five minutes after she had departed. He already knew where she was heading. Penny's voice had carried and he had heard her question about visiting the sea.

He was glad he had had the foresight to arrange for Perkins and Reynolds to be ready to accompany her if she should wish to ride out. There was no reason for her to suspect that these two men were other than they appeared. After the near catastrophe this morning he didn't want Penny upset again.

He knew exactly the direction she would take and was quite content to catch up with her at the bridge. She was in no real danger. He was just being overcautious. As he cantered through the sun-dappled avenue of trees he was smiling. There was good news for her; Reverend Plum had agreed to read the banns tomorrow at morning service.

*

The three riders slowed to a walk as they approached the narrow wooden bridge that was the only route down to the shore. Penny viewed it with disfavour.

'Phoenix will never cross that. I'd have difficulty persuading him on to a sturdier version. That looks decidedly rickety.'

Perkins dismounted and tossed his reins to Reynolds. 'It's perfectly safe, miss. I've been back and forth a dozen times. Why don't you get down and walk over it, see for yourself how safe it is?'

'Thank you. I'll do exactly that.' She didn't wait for the groom to assist her. She reached up and stroked the chestnut's head. 'You'll have to go across, my boy, if you're to have your gallop along the sand.' The horse nudged her shoulder leaving a trail of slobber down the shoulder of her smart green riding habit. Laughing, she rubbed it off with her glove. 'Stupid animal! Mary will be most displeased with you for smearing my jacket.'

Penny led her mount to the bridge and allowed him to sniff at the railings. 'There, you see, it's just a piece of wood. Now, you stand here with …' She looked at the groom.

'Perkins, Miss Coombs. Me name's Perkins.'

'So, you stand here with Perkins whilst I investigate this evil structure.'

She held on to the rail and jumped noisily startling all three horses. Reynolds, who had been distracted by something he'd seen in the dense undergrowth on the far side of the river, released his hold on his friend's horse and it galloped back down the path. Perkins managed to hang on to Phoenix, but had his feet trampled in the process.

'Buggeration! The varmint – he'll be home before we can catch up with him.'

'Mind yer language, Reynolds. Ladies present,' Perkins snapped.

Penny watched the unfortunate groom turn beetroot and turned away to avoid him further embarrassment. 'I do apologize,' she called over her shoulder, 'that was entirely my fault. I'm afraid I couldn't resist. When I was small my father used to take me to somewhere very similar and we would pretend there was an ugly troll hiding beneath the bridge. Only by jumping up and down would it be safe to cross.'

She heard the men chuckling and knew she had put matters right. She was to be their new mistress in a few weeks and did not wish to alienate the staff before she was even married to Edward. 'I shall walk sedately from one side to the other. I shall not make the same mistake again.'

From her vantage point on the far side of the river she watched the two grooms talking. They were obviously deciding whether it was worth one of them riding back to fetch the missing mount. She heard a rustling in the undergrowth but was not unduly worried. Being a country girl she was well used to hearing small animals in the hedgerows.

She looked longingly down the path that led to the sea. The waves were small, no sign of the huge breakers that had crashed against the beach that morning. A summer storm could be as ferocious as a winter one.

She turned spotting something glittering between the planks and, picking up her skirt, made ready to drop to her knees to investigate. Before she completed her descent the wood under her fingers moved and her heart jumped. Carefully moving into the centre of the narrow bridge, she flicked out the coin trapped in the mud between the planks. Perkins called her and she dropped her find into the pocket of her riding habit. She would examine it more closely later.

'Miss Coombs, your gelding's getting mighty impatient. If you still wish to cross we need to do it now.'

Penny hurried back making sure her boots made no noise this time. 'I think it would be better to leave it. Once Phoenix becomes upset only a gallop will settle him. I don't think it wise to risk the bridge today.'

'Very well, miss. I'll give you a leg up and then we can ride double. Luckily it ain't far.'

Penny quickly rammed her boot into the single stirrup iron before her horse could toss her to the ground. 'I must allow him to stretch his legs. On a single mount you can't keep up.' She saw the groom about to protest. Surely it was she who was the mistress here? 'I shall see you back at the stable yard. I noticed we passed a meadow on the way here; I intend to ride around that.'

Allowing them no time to voice further argument she touched her heel to her horse's flank and trotted down the path. It took all her expertise to retain control. She must keep to a collected canter until reaching the open field.

An overhanging branch whipped through her hair dislodging her hat; she laughed and rode on. Spotting the gate that led into the field she steadied her mount before urging him forward. They sailed over the obstacle with feet to spare. Phoenix felt the soft turf under his hoofs and danced sideways, eager to race ahead.

'Steady, boy,' Penny said, 'we mustn't take it too fast.' She slackened the reins a little and sat deep in the saddle. The horse lengthened his stride, breaking into a canter. She held him there for a few yards until he settled, before lowering her hands and giving him the office to gallop.

Hatless, her hair tore free from its pins and, by the time she pulled up, breathless but exhilarated, it was tangling round her face and hanging damply down her back. Her attempt to push it back from her mud-spattered face was ineffectual. Leaning forward she slapped her mount's sweating neck.

'Well done, boy, that was wonderful.' He whickered, swung his huge head and nuzzled her knee, leaving a second trail of slobber down her habit.

Penny gathered in her reins and clicked her tongue. 'Come along, let's go back to the lane.' She spotted a break in the dense hedge and jogged towards it. The gap was filled by another large five-barred gate, fastened securely with hefty rope. She peered at the knots in annoyance. There was no choice; she would also have to jump out. She leant forward and saw the path beyond was just wide enough for a safe landing.

She trotted Phoenix back, needing to give him the necessary momentum for his leap. Facing at the correct angle, she short-ened her reins, and leant down. 'Right, off we go.' He needed no further urging and broke into an extended canter and they flew into the air to land in a shower of mud, in the narrow lane.

*

Lord Weston, who was leading the missing mount, heard the approaching drum of hoofbeats and reined back, releasing his hold on the second horse as he forced his own hard against the hedge. He was only just in time. Phoenix hurtled through the gap, causing his stallion to rear and shy sideways, knocking him from his saddle and depositing him, headfirst, into the hawthorn hedge.

Penny struggled to keep her seat as her mount, startled to find the lane already occupied, reared, his flailing hoofs adding to the chaos. It was only when calm was restored and she was in full control that the significance of both riderless horses registered. It was Bruno – Edward's mount. Surely such an expert horseman had not taken a tumble?

Then, to her astonishment, the hedge parted and two hands appeared in the gap. 'Whatever are you doing in there, Edward?' No sooner were the words uttered than she wished them back. The language that greeted her ill-considered remark made her ears burn. She reached down, grabbed Bruno's flapping reins, and led him away from the heaving greenery, concerned the horses would take fright again.

She watched from a safe distance, as a head emerged followed by a pair of broad shoulders.

'I can't get free of this damn bush. The thorns have snagged me and I'm stuck fast.'

'As you can see, I'm not in a position to assist you, Edward. But Perkins and the other groom are not far behind me. If you remain still and be patient they'll be here in a moment.' She was having difficulty keeping her face straight. 'The more you wriggle the more embedded in the hedge you become.'

'I'm not standing in here like a tomfool. Take the horses away from me whilst I get myself out.'

Penny watched her beloved struggle, becoming more enraged as the thorns bit deeper. She was relieved to see the horse carrying both grooms approaching at a canter.

'Perkins,' she called, having to raise her voice to be heard over the crashing coming from the hedge. 'Can you get Lord Weston out before he has an apoplexy?'

Perkins slid expertly from behind the other groom. 'You get over there and help Miss Coombs with them horses. Lord Weston, you're scaring the beasts, sir. If you're quiet, my lord, I'll cut away the branches.'

Immediately Edward was still. 'You're right; my struggles are making the situation worse.' Penny watched Perkins unsheathe a knife that was tucked into his boot top and pull his gloves back on. The thorns were vicious and bare-handed he would be severely scratched.

'Hold still, sir, I don't want to cut you.' The groom started the laborious process of releasing his master. This task was only partially completed when the sound of a rider approaching from around the bend in the path was clearly audible.

'Good God! Am I to have an audience now? How much longer are you going to be?'

'Five minutes, my lord, no more.'

'Too long; I am coming out, stand clear, man.' With a herculean effort Edward wrenched himself free, the sound of ripping material made Penny wince. With a final oath he was out. His release so sudden he staggered across the lane and, losing his balance, fell face first in the dirt.

It took all Penny's skill to maintain her precarious grip on Bruno who skittered nervously, thoroughly alarmed by his owner's emergence from the bushes like a rat from its bolthole.

'Steady boys, steady. Stand quiet. Stand,' Penny soothed, holding her hands low and bringing her own weight forward, disturbed by the distinct possibility of Edward's imminent demise, crushed under the feet of plunging horses. Equally worried, Reynolds leant hard on his horse's chest, forcing it into the hedge and away from the man spreadeagled on the ground.

Edward rolled and in one movement sprang to his feet. She saw that his hands were shaking as he brushed the worst of the mud from his garments. She feared he did not trust himself to speak until he had his fury under control. She watched, feeling more worried by the second. It was not all her fault, but she doubted that he would see it quite like that. This was a different man to the passionate and gentle fiancé she had grown to love. He was a stranger to her.

At least aboard her horse she was relatively safe from physical retribution. The red head slowly lifted and she was impaled by a pair of arctic green eyes.

'What the devil were you playing at? Have you taken leave of your senses?' Penny opened her mouth to answer but thought better of it. 'Not only have I been plunged headfirst into a hawthorn hedge, but narrowly avoided being killed under my own horse's hoofs.' He stepped forward, his eyes not leaving hers. She swallowed; was he going to pull her from the saddle?

Edward froze as Mr Weston arrived on the scene. 'This will keep, Miss Coombs. But be very sure this is not the end of the matter.' His severe expression vanished to be replaced by a shiny smile as he turned to greet his cousin. 'James, what brings you this way? I thought you busy playing billiards.'

Penny's fingers slowly uncurled their death grip on the reins. She was safe, for the moment at least. Then it occurred to her that she could make good her escape whilst he was occupied with Mr Weston. Quite forgetting she was clutching Bruno's reins as well as her own, she clicked her tongue and dug her heel hard into Phoenix's side. The huge animal responded and, the riderless horse at her side, she raced off down the lane.

When her brain once more engaged in rational thought it was too late. They had left the others far behind. Penny reined back to a walk, horrified by her foolhardy action at a loss to know how to put matters right.

If he had been incandescent with fury before he would be baying for her blood now. She sat back, ready to continue her flight, but something stopped her. She could not let him walk the remaining few miles; he had suffered two accidents already today.

Reluctantly she turned the horses round and trotted back the way she had come, returning scarcely five minutes after she had left. Edward stood, arms folded, his face impassive. He was talking to Mr Weston but watching the path. How could he have known she would have the courage to return?

She trotted over to him an apologetic smile on her face. 'Lord Weston, I'm sincerely sorry for causing your fall. And I did not mean to take Bruno away with me.' She saw a flash of something in his eyes and prayed it was amusement. 'Am I forgiven, my lord?'

He held out his hand. Nervously she approached him, not sure if she trusted the gleam in his eyes. Penny was forced to stand in her stirrup in order to pass down the reins. She felt something grip her boot and the next moment she was falling headlong into his arms.

'My lord, you must not, we're not alone.'

She had no time to protest further before his mouth covered hers in a kiss that made her forget all sense of propriety. Her arms slipped around his neck and she buried her fingers in the silky hair at the base of his neck. She wanted the embrace to go on forever. It was Mr Weston who recalled her to her senses.

'Cousin, I think I am *de trop*. I shall continue my ride and leave you and Miss Coombs in private.'

Flushing painfully Penny struggled to remove herself from Edward's arms. 'Enough, my lord. Please let me go.'

'Never! You're my life and I intend to keep you by my side until the good Lord sees fit to part us.' His teeth gleamed as he reluctantly released her. 'You're an infuriating baggage who richly deserves to be put over my knee.'

'Edward!' Her horrified exclamation made him laugh out loud.

'This time you're forgiven, my love. Pray do not make a habit of tipping your future husband into a thorn bush if you wish to remain unpunished.'

Still chuckling he turned to apologize to Mr Weston, but he had vanished, along with the two grooms. 'Good God! We must have offended him by our behaviour.' He smiled ruefully. 'I'm deeply attached to my cousin, but unfortunately he has no sense of humour and a far stricter sense of decency than either of us. I shall have to do a deal of sweet talking to bring him round.'

'I like him too. It's strange that you're so similar in appearance but so different on the inside.' She reached into her pocket to find a handkerchief to remove some of the mud from her face and her fingers touched the coin she had picked up earlier. 'Look, Edward. I found this on the bridge. It's not often someone drops a silver coin and doesn't go back to look for it.'

Edward rubbed the mud from both sides and held it up to examine it. His breath hissed through his clenched teeth. 'This is a French coin, sweetheart. There's only one way it could have been dropped on the bridge: smugglers must be using *my* land and *my* beach.'

Chapter Twelve

'SMUGGLERS? HOW EXCITING – if I had known living here was going to be so thrilling I should have made a push to be invited sooner.'

'This is no cause for amusement, my dear. These men are murderous villains – not something from one of your romance novels.'

Penny schooled her expression to one of exaggerated apprehension. She pressed her fingers to her mouth and rounded her eyes before exclaiming, 'Oh, my lord, do not say so! It's gratifying to know that I've a strong protector to keep me safe.' She fluttered her eyelashes at him and saw his lips twitch. She didn't like to see him looking so grim.

'As I said before, my dear, you're a baggage sorely in need of restraint.' He smiled as he pushed a strand of hair from her face. 'Good heavens! You have no hat – no wonder poor James was shocked.'

She giggled. 'I lost it somewhere in the lane. Do we have to go back and search for it, or am I to be allowed to return in disarray?'

'I'm not going back to find a dratted hat. You look like hoyden and I'm forced to say that your behaviour matches your appearance.' Laughing, he tossed her back into her saddle and remounted. 'We'd better return, sweetheart. It's getting late. Let's not add tardiness to our list of faults.'

Two commendably straight-faced grooms were waiting for them in front of the house. Edward vaulted from his horse and was beside Penny before she had her boot removed from the stirrup.

He swung her to the gravel. 'Do you have another evening gown? I think tonight we both need to make a special effort.'

'I have three others, but none I like as well as the green.' She stood on tiptoe to whisper in his ear. 'Please, Edward, don't look round, but there are several faces pressed up against the drawing-room windows. I dread to think what Mrs Weston has been told.'

'Shall we shock them further?' His enquiry was teasing, but she recoiled in horror.

'You're incorrigible, my lord. Dear Aunt Lucy will be mortified at my wanton behaviour.' She stepped away, her cheeks flushed. 'I shall see you at dinner, my lord.' She dipped in a hasty curtsy, before gathering up the trailing skirt of her riding habit and hurrying inside.

Edward watched her go his eyes gleaming with appreciation. Why hadn't he seen how beautiful she was last year? Had he changed, or had she? He nodded his thanks to the grooms and strode into the house. He needed a stiff drink before going upstairs to change for dinner. His mouth curled, causing two footmen to step back in shock at the sight of their master actually smiling.

Nursing a full tumbler of brandy, he strolled across his study to stare out across the park. He needed to think. The silver coin found on the bridge proved beyond doubt that things had got out of hand on his own estate. These free-traders could well be involved in the gold smuggling. He had spent too long serving his country and had been neglecting his own property. This task would be his last for either Nosy or the government. In fact he would pen a letter at once to that effect to Major Carstairs, making his position quite clear.

He was just sanding his missive when he was interrupted by a sharp tap on the door. 'Come in, if you must,' he barked.

'Ned, a moment of your time, if you please.'

'James, come in. I have just finished.' Edward grinned at his cousin. 'I believe I owe you an apology, my friend. You must forgive Miss Coombs and I, we are so recently engaged.'

'No apology needed. It's I who have come to beg pardon for my curmudgeonly behaviour earlier. I have no right to frown on you – you are after all affianced.'

'And we're to wed in less than three weeks.'

James chuckled. 'Not a moment too soon, if you want my opinion.'

'I do not, Cousin. Now, if we're friends again there's a boon I wish to ask of you.' Edward waved towards an empty chair. 'I have reason to believe that an unscrupulous fortune hunter is trying to abduct my fiancée. I find myself inundated with estate business and don't have the time to be with Miss Coombs throughout the day.' He looked across at James. 'Could I prevail upon you to take my place when I'm occupied with other things?'

'I should be delighted, Ned. Miss Coombs and I have already become the best of friends. It will be no hardship to be her companion and escort her when you're too busy.'

'Thank you. I know there are grooms aplenty to accompany her, but I shan't be sanguine unless she has someone I can trust by her side.' He smiled warmly. 'Indeed, if I can't be there myself you're the next best thing.'

James stood up and bowed formally. 'If you'll excuse me, I must take my leave. Mama is expecting me to join her in the orangery for afternoon tea.'

'I shall tell Miss Coombs of our agreement and leave her to seek you out when she wishes to ride or drive into Ipswich.'

Edward folded his letter, sealing it carefully with a blob of wax and impressing his signet ring into the molten material before it cooled. Had he done the right thing asking James to be Penny's close companion? Was there a danger that she would come to prefer the younger man? James didn't have his fiery temper and autocratic manner and was far easier to jog along with. Well – it was too late too repine. He had made his decision and would just have to trust Penny's love was as strong and steadfast as his own.

He frowned as he leaned back in his chair to pull the bell-strap. She was so much younger than him – so innocent and unspoilt. Was it possible that she might compare and find his cousin the better man? His mouth curved in a wicked smile. There was one sure way to prevent her considering anyone else: he could anticipate his wedding night by seducing her into his bed. Then she would never wish to look at another man – his prowess between the sheets was legendary.

'Lawks, miss! Look at your hair!' Penny's abigail exclaimed in horror.

'I lost my hat, that's all. Do I have time to bathe before dressing for dinner?'

'Why don't you have a nice rest until your bath is ready? It takes a while to get the water up here.'

'Thank you, Mary. At least here they have a room especially for the bath and the dirty water does not have to be carried back downstairs as it does at home.'

Her maid deftly removed the soiled riding habit and Penny heard her tutting loudly about the state of it, as she returned to the dressing room. The shutters were open letting the late afternoon sunshine flood into her bedchamber filling the room with warmth and light. Ignoring the silk wrapper Mary had left her, she slipped on to her bed in her chemise and stretching out her bare legs she flopped back in to the waiting pile of pillows.

So much had happened in the last few days her head was in a whirl. She closed her eyes and let her mind drift, trying not to dwell on the more unpleasant incidents. Shivering as she recalled her fear when the balloon had ripped away from the ground. Then she felt a bubble of laughter at the recollection of her beloved headfirst in a thorn bush. She had never heard such profanities.

Smiling she sat up, too restless to remain still. For some reason whenever her thoughts turned to Edward she felt decidedly odd. What was it that made her limbs tingle and her feminine parts glow with anticipation? It was strange that thinking about Mr Weston, who was Edward's replica, had no such effect on her body.

The sound of laughter and clinking crockery outside in the

garden drew her to the window. Hidden in the shadows she peeped out. Under the shade of a large oak tree a table had been laid and sitting round it were Mrs Weston and her son with the Remingtons. Of the three aristocratic couples there was no sign. From her vantage point Penny watched the interplay between the families.

Mr Weston was putting himself out to be charming to the three giggling girls and they were responding accordingly. The two boys were awestruck at being in the presence of such a grand gentleman. She smiled noticing for the first time that Mr Weston's dress was similar to Edward's. He, too, was wearing a navy-blue superfine topcoat with a grey waistcoat and his cravat was tied in an identical arrangement to the one her fiancé favoured.

She heard Mary returning and moved away from the window. She knew very little about Mr Weston's financial circumstances apart from the fact that he was heir to the title if Edward should die without issue. She felt a wave of heat suffuse her at the thought of what might be involved in order for her to produce the requisite heir.

'Mary, guests are still on the lawn taking tea. I think I might postpone my bath until later and go outside and join them.'

'Very well, miss. The water's that hot it will keep warm for a good while yet. Shall I fetch your walking dress with the white muslin skirt and pink bodice? You've not worn that.'

'That's because I find I do not like the banded skirt – I much prefer a plain gown. However as it's in the first stare of fashion I suppose I shall have to learn to admire it.'

Penny hurried across the vast hall, glad she had agreed to slip a rose and white striped scarf around her shoulders for even with the elbow-length sleeves and demure neckline of her gown she was chilled. The sound of heavy footsteps alerted her and she paused to allow Edward to catch up with her.

He arrived at her side freshly garbed in buff trousers and royal blue top-coat. 'Sweetheart, are you going outside to join the tea party?'

'I am. I have hardly had time to further my acquaintance with

Mr and Mrs Remington and this seems an ideal opportunity to do so.' He was standing too close. She could feel the warmth of his breath brushing her neck. Nervously she stepped sideways wishing to put a safe distance between them. He matched her movement. This was too much! 'Lord Weston, kindly leave me room to breathe.'

He smiled down at her and her resistance melted. She swayed forward and his arms enfolded her.

'You're so lovely I cannot resist you.' He took her hand and placed it on his heart. 'Can you feel it, darling girl? It beats solely for you. I have waited ten years to fall in love and I burn to show you just how much I love you.'

Penny spread her fingers, burying them in the snowy folds of his immaculate cravat. He was so tall, so strong ... it was she who was making him tremble with desire. Slowly she raised her face and her lips parted to receive his kiss. Her feet left the floor and she felt a slipper drop to the tiles. She was lost in his embrace as eager as he to share their passion.

Edward, who was facing the open front door saw someone approaching and without putting her down spun round and headed for the privacy of his study.

'Put me down, please. Someone will see us.'

'Guests were approaching the hall, sweetheart. I had to remove us or we would have been discovered.'

'In that case, my lord, we're quite safe here and you may return me to my feet.' He ignored her request and she felt his arms tighten. She was having none of this highhanded behaviour. She pushed firmly against his unyielding bulk expecting him to release her. He didn't. 'Lord Weston, if you don't put me down at once I shall scream.' This remark had some result but not the one she expected.

He chuckled. 'Go ahead, my dear, if you have no objection to being seen as a wanton with no decorum.'

She had no alternative. She had given him an ultimatum and he had ignored her. Whatever the consequences she would not be ignored. Taking a deep breath she threw her head back and screamed as if her very life depended on it.

Edward dropped her to the floor as if she was on fire. As she struggled to regain her feet without his assistance, a gurgle of laughter welled at his expression of incredulity. However the sound of running footsteps and concerned voices approaching made all desire to laugh vanish. Deciding to leave explanations to her fiancé she fell back as if in a deep swoon.

With her eyes closed she could not see what was happening. Edward dropped to his knees beside her as if concerned by her collapse. He took one of her hands in his and she winced at his grip. Then his second arm slipped under her and she was hoisted into the air once more. This time if she was to maintain the pretence of being unconscious she could not protest at his rough handling.

'My lord, we heard the scream. Is Miss Coombs injured?' The anxious voice belonged to one of the guests.

'It was a ghost! Miss Coombs believed she saw a spectre appear at the far end of this passageway which then vanished through the wall. The sight was too much for her.'

Penny almost choked and decided it was time to make a miraculous recovery. He had other ideas and her face was firmly squashed against his chest giving her no opportunity to deny his ridiculous explanation.

She could hear the shocked exclamations and murmur of sympathy. They must think her a veritable pea-goose to believe such nonsense. Disregarding the consequences she sank her teeth into his chest and bit down. She felt him flinch but to her consternation, his arms remained locked around her.

'If you will excuse me, I must carry Miss Coombs up to her chambers in order to recover in more comfort.' He waited politely for his guests to step aside then marched back towards the hall. Even here he did not pause.

Penny had hoped he would allow her to run upstairs under her own volition but this was not to be. As if she weighed no more than a feather, he took the stairs two at a time paying no regard to her comfort whatsoever. She was tossed from side to side and the second time her knees cracked against the wall she squealed in protest.

'Be quiet! I have heard more than I wish from you this morning, Miss Coombs.'

The harshness of his tone and the roughness of his hold told her that this time she had gone too far. She prayed that Mary would be waiting for her in her apartment and not below stairs occupied with laundry and ironing because she knew that without an audience Lord Weston's fury would be unleashed on her without restraint.

Her father had never used corporal punishment when she had misbehaved. However bad her behaviour, he would admonish her verbally and then banish her to the nursery without supper. There she had to compose a suitable apology which would be offered when she was forgiven and eventually summoned to his study.

She knew the man holding her would not scruple to use physical retribution to stamp his authority. If she had not gone willingly into his arms, welcoming his kisses, none of this would have happened. What had possessed her to scream? To bite him? Why had she not lain still and been happy that his quick wit was smoothing over her appalling behaviour?

She felt her limbs begin to shake at the thought of what awaited on arrival at her rooms. She had behaved like a child in a tantrum – Lord Weston could not be blamed for wishing to punish her as he would if she was still in the schoolroom.

He halted briefly outside her parlour, leaning forward to release the catch. He did not push open the door, he kicked it. Penny's stomach churned and she felt scalding tears trickling down her cheeks. She waited to hear her maid rush into the room, but no one came to save her. She was alone with a terrifying stranger and must now face the consequences of her actions.

Chapter Thirteen

PENNY WAS DUMPED unceremoniously on to the small padded sofa that stood in front of the window seat. She shrank back, keeping her head lowered and her eyes closed, waiting for the storm to break. She heard him move away, there were some thuds and then silence.

She remained crouched and shivering for a while, before risking raising her head and opening her eyes. She was met by an implacable icy-green glare. The noises she had heard had been him carrying the chair she kept in front of her desk across the room and positioning it within arm's reach of herself.

She wanted to apologize – to break the interminable silence – but her mouth was dry and her words remained stuck in her throat. She could not look away. She was pinned to her seat like a butterfly to a board. Lord Weston slowly unfolded his arms and began to lean towards her. Panic held her frozen.

'You bit me,' he announced baldly. 'Not even as a child did anyone do that.'

Words finally tumbled from her mouth. 'I'm so sorry, my lord. I've never bitten anyone before. I don't know what came over me. You were holding me so tight and I couldn't speak and … and …' Her voice trailed away and her eyes filled. She gulped, wishing she had the strength to run away and hide.

He began in a conversational tone, no sign of his former anger apparent. 'What do you suggest I do? If one behaves like a spoilt brat should they not expect to be punished like one?'

'Yes. I deserve to be beaten and give you permission to do so.' Her voice was little more than a whisper.

'My dear, I don't need your permission. It's my right to administer whatever punishment I think appropriate.' Penny closed her eyes and waited, not bothering to search for a handkerchief to wipe away her tears. 'However,' he continued, 'I've never struck a woman or child and do not intend to do so now, however richly you deserve it.'

Her eyes flew open in astonishment. 'You don't wish to beat me?'

He smiled, his eyes alight with amusement. 'I didn't say I had no wish to beat you – I said that I wasn't going to. There's a distinct difference, my love. And you would do well to remember it.' He stretched out and lifted her from the sofa. This time she did not struggle. He nuzzled her ear and her pulse raced. Did he have a different kind of punishment in mind?

Placing his mouth directly over her ear he whispered softly. 'Be very sure, my dear, if you ever behave in such a way again I shall not hesitate to administer a spanking that will leave you unable to sit in comfort for a week.'

'I promise I shall be a model of propriety in future.' She wriggled, uncomfortably aware that she was in desperate need of the commode. 'My lord, please could you put me down? I need to go—' She stopped, her face fiery, appalled that she had been about to mention something so indelicate.

Without argument he placed her on the floor. 'I shall wait for you, Penny. There's something we need to discuss before this evening.'

She nodded, too embarrassed to reply. She turned, receiving a hard slap on her bottom to assist her on her way. She heard him chuckling hatefully as she rubbed the smarting area in the privacy of her bedchamber.

She returned to her sitting-room, face scrubbed clean and hair tidy, to discover the room empty. She looked at the bracket-clock and realized she had been absent for almost twenty minutes. Far too long to expect a lord to stand about. Disappointed, she walked to the window to stare across the garden.

It was too late to go down for tea and too early to dress for dinner. She would read her romance novel – it was one that had been recommended by her aunt. It was entitled *Pride and Prejudice* and the librarian had told her that it was very highly thought of by all the ladies who had borrowed it before her.

She was curled up comfortably on the window seat when there was a knock on the door. Before she had time to answer the door swung open and Edward appeared.

'Good – I apologize for deserting you, but I had business to attend to. Put your novel away, Penny, I wish to talk to you.'

Obediently she replaced her bookmark and closed the pages. 'I must beg your pardon for being so long. I was disappointed that you had not waited to speak to me.'

He strolled across and, placing one finger under her chin, tilted her head and brushed her lips with a gentle kiss. 'Sweetheart, may I join you here? Or shall we move to the sofa?'

'There's ample room on this window seat if I sit straight.' She prepared to remove her feet from under her. He prevented her by folding his length into the available space. Then he took her legs and rested them across his lap. She was certain having her limbs so close to his nether regions was not acceptable in polite circles, but she was content to leave things as they were.

'My lord, what is it you have to say to me that is so urgent it cannot wait?'

He ran his fingers lightly across her shins sending shock-waves of delight spiralling up her legs. Should she remove herself from his reach? When he was touching her she was unable to think clearly and was certain if her abigail walked in and saw them, she would be deeply shocked.

'I've asked Mr Weston to act as your escort when I'm unable to be at your side myself. I'm still not certain you're safe from harm. I've important estate business to attend to and cannot spend as much time with you as I should like. I hope this meets with your approval.'

His back was resting in the corner of the embrasure opposite to herself, his booted feet were crossed casually at the ankles and his cream britches clung to his thighs emphasizing their solidity. Penny could not tear her gaze away and failed to answer. She saw his fingers tense.

'This will not do, my love. I shall find myself taking shameful advantage if you continue to look at me like that.'

Her head felt heavy, her neck too slender to support it. Slowly she looked up to meet his quizzical gaze. 'I don't understand what happens to me whenever I'm near you. I feel so strange, as if I have a fever.' Her mouth curved mischievously. 'I'm beginning to suspect that you're making me unwell. Perhaps we should not continue with this engagement? I'm sure you don't wish to acquire an ailing wife.'

'Perish the thought!' Abruptly he pushed her legs aside and stood up. 'As soon as we're man and wife, I promise you, my darling girl, I shall cure what ails you. Believe me, I'm as afflicted as yourself.'

Penny scrambled from her perch to join him. 'You asked me something earlier, but I cannot quite recall what it was.'

'I told you that James will be your escort when I am not available myself.' He smiled and her toes curled in her stockings. 'The matter's not open for debate: it was a rhetorical question. As you are no doubt aware, I'm the lord and master here.'

She dipped in a low curtsy. 'I'm yours to command, my lord.'

'I agree that you're mine, my love, but I'm not sure how true the second statement is.'

'Are you suggesting that I'm disobedient? Surely not! I'm the epitome of docility and would not dare to go against your wishes.'

'As I've said several times before, sweetheart, you're a baggage. I shall see you in the drawing-room at seven o'clock.' With a nod and a wave he was gone, leaving the room feeling empty.

Several days later Penny was waiting outside the house with Mr Weston. They were discussing where to go for her morning ride.

'It's good of you to accompany me, Mr Weston. I'm sure you have better things to do than jaunt around the countryside with your cousin's betrothed.'

The young man bowed his head. 'On the contrary, Miss Coombs. I am only sorry that you have not felt the need to ask me until now.'

The clatter of horses being led around from the stables interrupted their conversation. Billy and Fred, Penny's own grooms, followed behind the stable boys.

Mr Weston stepped forward. 'There's no need for either of you to accompany us. Miss Coombs will be quite safe in my company.'

Billy looked to Penny for confirmation. She nodded. 'We're only riding in the woods. It's perfectly safe and I know that two of our carriage horses need shoeing. Lady Dalrymple and I wish to drive to Ipswich tomorrow so it's essential that the horses are ready.'

'Very well, miss.' Billy touched his cap politely and with Fred close behind returned to the stables.

Penny gathered up her reins, bending her leg to allow Mr Weston to assist her into the saddle. By the time she had the skirt of her dashing green habit arranged and her foot firmly in the single stirrup iron, her companion was mounted and waiting to leave.

Phoenix was, as usual, skittish and eager and Penny needed all her skill to remain aboard. Laughing she called, 'Shall we gallop round the park first?'

'I've a better idea. Follow me.' Without waiting for her reply, Mr Weston shortened his reins and his gelding shot off towards the path that led to the beach. Penny had no alternative, if she did not wish to be left behind, but to follow.

They thundered down the path and it was some time before she realized they were heading in the direction of the bridge across the fast-flowing river. She wasn't sure she wished to go there again, but had no option. She called out to Mr Weston, but her words were carried away by the wind.

Eventually the horse in front slowed its pace and she was able to bring Phoenix alongside. 'Mr Weston, I believe Lord Weston did not wish me to leave the park.'

'He didn't say so to me. I believe his only stipulation was that you remain within the confines of Headingly. Ned's land stretches several more miles in each direction so we're well within the estate.' He smiled. 'However, if you've no wish to continue in this direction, I'm yours to command. Shall we turn back and continue our ride through the woods in the other direction?'

'No, now we're so close it would be a shame not to go on.' Penny patted the steaming chestnut neck of her horse. 'But I must warn you, Mr Weston, Phoenix doesn't like crossing bridges of that sort. You'll have to take the lead.'

'If you wish, you can walk across and I'll lead your horse.'

What an idea! 'That won't be necessary, thank you. If I can't persuade him to take *me* then I shall take *him*.'

They rode side by side chatting companionably, and Penny was glad she had agreed to this excursion. Edward had said there were smugglers using his beach – she had never seen such a person and rather thought it would be thrilling to do so. She was smiling to herself at her absurdity when he spoke.

'Miss Coombs, do you care to share the cause of your amusement?'

'I was thinking that I should like to meet the smugglers who use this beach, which is nonsense, of course. No self-respecting free-trader would be abroad in daytime, would they?'

'Indeed not! What makes you think there're smugglers? I haven't heard that they're in this area.'

'Well, when I was here last time I found a French coin on the bridge. That's proof enough, surely?'

The path widened and the sound of the river racing towards the sea was clearly audible. Phoenix tossed his head nervously. 'Don't be silly; you've nothing to fear. The bridge is perfectly safe.'

'Are you sure you wish to remain mounted, Miss Coombs? Your horse seems a little unsettled by the noise of the water.'

Penny nodded. 'If you cross, I'll follow. Your beast is calm and can set a good example.'

She watched Mr Weston approach the narrow wooden bridge and almost wished that his horse would refuse to cross, that the whole expedition could be abandoned. She was to be disappointed as the grey walked on to the structure without hesitation.

Mr Weston reined in and turned to call back to her. 'Bring Phoenix along now, Miss Coombs. The closer he is to Trojan the easier it will be to persuade him to the other side.'

Penny sat deep in her saddle and urged her horse forward. To her delight Phoenix walked on to the bridge without hesitation. Mr Weston had been correct in his assumption. The grey walked on and she followed. She hadn't realized when she had crossed the bridge on foot that a rider was well above the safety of the wooden railing. She swallowed nervously as she glanced sideways and saw how far it was to the water below.

Phoenix, sensing her unease, stopped and his ears went back. 'Go on, stupid animal, it's only a bridge.' Penny urged him on knowing that her anxiety had caused his hesitation. The horse responded and began to move again. She looked ahead and saw, to her surprise, Trojan had increased his pace and was almost off the bridge. Why had Mr Weston not waited for her?

'Come along, Phoenix, we don't wish to be left behind.'

As she spoke, her horse reared up and lurched sideways. She clung to his mane and threw her weight forward, trying to force him back down. His front hoofs had barely touched the planks when for a second time he whinnied and shied. This time he crashed into the railing and Penny heard the wood splintering. The next thing she knew she was catapulted from the saddle and falling towards the raging torrent below.

Chapter Fourteen

L ORD WESTON WAS not happy. 'What the hell are you two doing here? Did I not give you orders to accompany Miss Coombs everywhere she went?'

Billy turned his cap in his hands, not daring to raise his head and to meet the basilisk stare of his lordship. 'Mr Weston insisted we weren't needed, my lord. He said as Miss Coombs would be quite safe with him.'

'And Miss Coombs said that we should go ahead and take the carriage horses to the smithy as she'll be needing them tomorrow,' Fred chimed in.

Lord Weston ground his teeth. First it was their mistress who ran roughshod over his authority and now it was her minions. 'Get out of my sight.' The two men slunk away, but he called them back. 'Wait! In which direction did they go?'

'Miss Coombs said they were riding in the woods, but that's not the direction they took. I saw them take the path over there, my lord. I'm not sure where that leads to.' Billy pointed and Edward followed his finger.

He smiled. Penny had decided to go down to the beach. It was closer than Home Woods; with any luck he would be able to ride back with them. He shouted to Reynolds and Perkins to saddle up and accompany him. He had not had time to have the area adjacent to the bridge searched for further evidence of the damn smugglers. Now was the ideal opportunity to put that right; he could direct his men and spend time with his favourite person. His wedding could not come soon enough. It was becoming damnably difficult to keep his distance, whenever Penny was in his arms he felt like a stripling again, not the jaded lover he had become.

Mounted on Bruno, his men behind, he cantered across the grass and on to the path that eventually led down to the beach. As they approached the clearing in front of the bridge his eyes narrowed and he pressed his horse into a gallop. There could be only one reason why the railings on one side were smashed. There must have been a terrible accident.

Wrenching his stallion to a rearing halt he flung himself from the saddle and raced to the bridge. Standing precariously on the ruined structure he searched the banks on either side for any sign of life. There were no horses or riders. Desperately he shouted out their names.

'Penny! Penny! Can you hear me? James! James! Are you down there?' His voice ricocheted across the chasm. He received no reply.

Perkins arrived at his side. 'Something havey-cavey about this, sir. Look across the river, them bushes looks as if they've been disturbed, and not by no rabbits neither.'

For a moment Edward was unable to accept the evidence before his eyes. It was too awful to contemplate. One, or both, of the horses had crashed through the wooden side of the bridge and plunged thirty feet into the icy torrent below. He prayed it hadn't been Penny. Wearing a heavy skirted riding-habit would mean certain death. Not even the strongest swimmer could stay afloat dragged down by that weight. Whatever had happened he must be strong and not stand dithering like a coward.

In the few seconds Penny had before she hit the water she was aware that a massive shape was also hurtling down beside her. Phoenix had fallen too. She hit the water backwards, giving her precious seconds to take a deep breath and shut her mouth before the river closed over her head.

She was tumbled head over heels, her skirts blanketing her, pushing her down. Frantically she kicked her feet clawing at the sodden material, trying to find the strength to reach the surface before her breath was exhausted.

She managed to release one hand and, grabbing a fold of skirt, wrenched it down and her other hand came free. She prayed that, with both arms to assist her, she could fight her way up and take a gulp of air. From somewhere she found the strength to resist the deadly pull of her habit and for a brief, lifesaving moment, her face broke the surface of the water.

Only a miracle could save her, she was going to be dragged under again and this time would not be able to swim back up. She drew in what she believed would be her final breath and closed her eyes. As she started to sink she was aware that she was not alone in the river, Phoenix was swimming strongly just ahead of her.

His tail! If she could grab it he would pull her to safety. From somewhere came the energy to throw herself forward and her flailing hands succeeded. She twisted the wiry hair around her wrists and hung on, knowing this was the miracle she'd prayed for.

She was towed behind the powerful animal as he swam, unbothered by the extra weight, towards the bank, her knees bumped against the river-bed and she was safe. Half drowned and frozen she stumbled behind her horse until he stopped.

Forcing her eyes open to see she was kneeling a mere yard from the bank. Had Phoenix sensed that he might injure his mistress by heaving himself out of the water? She attempted to unravel her hands from his tail, but for some reason they refused to function. Was she to perish so close to safety?

'Miss Coombs, Miss Coombs, hang on a moment longer. I shall be with you. For God's sake don't let go.'

It was Mr Weston's voice. She felt her remaining strength ebbing. He was here to take care of her now. Vaguely she was aware of splashing and then two strong arms were lifting her and she knew her ordeal was almost over. She heard him babbling over and over. 'I'm sorry. I'm sorry. I should have jumped in after you but I cannot swim and then we both would have drowned.'

She hadn't the strength to answer. She could no longer fight the blackness that was sweeping over her.

'We must get down there. There's a path that runs along the river-bank on the far side. I shall take that. Perkins, try and find a way down this side. Reynolds, come with me.'

Edward pounded across the bridge his footsteps echoing hollowly on the wood. He knew it would be foolhardy to attempt to take the horses across. Without the support of the railing it might well collapse. With his man at his heels he forced his way through the undergrowth and within moments was on the narrow sandy path.

He ran, knowing every second counted. As he raced he scanned the water and the far bank, but there was no sign of either his cousin or his fiancée. He felt a solid lump of fear settle in his throat. If anything had happened to his darling girl his life would be meaningless. Without her he might as well be dead. He knew with a piercing certainty that if he would never marry another even if it meant his estates and title were forfeit on his demise.

The two men rounded the bend; first he saw Trojan, his cousin's grey, standing unharmed by the river's edge. The pain he felt as he realized the significance doubled him up. He could not go on. He could not bear to know for certain that Penny was dead. He received an ungentle shove in the back.

'No, sir, it's not what you think. Look. Ahead of us. On the bank – it's Mr Weston and he has Miss Coombs safe in his arms.' Reynolds had seen what he hadn't.

Edward straightened his heart exploding with joy. James was sitting on the edge holding Penny wrapped snugly in his topcoat. 'James – thank God! I thought you both dead.' With renewed vigour he bounded towards them. 'She's alive. She's alive.' He repeated to himself, his eyes filling as he sent his thanks to the Almighty.

James shouted back. 'Miss Coombs is alive, Ned, but only just. If we don't get her out of these sodden garments and into the warm she might still succumb to congestion of the lungs.'

'Here, James, let me remove her skirt and jacket. Without that she will be much warmer.' He was surprised his normally quick-thinking cousin had not reasoned this out for himself. 'Penny, sweetheart, I'm here to take you home. Stay awake, my love, you must not go to sleep, not yet, not until you are warm and dry.'

Expertly he unbuttoned her skirt knowing she would have another, made of lighter stuff, underneath. Within five minutes he had removed her outer garments and enveloped her in his own coat. Reynolds steadied his arm as he swayed to his feet holding his precious burden tight against his chest.

'Edward? Phoenix saved me. I should have drowned if he had not towed me to safety.' Her voice was so faint he didn't catch her words.

'You're safe now, sweetheart. I'll have you home in no time.' He turned to Reynolds. 'Assist Mr Weston; he must be exhausted too. You'll have to ride along the beach and come home through the village; the bridge isn't safe for horses. Ride the chestnut, but take it slowly, the poor beast is almost done.'

Knowing that his orders would be followed, he retraced his steps, talking softly all the while, forcing Penny to respond. Perkins was waiting at the bridge to escort him over.

'This is a bad business, my lord, the railings have been tampered with. That's why they gave way. And some bastard was hiding in them bushes. This was no accident, I'm certain sure of that.'

'I half suspected as much. This bridge is regularly maintained. Stay here and have a look around. I'll send more men out to help you and carpenters to mend the railings.'

Reluctantly he handed Penny to his man whilst he vaulted into the saddle. 'Here, give her to me.' He settled her safely across the pommel and nodded. 'Take care; we're dealing with something here that I don't understand. How can the traitor believe killing Miss Coombs will divert attention? It makes no sense, but I shall fathom it out and when I do, I shall kill whoever did this.'

Penny heard his words and knew it was no idle threat. She was so cold; maybe if she wriggled closer Edward's body would warm her. She shifted closer and his arms tightened.

'Darling, keep still, Bruno is not accustomed to a double burden.'

She buried her face in his mangled stock. He smelt of damp and sweat and … she breathed in deeply … yes, she had it now. It was a faint hint of lemon. She loved his smell. She sighed. She loved him – every bit of him. She began to feel far warmer than before. For some reason her blood was racing round her body and she turned her head to gaze up heavy-eyed. His eyes blazed and darkened. His cheeks flushed and then he swore.

'Bloody hell! Don't look at me like that, darling. Bruno will have us both pitched to the floor in a moment.'

She stared longingly at his mouth. She wanted to feel it pressing against her own. She had so nearly died and only his passion could melt the ice of fear. 'Kiss me, darling. I shall not feel safe until you do.'

'I will, my love, but not right now. As soon as we're back and you're warm and dry I promise that I shall be at your side and you shall have your kiss.'

'I'm burning up – and my clothes are almost dry. Couldn't we stop for a while?'

'Don't tempt me! However warm you think you are, I know different. You're frozen; I can feel the cold seeping through my shirt. The heat is an illusion, my dear, caused by your desire.'

Suddenly too tired to argue, she shivered and he drew her closer. She was more asleep than awake for the remainder of the journey and was barely aware of being handed down to another pair of male arms and then being restored to her rightful place.

She heard the murmur of voices, loud exclamations and cries of distress. Was someone hurt? Had there been another accident? She felt the softness of her bed beneath her limbs but did not open her eyes. She heard Mary's voice and felt her wet clothes being removed then she was wrapped in something soft and warm. It was blissful to be so snug and comfortable at last.

'Don't go to sleep, Penny. A bath is being prepared for you and a hot drink is on its way.'

Edward was back. She answered sleepily, 'As long as it's not alcohol, it will be very welcome.' She felt the blanket part and strong hands began to rub one foot. Her eyes flew open. 'What are you doing? Edward, you must not, Aunt Lucy will be here at any moment.'

'I'm showing your maid how to restore the blood to your extremities, nothing indelicate. Your temperature has fallen drastically and without this treatment you could become extremely ill. Your maid is standing right beside me, watching my every move.'

She tried to relax; she was so tired. Being almost drowned was an exhausting experience. Why wouldn't Edward let her sleep? He had a penchant for pummelling her. Gradually a tingling feeling spread along her ankle and up her calf. Different hands took over the task and she was able to relax. It made her feel decidedly odd having him so close to her when she was unclothed beneath the blanket.

She heard her bedchamber door open and close and knew he had gone. Not a moment too soon as Lady Dalrymple hurried in.

'Good heavens, my dear, whatever next! This is your second accident involving water in less than a week. It is a good thing Mr Weston was able to swim out and save you.'

'But he didn't, Aunt Lucy. I managed to grab hold of Phoenix's tail and he towed me to safety. Poor Mr Weston was beside himself with anxiety, but was unable to jump in as he can't swim. I believe we should keep this between ourselves. He's a kind man and I would not wish to embarrass him. He waded out and carried me to the edge; without his assistance I might not have been able to clamber up the bank.'

Lady Dalrymple came round to sit on the far side of the bed, leaving Mary free to continue her rubbing. 'Well, everyone thinks that he saved you and he has not denied it. Although when I think about it he did say that your horse had played a part.'

Penny glanced at her maid. 'Make sure that our version of events is what is talked about downstairs, Mary.'

'Of course, miss. It's not Mr Weston's fault that he can't swim. Not many folk can, and I don't blame them. Water is nasty cold stuff unless it's in a bath tub.' The abigail, her task completed, folded the red flannel around Penny and drew over a warm quilted coverlet. 'There, miss. You stay put until I have your bath ready.'

Penny grinned. 'I can hardly do anything else, wrapped up like an Egyptian mummy.' Lady Dalrymple smoothed the covers and Penny could see tears glittering in her eyes. 'Please, Aunt Lucy, don't be upset. I have had three brushes with danger and death and you know what everyone says?'

'What is that, my dear?'

'That things go in threes, Aunt Lucy. Now I shall be safe.'

'I'm wondering, my dear, if we should return to Nettleford for the time being. No such accidents befell you there. We can return for the ball, of course.'

'And my wedding to Lord Weston? Are you having second thoughts about that?'

'No, but I do consider an engagement of scarcely three weeks is indecently short. Perhaps it would be better to postpone your marriage until later in the year.'

Penny was about to tell her elderly relative that even two weeks was too long. That she was eager to spend her nights with Edward learning how to be a wife, but it would be wise to keep such information to herself – this admission might cause her aunt to have an apoplexy!

'I think you'll find Lord Weston would not allow it. He's determined that we shall be man and wife as soon as the banns are called.'

'Very well, I shall not interfere. By the by, Penelope, Weston asked me to tell you he would be up to see you later this afternoon. You are to send word when you wish to receive him.'

A long soak in hot water completed the job of restoring her circulation. She insisted that she would get dressed again and Mary could not persuade her otherwise. Penny consumed a hearty luncheon brought to her on a tray and by two o'clock was more than ready to see her beloved Edward again. She felt the all too familiar heat travelling around her body as she recalled his promise. Was that why he had asked her to send for him? She shivered in anticipation and wished that she had not insisted on wearing a long-sleeved tea dress with a decidedly demure neckline.

'Mary, I shall not require you any more until I dress for dinner later.'

The maid bobbed a curtsy and with a rustle of starched petticoats and crisp white apron she returned to her duties elsewhere. Penny stretched out on the *chaise-longue*, carefully arranging her skirts to cover her ankles. It would not do to give him too much encouragement.

She was still smiling at the thought, when the expected knock came on her door. 'Come in, Edward.'

Chapter Fifteen

LORD WESTON WATCHED his butler's bushy eyebrows shoot up in shock at his disreputable appearance and decided he had better return to his chambers and put on a fresh neckcloth and jacket. Upsetting Foster had repercussions! The last time he had ignored such a gesture, his dinner had appeared cold for three nights in a row. He had been intending to go straight from Penny's apartment to the stables to get things organized.

'I need a fresh stock and another coat,' he roared, as he entered his rooms. His valet was waiting with both items by the time he got to his dressing-room. 'Make sure Mr Weston has everything he needs. *His* man is totally inept.'

That was as close to a compliment as he got. The valet bowed and stepped back to allow his master to continue on his way.

Edward arrived in the stable yard to discover Phoenix tied to the iron ring outside his loose box. Two stable boys were busy rubbing him dry with handfuls of folded straw. He noticed that the grey James rode was in his box contentedly munching his feed. It had not taken as long as he'd anticipated for them to return along the beach.

Perkins met him, touching his forelock politely. 'My lord, come and look at this. See what you think.'

Edward examined the chestnut horse. There was no mistake. The animal had two deep cuts on his left rump. 'A catapult and stones, do you think, Perkins?'

'Something like that, sir. Poor beast had no chance. With the railings tampered with, when he shied sideways, he would have lost his balance.'

'How could the attackers know Miss Coombs would be riding over the bridge that morning? I doubt they would have hidden there every day on the off chance.' His expression darkened and he glared around the yard. Every groom and stable boy became feverishly occupied. 'We've an informant in this yard, Perkins. There's no other way they could have known.'

He drew his man aside, away from prying ears. 'Find out who it is. It will be one of the younger men, no doubt up to his ears in debt and prepared to take dirty money in order to clear himself.'

Perkins shook his head doubtfully. 'Beggin' your pardon, my lord, but I doubts anyone working here would risk their position for a bit extra. I reckon there's someone watching the stables and the house and it's them what takes the message.'

'I hope you're right. Get the men to check for evidence of hidden watchers, but also make a few discreet enquiries, see if any of the grooms have had an unexpected windfall lately.'

'I'll do that. It's going to be a high tide and a full moon next week. We'll all have to keep our eyes peeled for the next ten days.'

'Indeed. I want four men with Miss Coombs wherever she goes, even when she's in the park. I've no idea why she's been targeted in this way, but until we have captured the traitor and his gold we will have to be extra vigilant.' He beckoned Reynolds over. 'Ride to Ipswich and ask the militia to make their presence felt along the beach and the surrounding area.'

He instructed Perkins to take several men to search around the bridge and sent a message to his estate manager to arrange for the immediate repair of the railings. Satisfied he had done all that was necessary he returned to his study to write a letter summoning Major Carstairs. He needed a second opinion on this matter. For the first time in his life his full attention was not on the task. How could he concentrate on government business when Penny appeared to be in mortal danger? The missive was complete when Foster tapped at the door. At last – Penny was ready to see him.

*

The door opened and Penny felt a frisson of excitement ripple through her already overheated body. She had been in company of other more handsome men, but it was only her darling Edward that made her feel like this.

She noticed her smile of welcome appeared to have the same effect on him. His eyes reflected his desire and she revelled in her power. 'Edward, come and sit next to me. There's plenty of room.' She bent her knees to give him the space he needed.

He shook his head as he ran his finger impatiently around his stock. 'No, sweetheart. I think it would be unwise for us to be within touching distance. I have serious matters to discuss with you.' He collected the same upright chair he had used a day or so ago, but this time he swung it round and straddled it.

Her pleasure in the moment began to fade at his sober expression. 'What is it? Have you more bad news?'

'What I'm going to tell you is in the strictest confidence. It must never leave this room. Both our lives depend on it.'

Penny forgot her coquettish behaviour and placed her feet firmly on the carpet, her face as serious as his. 'I promise, Edward. Whatever you reveal, I shall not pass it on, even to Aunt Lucy.'

'Good girl. I'm not what I seem; I'm a government agent and have been so since my majority. That is why I have never set up my nursery. A man in my position can't allow himself to be distracted.'

'Is that why you left me so abruptly in London? You were called away?'

He grinned ruefully. 'As I'm being totally honest, my dear, I'm forced to admit that I never had any intention of offering for you last season. I used you as cover.'

She stared at him, appalled. She drew breath to comment and he raised his hand in supplication. 'Please, sweetheart, hear me out without interruption. I have more to confess. I wish to get matters absolutely straight between us.'

'Very well, I shall be silent until the end.'

'I selected you from the list of debutantes precisely because you're intelligent as well as beautiful. Even for King and country

I could not spend my time escorting a ninnyhammer. When I was asked to root out the traitor believed to be travelling with this balloon party it was suggested I renewed my association with you, letting people believe that I was about to make an offer.'

She had heard enough. Whatever she had promised she had no intention of hearing any more. She jumped up, tears of anger and disappointment glittering in her eyes. He faced her and she knew he would not let her run away.

'Sit down, Penny. You must hear the whole before you decide if you wish to break the connection between us.'

She subsided her face stony. Whatever he told the next, her mind was made up. She would have none of him. However much she loved him he had treated her abominably.

He resumed his story, his face watchful. 'I'm convinced the traitor is Count Everex.' He rested his chin on his folded arms and fixed her with his penetrating stare. 'I agreed reluctantly to set up a house party and invite both you and Ducray. However, everything changed when I saw you again. Before I realized what was happening I was head over ears in love with you.'

He reached across to capture her hand; she was tempted to snatch it back. 'Please, don't look at me like that. I love you. You're the most important thing in my life. I have already written my letter of resignation and I intend to devote my life to you and any children we might have together.'

Her heart melted. His every word rang with sincerity. How many other men would be brave enough to admit their faults? She sprang to her feet and before he could refuse her she was on his lap with her arms tightly wound around his neck. 'I forgive you, Edward. You used me abominably, but at least it was not for personal gain. And, my love, you have a promise to keep.'

She tipped her face and, as his lips covered hers in a tender kiss, she pressed herself closer. Eventually it was he who called a halt. He stood up, placing her firmly away from him. 'Sweetheart, that's enough. If we continue making love like this I shall lose control. Holding you in my arms is exquisite torture.

I ache to take this to its conclusion – as I'm sure you're aware.'

Penny had no idea to what he was referring. Her knowledge of what actually took place between man and his wife was sketchy. She had seen animals mating but could not credit that the same extraordinary practice occurred between human kind.

'Sit down in the window seat with me, my love. As usual you distracted me and there are still things we must talk of.'

She took the place he indicated and he sat sideways, the tails of his coat flicked aside to rest across his lap. She supposed he did not wish to crease them. When she was comfortable he returned to the subject of his government work.

'As I told you, I'm convinced that the Frenchman is the traitor. It's he who is orchestrating these attacks on you.'

'Attacks? Are you saying that today's incident was no accident? That someone deliberately caused Phoenix to rear and throw us into the river?'

'I'm afraid that I am. Until this matter is resolved I must ask you to stay within sight of the house. The trip to Ipswich tomorrow must be postponed.'

'Of course, I shall do everything you ask. I believe we shall defeat the evil that's stalking us. The count cannot be working alone. Who else is involved in this, Edward?'

'Smugglers, my dear. There are many of them hereabouts and any one would happily slit your throat for a gold coin. Thousands of gold coins are involved in this.'

By the time he had explained everything to Penny she knew exactly what she could do to help.

'Allow me to charm the count; he's a venial man and has already made overtures to me. If I pretend to be interested in his flirtation then it's possible he will inadvertently reveal his true self.'

'And it's possible that he will murder you. I absolutely forbid you to attempt any such thing. It's far too dangerous.'

'I'm not suggesting I promenade with him alone. I thought I could spend some time with him after dinner, and over the supper tray. I'm not a goose. I should do all this in full view of your guests.'

He laughed. 'In which case I agree – you may try and charm some information from him. But, have you considered how the rest of the house party might view your antics? Don't you think they might expect me to call him out?'

'Now you're being silly. I shall do no more than I've seen the other ladies do when they have been conversing with him. A little fan fluttering and a few fulsome compliments was all I had in mind.'

He patted her knees and stood up. 'I must take my leave, darling. Remember what we've spoken about is a secret between us. The gold bullion is expected to arrive before the high tide next week. Until then we must be extra vigilant.'

'Thank you for taking me into your confidence, Edward. I don't believe there's a man anywhere in England who would have done the same. I consider myself privileged to be part of this and blessed to be marrying you.'

She saw him hesitate and his eyes burned with passion, but somehow he found the strength to turn away and did not speak until he was opening the door. 'I'm the luckiest man in Christendom to have such a woman at my side. I promise you, my love, that when this wretched business is over I shall show you just how happy you make me.'

That evening Penny chose to wear the same evening gown that had prompted Edward to declare himself. Then she had been so caught up in the announcement of her engagement, she had been unaware of anyone apart from her fiancé. Tonight it would be different. She felt like an actress in a play; whatever she did would be done by someone else. She was going to perform her part, as an irresponsible young lady, to perfection.

Knowing she looked her best she didn't bother to check her appearance before gliding downstairs, her eyes sparkling with excitement. She could hardly believe that she was the only one who knew the austere and irascible Lord Weston was in fact a government agent. He had trusted her with his secret, indeed possibly with his life and she would not let him down.

What would dear Aunt Lucy think of her behaviour? Her

reputation for being a well-brought-up young lady could well be in tatters by the end of this evening. It did not occur to her that when Edward had agreed to her forming a liaison with the handsome young Frenchman, he had not actually believed she would have the courage to carry it out.

She nodded regally at the two footmen waiting to direct the guests out on to the lantern-lit terrace. Edward had not told her they were to gather outside tonight. She had not brought her diaphanous Indian silk wrap and the deeply cut *décolletage* and short cap sleeves of her gown would offer no protection from the chill of the evening.

She beckoned one of the footmen over. 'Kindly go to my chambers and ask my maid to bring down my wrap.'

The young man bowed and vanished through an invisible door in the wall. She smiled and shook her head. Would she ever get used to the way the staff appeared and disappeared as if by magic? She could hear the sound of tinkling crystal and voices drifting in through the open French doors of the drawing-room.

She walked gracefully across the room, unaware that there was someone watching her with malevolent eyes from the depths of a deep-seated armchair. Yet another uniformed young man bowed her through the door and out on to the terrace. She was not the last to arrive, neither the count, nor Mr Weston were amongst the people chatting and drinking champagne.

'Sweetheart, you look *ravissante*.' Edward took her hands and raised them to his mouth. The desire in his eyes made her knees tremble. How was she going to pretend she was interested in anyone else when she burned for him?

'And you look wonderful, as well. Black and white does not suit every gentleman – but on you evening dress looks magnificent.' She saw his throat convulse and she winced as her fingers were crushed. Instantly he released her.

'I apologize, my love. You see how even a compliment from you affects me.' He pulled her arm through his and led her over to join his guests. All the conversation was about her narrow escape and whether she was fully recovered from her experience. Penny was heartily sick of the subject and was relieved when Edward excused himself and went across to talk to another lord, leaving her to her own devices.

The count had arrived shortly after her and was watching her from the edge of the circle. It was the perfect opportunity to begin. As she drifted towards him James Weston appeared in the doorway and hesitated, as if reluctant to come in. She imagined he was embarrassed, as she was, by all the attention and feared everyone would be talking about his failure to jump in and save her.

She must reassure him that his secret was safe. 'Mr Weston, how are you this evening? As you can see, I am fully recovered from my experience. I'm afraid that the sole topic tonight is of our exploits.' She smiled at him, hoping to reassure him. 'You're the hero of the hour, and no one, not even Edward, will hear anything different from me.'

She saw the relief on his face. 'Thank you, Miss Coombs. You're as kind as you are beautiful. You have no lemonade. Would you like me to fetch you some?'

'Yes, that would be delightful, Mr Weston. You shall find me talking to Count Everex.'

Penny drifted across the terrace, the lantern light making her sarcenet overdress sparkle. She saw her quarry's eyes widen in appreciation as she dipped in a formal curtsy before him. 'Count, I have spent too little time in your company. It's something I intend to address this evening.'

The Frenchman took her hand and raised it to his lips. Penny held her breath. Would he dare to kiss it? As his mouth grazed her knuckles she felt nothing and had to restrain herself from wiping the area on her skirt. Determined not to display her distaste, she lowered her eyelashes and peeped provocatively through them. The count was not the only one to react to this flirtatious gesture; Lord Weston's expression was murderous.

Chapter Sixteen

'My dear, Miss Coombs, I have been waiting with commendable patience for you to acknowledge my existence. I am yours to command.' He attempted to gently guide her away from the main group, intending to continue their conversation somewhere less public.

Penny hid her discomfiture under a trilling laugh. 'La! Count Everex, you speak such excellent English. I would not have known that you are a foreigner.'

'I attended school in England, Miss Coombs. It was this that coloured my feelings for your so beautiful country.' His expression was open but his eyes were hard. She had the distinct feeling that the count had not enjoyed his schooldays. Perhaps that was why he was now collecting money to help Bonaparte.

With some relief she saw Mr Weston returning with her drink and greeted him rather more warmly than he was used to. 'My dear Mr Weston, I'm most obliged to you for fetching my drink. It's so very kind of you.' She saw his expression change to one of disapproval and she knew she had overdone it. He must think her a widgeon to be simpering and preening to every man in sight.

'Miss Coombs, allow me to escort you in to dinner.' Edward's tone was decidedly chilly and the rigidity with which he held himself filled her with a sense of foreboding.

'My lord, I'm acting the part we agreed upon. Was it not our intention for me to inveigle Count Everex to reveal vital information? I'm merely fulfilling my role as your assistant.' She made sure her voice was so low the couple behind them, could not overhear.

She felt the muscles of his forearm relax. 'My dear, I had for the moment completely forgotten your ridiculous suggestion. I wish you had reminded me before you began to flirt so outrageously with someone else.'

'I do believe that you're jealous, my lord.' She squeezed his arm and smiled up at him beguilingly. 'I can assure you, you've no reason to worry on that score. I find his fulsome compliments and touch quiet repellent. It was all I could do not to snatch my hand back when he kissed it.'

'In that case, my love, you're forgiven.'

He had no time to finish his sentence as they had processed into the grand dining-room. Foster had decided to place Penny at the far end of the table, in the position reserved for the hostess – as far away from Edward as it was possible to be. Disappointed that she was unable to continue their *tête-à-tête*, she sat in her designated seat resigned to the fact that whenever they dined in company she would be expected to entertain the guests at this end of the table whilst her husband-to-be did his duty at the other.

To her delight, she discovered that her quarry was to be seated on her right. She would be able to continue her clandestine investigation under the cover of general dinner conversation. She carefully avoided looking directly at her fiancé knowing he would try and discourage her. He had said her idea was ridiculous! By the end of the evening she had every intention of proving him incorrect.

The count was charming and circumspect and revealed nothing of interest. However, Penny pretended to be slightly enamoured and agreed to spend further time with him the following evening. When the final cover was removed and the port about to be placed on the table for the gentlemen, she rose and led the ladies through to the drawing-room. Mrs Remington followed her out on to the terrace, her two giggling daughters not far behind.

'Miss Coombs, we do so admire your gown. Such an unusual

shade for a young woman, but it is the perfect match for your green eyes.' The middle-aged lady nodded vigorously sending her many egret plumes bobbing. 'Who is your modiste? Surely you don't have your gowns made up locally.'

'I do indeed, madam. I should be delighted to pass on her name and whereabouts to you and your daughters.'

The remainder of the evening passed pleasantly and even the return of the gentlemen failed to stop the lively conversation. It was decided that the following day there should be a picnic to the beach, if the weather stayed clement. It did not occur to her to inform Edward of the excursion.

Penny had no further contact with either Edward or the count, but retired to bed her head full of plans for the coming picnic and the ball that was to precede her marriage. Her aunt and Mrs Weston appeared to have matters well in hand and she was happy to leave it to them. She had not seen her elderly relative so animated for years.

'Will you join me for a game of billiards, gentlemen?' Edward asked, as he watched his beloved lead the ladies from the drawing-room.

'If you'll excuse me, Ned, I'm for my bed. After the exertions of this morning I find myself in need of a good night's sleep.'

Edward embraced his cousin. 'Goodnight, my friend. I shall never forget what I owe you.'

'It was nothing. No more than any man would have done.'

Edward turned to the other gentlemen. 'Well, sirs, are you game?'

Followed by Mr Remington, the count, and two others, he led the way across the spacious corridor and into the billiard room. He hoped that he might be more successful than Penny in his conversations with the Frenchman.

'Count, Monsieur Ducray does not join us?'

'No, my lord, he said he had to return to the barn to speak to his men. It appears he received a message earlier that it's likely the balloon is going to require a new valve in order to repair it and he has gone out to confirm this.'

'I'm sorry to hear that. I suppose that would mean the enterprise is stalled for the moment? What will you do if you're no longer needed for a co-pilot in this enterprise?'

'I'm not intending to stay much longer with the party. I have business in London.'

'Is it possible that you can postpone your journey until after the ball? There's always a shortage of eligible bachelors on these occasions. I believe Miss Coombs would be quite put out if you go before then.'

'In that case, I shall accept your kind invitation.'

Edward, satisfied he had achieved his objective, turned his attention to the other gentlemen and soon had a noisy game under way.

It was well after three o'clock when his guests finally staggered off to bed. As soon as the last of them had bid him a drunken farewell, Edward straightened and his eyes lost their glazed expression. He was confident no one in the group had been aware that he was quite sober. His brandy had been surreptitiously tipped into a handsome porcelain vase that stood on a pedestal by the mantelshelf. He'd sent the footmen to bed long ago, so the task off extinguishing the many candles fell to him.

During the evening the count had become less guarded and Edward was sure the man did not suspect him of being any more than he appeared. The smugglers' attempts on Penny's life had to be a cruel diversion. The bastards obviously believed that trying to kill her would take his mind off the next high tide and the prospect of a French ship being able to sail in under cover of darkness.

He made his way to his own apartments on the ground floor at the rear of the house. This meant he could come and go through his own door with no one any the wiser. Pale dawn light was filtering through his shutters when he eventually closed his eyes.

The picnic party gathered in the drawing-room at eleven o'clock. Penny spotted her aunt, resplendent in burgundy cambric, holding court from a high backed chair by the open French doors.

'Aunt Lucy, this is so exciting. I can't remember the last time I went on a picnic of any sort and I've never been on one so grand.' She stared around the small group, which included only the four Remington youngsters and the ladies. 'Where are the gentlemen? Are we to go on this outing unescorted?'

Mrs Remington overheard her comment and called out cheerfully, 'My dear Miss Coombs, Remington did not go to his bed until dawn and he was a trifle bosky. I think the game of billiards continued well into the night and a great deal of brandy was consumed by all.' She beamed. 'I doubt any of them will be abroad before noon at the earliest. We shall have to go on alone; they can join us later.'

Penny frowned. Edward had been quite specific about her not leaving the grounds without his permission and his escort. She glanced around the circle of expectant faces, all eager to leave. How could she explain to them her reasons for delaying? As far as they were concerned, she had been involved in a series of unfortunate accidents. Her aunt believed the attempted ambush had been orchestrated by a fortune hunter, and she had not been told that the balloon and river incidents were more sinister.

She had no choice. She would accompany the group to the beach, but before leaving would write a note to Edward explaining why she had been obliged to leave without him. Good grief! He knew nothing of the picnic, unless one of the other men had mentioned it to him.

'Mrs Remington, did you tell your husband about the picnic?'

'No, my dear, I had no opportunity. I left instructions with my maid to tell him as soon as he wakes.'

Penny looked round the circle of waiting guests. 'Ladies did you speak to your husbands about our plans?' Both ladies shook their heads. 'I'm not sure if we should leave without any of our menfolk to escort us. Lord Weston believes there might be smugglers using his beach.' Penny hoped the mention of free-traders would scare the ladies sufficiently for them to wish to postpone the picnic until later on.

Unfortunately it had the opposite effect. 'Smugglers? How thrilling!' One trilled. 'I have always wished to meet a smuggler.'

'I had no idea Lord Weston lived with such excitement on his doorstep. But he's the local magistrate, is he not?' Another added, her expression animated. 'I'm certain this picnic will meet with his approval. No villain will dare to accost us, knowing where we come from.'

Penny was undecided. She knew what Edward was like when he was angry and she had no wish to be on the receiving end of a tongue lashing, or even worse. Lady Dalrymple settled the matter for her.

'Penelope, you refine too much on this matter. We are travelling on Weston's land at all times, are we not?' Penny nodded. 'Very well, then as the most senior member of this group it shall be my decision. It is a beautiful, balmy day – far too good to stay indoors when we have the opportunity to spend it sitting by the sea.'

Relieved the decision had not been hers, Penny nodded her acceptance. 'I shall speak to Foster before we depart. He can inform Lord Weston for me.'

The sound of carriage wheels crunching on the gravel outside heralded the arrival of their transport. The Remington boys had opted to ride alongside which meant only two open carriages were needed to accommodate the seven ladies.

'Aunt Lucy, will the picnic travel with us, or have you arranged for the staff to be there to greet us?'

'I spoke to Mrs Brown last night and she has the matter in hand. She suggested a suitable spot and will have sent everything we need ahead of us.'

'In which case the butler will already be aware of our plans. Nothing happens here without Foster knowing of it. Excuse me, Aunt Lucy, I shall speak to him myself before we leave.'

Penny rang the bell. 'Please, everyone, go out and get settled. I shall join you very shortly.' A footman appeared in answer to her summons. 'I wish to speak to Foster.'

The elderly retainer appeared with alacrity and Penny made sure the information would be given to Edward as soon as he rose from his bed. There was no more she could do so she hurried after her guests.

All her reservations vanished when she saw who was to accompany the outing. Her two men, Billy and Fred were there and also Edward's men, Reynolds and Perkins. There were two footmen standing behind each barouche which meant a total of eight strong men to protect them. Surely even Edward could not object to her going on this picnic now?

To the sound of several parasols being opened the carriages rolled away. Penny settled back against the squabs prepared to enjoy her outing. She was seated next to her aunt. 'Aunt Lucy, I do hope Lord Weston is not vexed with me for going out without his blessing. He was adamant that I must not go anywhere without his permission.'

'Fustian! You are not married yet, my girl. He has no right to restrict your movements in this way. I must say I had no idea his ideas on matrimony were so antiquated. I thought him a modern man – that he would allow you to be yourself and not insist on his legal rights.'

This conversation was conducted quietly, making it impossible for the other occupants to overhear.

'His motives are good, Aunt Lucy. He's anxious to keep me safe, not cause me any distress.' Penny wished she could explain why Edward was so worried about her safety, but she was sworn to secrecy.

Her aunt sniffed. 'Well, my dear, if you are satisfied with how things stand, then it is not for me to criticize.'

Penny was relieved the subject had been dropped. She turned her attention to the other ladies sharing her carriage. It was only then she realized the Remington family were travelling alone. Her eyes narrowed, angry that her new friends had been slighted in this way. She would ensure that she travelled back with them.

The carriages bowled along the narrow lane screened on one side by a hedge which gave a welcome shade from the sunshine which was already almost too warm for comfort. Glad she had decided to wear her flimsiest muslin and leave her spencer behind, even so she was decidedly hot by the time the vehicles slowed to a walk.

'Miss Coombs, may I speak with you?' Perkins was alongside and his quiet request went unnoticed by all but Penny.

She swivelled in order to hear him better. 'Yes, what is it?'

'To reach the beach you'll have to walk along a narrow path. The carriages can't go much further. Beggin' your pardon, miss, but I'd like you to walk in the centre of the group; that way you have the most protection.'

'Of course, I shall do whatever you suggest, Perkins. I know his lordship trusts your judgement and I shall do the same.' She glanced around nervously. 'Surely with so many men around us we must be safe?'

His expression was not encouraging. 'Them as tried to ambush you had rifles, miss, they can hit their target from a distance.'

Hardly reassuring news, but she was determined not to allow this man's gloom to ruin her day. 'I'm sure between you I shall be in no danger. I take it the path is only exposed on the side that faces the shore?' Perkins nodded. 'In that case if you walk on the other side of us we shall be quite safe.'

The coachman drew the carriage to a smooth halt and the ladies climbed down. Obediently Penny found a spot between the two Remington girls and the small group set off towards the sea.

'I can hear the waves breaking on the shore,' Miss Charlotte Remington squealed. 'I do so love the water, don't you, Miss Coombs?'

'Indeed I do, Miss Charlotte, but I have rarely ventured in to swim.'

'I did,' Miss Remington said, eager to join in the conversation. 'When we went to Brighton last year we all took a dip in the sea. It was most unpleasant and I shall not be repeating the experience.'

Penny laughed. 'I have had more than enough of cold water these past few days and can quite understand your dislike of being immersed.'

With Lady Dalrymple leading the group the short walk took rather longer than it should have done and all the ladies were complaining of sand in their slippers by the time they reached their destination.

'Look at that! How pretty! I should have known Lord Weston's staff would do us proud.' Lady Dalrymple clapped her hands in delight.

Penny slipped past the others in order to see what her aunt was so pleased with. 'Good heavens! Tables and chairs, parasols and cushions! We've every luxury here.' She placed her arm under her aunt's elbow and prepared to lead the way across the sand to the oasis of maidservants and the footmen awaiting them at the water's edge.

'She's gone where? God damnit! A bloody picnic! After all I told her about staying close to the house she's taken all the ladies on a bloody picnic!' Lord Weston was not amused. In fact he was furious. The last thing he wished to do was gallivant down to the beach and eat a picnic.

Chapter Seventeen

PENNY FOUND IT hard to relax and enjoy herself. She expected Edward to arrive at any moment in a frightful temper. Perhaps if she spoke to Perkins, made sure he knew she'd had no choice in the matter, *he* could explain it to him.

She leant across to speak quietly in Lady Dalrymple's ear. 'I'm going to find Perkins. I shall be back before they serve the food.'

Her aunt knew why she was anxious. 'Go ahead, my dear, you are as jumpy as a kitten at the moment. I shall be perfectly content sitting here watching the others paddle.'

The beach was uneven and several times Penny lost her footing and her slippers were soon full of sand. There was nothing for it. She would have to remove her stockings and shoes as the other ladies had. She sat down on a convenient tussock of sea grass and surreptitiously slid one hand along her ankle until her questing fingers reached the ribbon. Deftly untying it she rolled down her right stocking and took it off.

She was in the process of removing the second when she heard the sound of male voices and the thud of hoofbeats in the sand. Too late! The gentlemen had arrived. Hastily restoring her skirt so that it covered her feet she stood up, her rolled-up hosiery tucked into her slippers. It wasn't Edward: it was the count. Her broad smile of relief, that she might still have time to speak to Perkins, was misinterpreted.

The Frenchman rode his mount so close to Penny she was obliged to take a hasty step backwards, allowing him to see her bare feet beneath the hem of her dress. He dismounted with his customary elegance and, using the bulk of his horse to screen them from prying eyes, bowed low. As he straightened, he ran his eyes from her toes to her crown, a lascivious gleam in his eyes.

Now what had she started? She was mindful to give him a sharp set down for his effrontery, but she did not wish to appear standoffish. Perhaps this would be the perfect time to discover his intentions. Gritting her teeth, Penny returned his bow with a deep curtsy, remembering too late that her dress was cut low across the bosom and today she had discarded her *fichu*.

Her face flushed. She was not finding this dissembling to her taste. She wished she had never offered to charm this man for she believed she was in danger of becoming embroiled in something unsavoury.

'My dear Miss Coombs, may I say how enchanting you look today. Have you been dipping your pretty toes in the sea?'

'I was just about to do so, sir, when you interrupted me. Could I ask you to remove your horse?' She did her best to simper like a silly debutante. 'The smell, you know, a trifle overpowering in this heat.'

Instantly apologetic for his lapse in manners, the count led his sweating mount away promising to return immediately. This small reprieve gave Penny the opportunity to pick up her skirt and run down to the waves and mingle with the other ladies. Surely here, she would be safe from his attentions?

The grey water of the North Sea was cold and brought back unpleasant memories of the near fatal balloon incident. How could the other ladies walk around as though they were enjoying it? 'Ladies, this is far too unpleasant for me. I am returning to sit with Lady Dalrymple. The picnic is being set out on the tables as I speak so please join me as soon as you're ready.'

Her feet were coated with sand by the time she reached her aunt. She scowled down at them, wishing she had not agreed to come on this excursion.

'Penelope, do not frown, my dear, it does not suit you.' The old lady chuckled. 'I believe you had forgotten just how much you dislike having sand between your toes. Sir John and I never brought you to the beach for that very reason. That is why I insisted that the picnic be set out on the grass.'

Penny dropped into the chair beside her aunt before answering. 'I do remember, now you mention it, Aunt Lucy. I sincerely hope Mary has brought the wherewithal to remove this unpleasant gritty substance from my feet.'

Before she had finished her sentence she saw her maid, accompanied by a footman carrying a bamboo screen and another, with a jug and bowl, approaching her. Everything had been thought of.

'Mary, I can't tell you how pleased I am to see you. The sooner my feet are clean the happier I shall be.'

The screen was positioned around her chair giving her the necessary privacy whilst her feet were washed and dried. It was unfortunate that this also hid her from view.

Edward glared at his unfortunate butler. 'How long ago did the ladies leave, Foster?'

'They left at eleven o'clock, my lord, over an hour ago.'

Edward's jaw tightened. He did not need his butler to tell him how long had elapsed. 'Are any of the gentlemen about yet?'

'They are, my lord. They're in the breakfast parlour.'

Edward strode down the corridor determined to inflict the misery of a picnic on the rest of his guests. The footman waiting by the door scarcely had time to open it for him. The room was full of the sound of clattering cutlery and loud conversation.

'Good morning, gentlemen. Did you know that our ladies have taken themselves out for a picnic on the beach?'

One nodded, his mouth too full of ham and coddled egg to answer, another shrugged as if not surprised by the news. It was Mr Remington who eventually spoke.

'Yes, my lord, and we're all aware that we shall be obliged to join them there. I'm in no hurry to do so, I can assure you.'

A general murmur of assent greeted this remark. Glad he was not the only one who found the notion repellent. Edward grinned. 'Unfortunately we must make a move quite soon if we are to arrive before the tide turns and the picnic party is obliged to return.' Then he noticed one of their party was missing from the table.

'James, have you seen the count this morning?'

'I saw him heading for the stable a while ago. Perhaps he is more fond of picnics then the rest of us.'

Edward frowned. He didn't want that Frenchman anywhere near his fiancée, but he could hardly dash off having said his guests had time to finish breaking their fast before leaving. Hiding his disquiet, he strolled across to the groaning sideboard and selected a few slices of ham and some bread. As soon as he was seated a footman came over to fill his cup with coffee.

'Have you heard about the ball and garden party that I'm holding to celebrate my marriage?' He smiled around the table and received looks of commiseration. 'It won't be so bad, you know. At least Lady Dalrymple and Mrs Weston are not insisting on costume.'

Mr Remington tossed his napkin on the table. 'I cannot abide being obliged to dress up like a Roman or some such nonsense. But, we aim to please our ladies. Weston, you're a lucky man. You have found the perfect match.'

'Thank you. I'm well aware of my good fortune. I had no intention of marrying until I met Miss Coombs.' He looked a little shamefaced as he continued, 'And even then it wasn't until we renewed our acquaintance that I was sure I had made the right decision. I'm a lucky man indeed that she was prepared to give me a second chance.'

'Not giving her the opportunity to change her mind, Weston. And I don't blame you – I'd not let such a delightful girl get away either.' Mr Remington pushed back his chair and prepared to leave the breakfast parlour.

'Shall we convene outside in twenty minutes, gentlemen?' The assembled guests nodded in agreement.

It was nearer the half-hour before the horses cantered out of the park following the lane that the carriages had taken previously. Edward knew that his men had accompanied the ladies to the beach and was feeling more sanguine about the whole episode. Penny could come to no harm surrounded as she was by ladies. He smiled grimly. It would be hard for even the most skilled of marksmen to distinguish his beloved from a group of other similarly dressed women.

The place that had been selected for the picnic was ideal. It was a secluded part of the coastline only accessible by this one path and no self-respecting free-trader would dream of landing his contraband in such a place. In order to reach this particular beach they would have to lead their donkeys within a few hundred yards of Headingly.

He felt almost carefree as he led the group along the narrow lane. Captain Smith and his militiamen had patrolled the shore and found nothing untoward. There were rumours in the coastal villages about an expected visit from a ship bringing French brandy and other illegal items, but so far his spies had not discovered the exact date or whereabouts of this event.

He had spread his net wide and found no trace of any gold or talk of strangers in the vicinity. When they came, he was ready for them. He was determined to complete his last mission successfully, then could devote the rest of his life to being a husband and father.

He pulled up and turned in his saddle to speak to the four men riding behind him. 'Shall we complete this journey along the sand? The tide is out and sand will be perfect for a gallop.'

'Excellent notion, Weston. My mount is fretting to stretch his legs,' Mr Remington called back. A chorus of agreement followed from the other three.

'Follow me. The path is steep but manageable.' Edward turned Bruno into a narrow gap between the bushes and moments later emerged on to the shore. His horse threw his head up and danced sideways in eager anticipation of the treat to come.

Edward held him back until they reached the wet sand. He glanced over his shoulder to check that all his party were safely behind him before giving Bruno his head. He had defied convention and rode bareheaded. The wind whipped through his auburn hair and his eyes streamed. He scanned the beach ahead, looking for the ladies.

Yes! They were exactly where he'd been told they would be.

Safely ensconced on the grass that ran along the edge of the sand. The thick hawthorn hedge sheltered them from the wind and also from being seen by anyone lurking in the boggy land that ran behind it. He stood in his stirrups, ready to wave to Penny, but couldn't see her.

He saw the other ladies picking their way back towards the tables and chairs; saw Lady Dalrymple talking to one of the maids, but there was no sign of his betrothed. He'd seen the bamboo screen, but in his frantic search had not recognized its significance. Where the hell was she? And, more to the point, where was that bastard Everex?

He realized that Perkins and Reynolds were missing also. This was not good. In fact it was very bad indeed. His heart hammered in his chest and he kicked Bruno hard, urging him faster. He had temporarily forgotten he was being closely followed by four other riders.

Penny heard the galloping horses and jumped up upsetting both the basin and the screen. The chambermaid attempted to grasp it and managed to catch one corner. A sudden gust of wind lifted it into the air and with a scream of despair the girl was forced to let go.

Penny watched in horror as the flimsy object flew across the beach directly in the path of the approaching riders. Why Edward had chosen to arrive so precipitously she had no idea, but given the speed he was travelling the result was inevitable.

Bruno seeing the screen flying towards him swerved side-ways and leaped into the air. His rider flew in the opposite direction. In the resulting confusion Mr Remington and Mr Weston were the only two lucky enough to remain in the saddle.

With her fingers pressed over her mouth to hold back her laughter, Penny stood and watched knowing it would he fool-hardy to venture nearer. Edward was already on his feet and was attempting to ring out the water from his jacket. His two friends were similarly occupied. What was wrong with Mr Remington and Mr Weston? Why were they both doubled up across the necks of their horses?

They were laughing. She was shaking, tears streaming down her cheeks when the other ladies joined her. Unable to speak through her giggles she gestured wildly towards the group of gentlemen; three wet and horseless, the other two incapable with mirth.

'Good heavens! Whatever next! My husband never falls from his horse.' The lady showed no inclination to rush forward and offer her spouse comfort in his hour of need. 'I do hope he will not wish to sit by me now he is all wet and sandy.'

The second shook her head in disbelief. 'How did that bamboo screen end up so far away? It's most vexing – I have no wish to replace my stockings without a modicum of privacy.'

Lady Dalrymple called down from her vantage point on the grass above them. 'The wind took it, my lady. It was that, that caused the horses to unseat their riders. Penelope, shall I send a footman to recover it?'

Through her splutters Penny managed to answer, 'I doubt if it will be any use, but we cannot leave it to spoil the beauty of shore, so yes, please send someone.' Her voice shook as she added, 'I should ask for a volunteer, Aunt Lucy. Tell them, whoever is brave enough to go down there and collect it shall be well rewarded.'

She turned to the group of interested spectators. 'Ladies, I think it would be wise to go and seat ourselves at the tables. Let us leave the chairs down here on the sand for the gentlemen.'

By the time they were settled she could see that Perkins and Reynolds had rounded up the three loose animals and the gentlemen were remounted and heading in their direction. She was grateful to be surrounded by guests and staff. Edward was too much the gentlemen to make his displeasure known in public.

It wasn't her fault he had taken a tumble. If he had been travelling at a suitable speed and not thundering down the beach as if he was leading a cavalry charge, none of this would have happened. As the lemonade was being passed around the tables she noticed that one of their number was still absent. Where was Count Everex? She could hardly credit that he had not appeared to join in the general amusement.

'Mrs Remington, have you seen the count anywhere? He arrived some time ago and spoke to me before leaving to tie up his mount.'

'No, I'm sorry, I haven't.' The older lady smiled. 'I expect Charlotte will know where he is. I believe she has developed an infatuation for him.' She turned to speak to her daughter who was sitting on her right. 'Lottie, did you by any chance see where the count vanished to?'

Her daughter blushed and looked uncomfortable. 'Mama, I don't know if I should mention it, but I saw him take his horse behind the hedge.'

Mrs Remington looked puzzled. 'Why should you not mention that, my dear? Is there something you're not telling us?'

The girl nodded. 'I shall whisper it to you.'

Penny watched the girl's head disappear inside the brim of her mother's bonnet. Although Charlotte whispered Penny heard quite clearly what she said.

'He did not go alone, Mama, one of the girls went with him.'

Mrs Remington's shocked exclamation caused several interested heads to turn their way. 'How scandalous! And I thought him a well-behaved young man.'

The conversation was rudely interrupted by the arrival of three wet and disgruntled gentlemen accompanied by two others, who were dry and in the best of spirits. Lord Weston dropped on to one of the slatted chairs the ladies had left ready for them.

Penny observed him hold out his boot to Perkins who tugged it off. The boot was full of water. She watched as the second Hessian was removed and this too was solemnly emptied. She felt a bubble of laughter welling up inside her. She tried to stifle it by clasping her napkin over her mouth, but the ridiculous sight of her top-of-the-trees fiancé reduced to such a state overcame her. Edward obviously heard as he instantly swivelled. Her desire to laugh trickled away like sand through her fingers as she met his fulminating glare.

Chapter Eighteen

LADY DALRYMPLE HAD no such qualms. Her bark of merriment was clearly audible to the three wet gentlemen. Penny couldn't stop herself from joining in. Soon the entire table was hiccupping and spluttering. Before long the laughed at were laughing too.

Edward made no attempt to replace his boots or stockings but handed them, to Perkins. 'Get these dried out a bit before I return.' He grinned, looking years younger. 'Try hanging them over the hedge.' He rose and sauntered up the sandy incline and nimbly hopped on to the grass platform upon which the giggling group of ladies were seated.

Penny stood up and came to meet him, ignoring the interested spectators. 'My lord, I'm sorry you took a tumble and am relieved that no more than your clothes were damaged.'

'Apart from my pride, of course.' He held out his hands and she placed hers in his feeling the rasp of sand on his fingers.

'Why were you in such a hurry? Were you racing each other?'

He lowered his head in order to speak directly into her ear. 'No, my love, we were not. I became anxious about your safety and I could see neither you nor the Frenchman.'

She blushed. 'I was behind the screen ridding my feet of this wretched sand and the count went behind the hushes with one of your maids.'

'I am relieved that it wasn't you.' His tone was playful but she detected a clear warning in his eyes. 'However, the girl shall be dismissed.'

'But …' His raised eyebrow and slight shake of his head made

Penny reconsider her protest. Plenty of time to discuss some things when they were in private. Instead, she grinned down at his bare feet, now liberally encrusted with sand. 'I believe we're a matching pair, my lord.' In her hurry to reach the sanctuary of the picnic tables she had not waited to replace her hosiery.

'Good grief! Now we're an encampment of vagabonds indeed.' Chuckling he gestured towards the hedge from which three pairs of men's stockings were hanging.

'Come and join us, my lord. After all the excitement you must be ravenous.'

The outing was declared a resounding success by all who attended, even the three fallen riders. The party reached home in good spirits by mid-afternoon and then returned to their various apartments to change.

Penny promised to join her aunt in her private parlour later, before changing for dinner, in order to finalize details of the celebrations that were being held to mark her nuptials. Edward was organizing the ceremony itself, and the wedding breakfast that would follow, and she was happy for him to do so.

She could hardly believe that in just over two weeks she would be a countess: Lady Weston – no longer plain Miss Coombs. However, she knew she must concentrate on helping Edward to catch his traitor and put all frivolous thoughts about parties and balls to one side until this matter was concluded successfully.

Having removed the hateful sand from her person, she allowed Mary to dress her in a favourite half-dress of pale blue and light sarcenet, shot with white. Both the back and front of the bodice were of a particularly delicate white lace that had come all the way from Brussels and she knew she looked her best in it.

'Put out the rose-pink silk gown for tonight, Mary. It is the only one I haven't yet worn.'

Still having three-quarters of an hour before she was to present herself at her aunt's chambers, Penny decided to seek out Edward. There was the matter of the misbehaving maid to be discussed before he had her sent away without a reference.

It was so unfair! The poor maid might well have been given no choice in the matter and yet it was she who would carry the blame. The detestable count would continue to behave disgracefully and no one would think the worse of him. Which room should she investigate first? Edward could be in his study, library, or perhaps playing billiards with the other gentlemen. She heard voices approaching from the direction of the billiard room.

'Mr Weston, how delightful to see you. Have you just left Lord Weston, by any chance?'

He bowed. 'No, Miss Coombs. I believe he's dealing with his correspondence in his study.'

'Thank you. I shall seek him out there.' She smiled at the lanky Remington boy who was with him. 'I shall see you both in the drawing-room before dinner.'

Outside the study she hesitated. If Edward was busy, would it be wise to interrupt him? Yes – she believed he would be pleased to see her. She was always thrilled when he appeared, and hoped that he felt the same. She knocked and receiving no immediate reply, rapped more sharply. This time he responded.

'Come in, if you must.'

This was the one occasion when she would have liked to have been accompanied by a footman. She turned the handle and stepped inside. Edward was sitting at his desk, papers spread all over the surface. His brow was furrowed and he didn't look up.

'Edward? Should I go away? I shan't mind if you are too busy to speak to me at the moment.'

Instantly he was on his feet, his face transformed with pleasure. 'Darling girl, I'm always pleased to see you. I must apologize for my rudeness. I didn't know it was you disturbing me.' He led her to an armchair positioned close to the desk. 'Sit here, you can be my muse.'

'Have you had bad news from London? Mr Weston said you were dealing with correspondence.'

'Not bad news, exactly. But you're right, it is from London. Major Carstairs is unable to join us. He's been sent to France. I shall have to sort this out without his expertise.'

'I'm here to help you, Edward. I intend to continue my ploy

with the count tonight.' Her mouth pursed in disgust. 'I can assure you I'm not relishing my role after his disreputable behaviour this afternoon.' She thought she had introduced the tricky subject of the maidservant rather cleverly.

'I've had a word with him. He will not step out of line with any of my staff again.'

'I'm glad to hear it. And the girl? What of her?'

'I left the matter with Mrs Brown. It's up to her if the girl is dismissed. I have no further interest in it, and neither should you.' He was perching on the edge of his desk, his legs crossed casually. His next words took her by surprise. 'I absolutely forbid you to spend any time with the count. I'm certain he's the traitor. Your involvement is at an end.'

Penny lowered her eyes demurely, the picture of innocent obedience. He was not fooled for one moment. She found herself hemmed in by his arms resting on either side of her chair.

'I mean it, Penny. That man's dangerous: surely you saw him for what he is this afternoon? I want your word on this.'

She ventured a glance upwards and met his steady gaze. The protest she had been about to make remained unspoken. An all too familiar heat flooded through her. She saw his expression soften and he dropped to his knees in front of her. Stretching out she traced the outlines of his face with her fingertips loving the way he trembled under her touch.

Her eyes were huge; her lips parted expectantly waiting for his kiss. His hands came up to cover hers, pulling her gently from the chair.

'This is madness, my love. I vowed to keep my distance until we're married, but when you look at me like that I can't resist you.'

Penny sighed and settled herself into his arms, breathing in his musky male scent. His arms tightened, pressing her breasts hard against his chest. Her head was spinning, her reserve rapidly breaking down as her desire spiralled out of control.

She buried her fingers in the hair that curled just above the high collar of his waistcoat. Tilting her head back she waited for his lips to cover hers.

'No, darling, we must not. Once I start kissing you I'll not be able to stop.'

His hands gripped her arms and she was lifted to her feet and placed firmly away from him. For some reason he turned his back on her and marched over to stare out of the window.

'Go away, sweetheart. I shall see you at dinner. I have work to complete.'

She stared at his back, not sure if she was vexed or puzzled by his bad manners. She sniffed loudly. 'Very well, Lord Weston. I shall go. Please do not bother to bid me farewell.'

His rich laugh filled the room. 'Out – immediately, before I change my mind and it will be a different kind of work that we complete together.'

Scampering from his hateful laughter she arrived pell-mell in the Great Hall severely startling the butler and two footmen. Skidding to a halt she attempted to look dignified, but was sure her hair had begun to come down and her cheeks were decidedly flushed. Ignoring the three of them she sailed past and ran lightly up the stairs.

As soon as she was out of sight she paused to straighten her skirts and re-pin the errant strands of hair that had escaped during her time in the study. Satisfied she was tidy enough to visit her aunt she headed up the second flight of stairs to arrive exactly on time at Lady Dalrymple's sitting-room.

'I shall be late, Mary. There's nothing we can do about the neckline.' Penny stared dubiously at the unnecessary expanse of creamy white flesh that was exposed by her evening gown. 'I don't remember this gown having such a low *décolletage*. I shall feel half naked going down in this.'

'The garnet necklace fills a deal of the space, miss. And the matching string of stones I've threaded through your hair look a treat. That pink sets off your dark hair and makes your eyes sparkle. I'm sure everyone will notice.'

Penny rather thought it was her bosom that was going to be noticed, especially by the gentlemen. She enveloped herself in the matching wrap; at least she could remain hidden until they went into dinner. If she refused a drink, she would not have to allow her shawl to slip down to her elbows.

She met the Remingtons in the passageway and their unaffected good humour made her forget about her low-cut evening gown. The two girls were dressed identically in diaphanous white sprigged muslin. Dainty white evening slippers peeped out from below their flowing skirts.

Charlotte spoke for her quieter sister. 'Miss Coombs, that's a beautiful gown. Mama will not allow Elizabeth and I to wear any colour. She says colours are unsuitable for girls of our age.'

'Thank you. Miss Remington. I also spent a season dressed entirely in white and pastels. However, now I please myself.'

Penny smiled inwardly as she led the procession down to the drawing-room. She was sure that the Remington girls were only a year or two younger than herself. Obviously her status as a future countess gave her added maturity in their eyes. She dreaded to think what the reaction would be when she removed her wrap.

When dinner was announced Edward took her arm and they walked together into the dining-room. It was the first time that evening they had had the opportunity to speak privately.

'You look enchanting tonight, my dear. That colour is perfect on you. If I had known you were wearing that gown I would have given you something more suitable to wear around your neck.'

'These garnets belonged to my mother, Lord Weston. I am quite content to wear them and require nothing else.' Her voice reflected her hurt at his disparaging remark. He had no time to beg her pardon before they were ushered, as always, to either end of the long table.

Penny sat down first and, still smarting from his thoughtless comment, dropped her shawl revealing for the first time just how low her dress was cut. She raised her head and stared down the table defiantly. She was a woman grown, the other ladies had gowns as revealing as hers.

Edward regretted his casual criticism as soon as he had spoken, but was given no opportunity to put matters right before he took his place at the head of the table. He had not meant to cause distress – the garnets were lovely but the family rubies were even better. In fact, he would fetch the rubies from the safe in his rooms and give them to her before she retired for the night.

He glanced down the table and his jaw dropped with incredulity. Sitting facing him was the most beautiful woman he had ever seen. How could the young girl he'd first met have metamorphosed into this amazing creature? It was not just the deep neckline, nor the sophisticated hairstyle – it was something else. Penny was staring at him with a look of such disdain he felt his toes curl in his shoes.

He was a lucky man; looking as she did she could have anyone she wanted. The servant had already filled his crystal glass with claret and he raised the glass and toasted her. It was a gesture that acknowledged her beauty and that she was a woman grown. A woman well able to run his home and raise his children.

He knew that his relationship with her was changed. From this point forward he would treat her as an adult – allow her to have an opinion of her own. His mouth curved involuntarily. What was he thinking? His darling girl was already quite capable of making her feelings known. He bowed his head, then placed the glass against his lips, holding her captive by the power of his gaze.

She reached out to slowly bring her own glass to her mouth, there was an uncomfortable tightening in his trousers as she pressed the rim to her lips, returning his salute. He wanted to slam his chair back and carry her to his bedchamber. So much for his vow to keep his distance!

There was a presence at his left shoulder and he glanced round, Foster wished to speak to him about the wine. When he looked back, his eyes narrowed and his face assumed a look of such ferocity that the lady, who was seated on his left visibly recoiled.

God damn it! Why hadn't he thought to rearrange the table seating and put that bastard Frenchman well away from Penny? If that man had the temerity to touch so much as a hair on her head he would not wait until he was certain he was dealing with a traitor but would kill him now. Someone touched his elbow and he was obliged to transfer his attention from the far end of the table.

'Weston, have no fear my friend. Miss Coombs will not be taken in by that man. Remember she is your hostess and it is her duty to entertain your guests.'

Edward ground his teeth, biting back a pithy retort. Forcing himself to relax he smiled at his neighbour. 'Of course, my friend, you're quite right. I must learn to trust her judgement.'

'Your fiancée is a beautiful young woman, my lord, it's inevitable that she will attract the attention of any gentleman who is not in his dotage.' The lady next to him gestured with her fan. 'See how she shines like a beacon at the end of the table. I can't believe it's the same quiet girl who had her come out only two seasons ago. She is a diamond of the first water, an incomparable.'

Mr Remington chuckled. 'If Miss Coombs was making her debut now, you wouldn't have had a chance, my friend. I've no doubt she could have had a duke, or a marquis at the very least.'

Edward knew himself to be a fortunate man. He had won her heart and couldn't see why she had stayed true to him after his callous treatment. He didn't deserve her love, but by God, he was going to keep it. Hostess or not, if either the Frenchman or his cousin paid her too much attention they would have him to deal with.

The dinner was served *à la Français*, the dishes placed down the centre of the table allowing the gentlemen to serve the ladies either side of them with the choicest morsels. There were several removes and by the time the fruit and nuts arrived, Edward noticed it was full two hours since they had sat down. He had kept his basilisk stare on the far end of the table and was certain nothing untoward had taken place between his beloved and the Frenchman.

He smiled at Penny as she rose gracefully, preparing to lead the ladies into the grand salon. As she swept past him, she glanced in his direction giving him a saucy wink. He raised an eyebrow and he heard her delighted chuckle as she left the room. He decided the gentlemen would not linger over the port tonight. He wished to slip along to his apartments and find the ruby parure that had been in his family for generations. Before Penny retired, he would draw her to one side and present her with the jewellery.

Less than half an hour after the ladies had left, Edward pushed his chair back, cutting short the conversation about the relative merits of a high-perch phaeton against a racing curricle.

'James, I have some urgent business to attend to, would you be so kind as to take the gentlemen through?'

His cousin smiled. 'Delighted to help: come along, gentlemen, we have been given our instructions. It's more than my life's worth to gainsay my cousin.' This sally was greeted by general laughter, but no one argued or demanded a third glass of port.

Still smiling, Edward hurried down the well-lit corridor to his chambers. The candle-filled sconces flickered as he dashed past. It took him longer to locate the box he wanted than he'd anticipated. Eventually he found it underneath a pile of documents right at the back of his strong box. Flipping the lid open he checked the contents were intact. His mother had never worn the rubies; in fact he had never seen them where they ought to be, around the neck of a Countess of Rushford.

The drawing-room doors were open and he could hear laughter and the sound of someone playing the piano rather badly. He hoped it wasn't Penny doing so. He realized there was still so much he didn't know about his fiancée. Was she musically gifted, or like him, tone deaf? Could she paint a pretty watercolour and embroider a cushion cover? The thought of her doing either made him smile at the absurdity, Penny was an outdoor girl, a bruising rider and more interested in growing plants than painting them. He strolled back in to join his guests, his eyes eagerly scanning the room. He stopped, his smile fading. There was no sign of either Penny or the count.

Chapter Nineteen

Penny hoped the gentlemen would not spend too long passing the port as she had learnt one or two interesting facts about Count Everex and she wished to share them with Edward. Although he had ordered her not to continue with her investigation, she felt sure anything gleaned over the dinner table was allowable.

She circled the room for a while doing her duty as hostess before pausing by her aunt. 'It's such a beautiful evening I'm going to stroll on the terrace and listen to the nightingales. Could you direct Lord Weston to me when he arrives?' She also wished to get as far away as possible from the excruciating noise of Miss Elizabeth on the pianoforte.

'Put your wrap around you, Penny. It's only the end of May.'

'But it's unseasonably warm, Aunt Lucy. However, I'm happy to do as you ask. I have attracted more than enough attention this evening.'

She wandered outside and the trills of a late blackbird resting in the honeysuckle that grew close by attracted her attention. It was pleasantly cool after the heat of the drawing-room. It was good to have the room well lit but so many candles made the room over warm.

She leant against the stone balustrade letting the liquid sound envelop her. It was so beautiful here; she could hardly believe this was where she was going to spend the rest of her life. She heard male voices mingling with the plink plonking of the piano and the laughter of the ladies. Smiling she turned to greet the man who came to join her on the terrace.

'Count Everex. I was not expecting you to join me. Lord Weston would not approve of us being out here alone.'

'My dear, Miss Coombs, when Mr Weston told me you were out here I could not resist the opportunity to continue our conversation.'

He remained a correct distance from her, making no attempt to crowd her or take liberties with her person. Maybe she had misjudged him; perhaps he was a gentlemen who just happened to be a traitor.

'Then you're welcome, sir. I'm waiting for it to be quite dark because the nightingales don't sing until the blackbirds have stopped.'

'You're a lover of nature, Miss Coombs. My main estate, on the Loire, would please you mightily. We have dozens of songbirds in the grounds, also deer and wild boar.'

'It sounds delightful. You must be so sad to have had it removed from your family by that upstart Napoleon Bonaparte.'

'I am one of the fortunate few, Miss Coombs, who has been allowed to keep his land. It is in name only at the moment, as all the revenues go to the government. However, I anticipate that I shall be able to return home very soon.'

Penny felt a tingle of excitement. Was she about to learn something really important? She moved closer, as if attracted by his conversation. 'What is your home like? Is it as grand as Headingly Court?'

'Far grander; in fact it is a palace. Imagine the castles in your fairy-tales and you will know what my *château* is like. I'm about to become a very rich man.' He lowered his voice and bent his head in order to whisper the next piece of information. 'In a week's time I shall receive a message from London and it will tell me that my fortune has been restored to me.'

'Good heavens! How very mysterious. Have you an elderly relative about to meet his Maker who has made you his beneficiary?'

The count shook his head and she smelt the pomade he used on his hair. It was unpleasant; she much preferred the fresh smell of lemons.

'I am not at liberty to tell you the details, Miss Coombs, but I shall be far richer, far more influential than Lord Weston. Would you not reconsider your attachment to him?'

In his determination to convince her of his sincerity he snatched her hands and held them to his chest. Penny was speechless with mortification. How could she extract herself from this situation without offending him? She let her hands go limp in his and looked directly at him.

'Sir, I believe you have misunderstood the situation. I have no interest in either you or your *château*. I am betrothed to Lord Weston and happy to be so. Please release my hands at once.'

He did so, stepping back his eyes wide with embarrassment. 'I beg your pardon, Miss Coombs. I have allowed my partiality to overcome my good manners. Pray excuse me; I shall not bother you in this way again.' Then he was gone, melting into the night, his black evening clothes making him invisible in the darkness.

A movement at the French doors alerted her to someone else's presence. She knew with a sinking certainty that it would be Edward standing there, and that he would have seen the whole. She braced herself for the inevitable reckoning. He had warned her not to continue her game and she had chosen to ignore him.

She kept her back firmly turned as he approached on soft feet behind her. She almost smiled as it occurred to her it could be someone else entirely. Then she would be in a worse position than before. No – it was he. She would recognize his distinctive aroma anywhere. She shivered and it wasn't from cold.

'Miss Coombs, would you be so kind as to accompany me to my study? I have pressing things to discuss with you that cannot be said in public.' Edward did not wait for her reply. She felt his arm, like a band of iron, close about her waist and was given no option but to go with him.

He marched her down the terrace to a second pair of French doors which were conveniently ajar. His free hand reached out and pulled them open and she was bundled inside the pitch-dark room. She heard the distinctive click as he locked the doors behind them. She was standing by herself somewhere in a room she had not visited before.

She would not be intimidated. She was not a child to be chastised for disobedience. Was he hoping to demoralize her by making her stand in the dark waiting for him to pounce? It was ridiculous! It was like something in one of the Gothic romances she used to read. From nowhere came the irresistible urge to giggle.

Desperately she tried to stifle the sound with her fists. Laughing at him might not be the best action in the circumstances. She knew enough about jealousy to realize it might have caused him to misconstrue what he saw and believe she had encouraged the count to take liberties.

Taking several calming breaths she decided her voice was steady enough to speak. 'My lord, is it your intention to hold this conversation in the dark? I have no objection, but would prefer to be seated before we begin.' She felt the giggles coming back. 'I have a tendency … have a tend … ency to lose my balance when I cannot see.' She gulped and knew that she could hold them back no longer.

His hand reached out and rested lightly on her shoulder. 'Are you laughing at me, by any chance, Miss Coombs?'

His voice was soft and she found it impossible to judge his mood. Was he still angry? She had no idea and without being able to see him, could not decide. She decided to risk a light reply.

'Not at you, my lord, but the situation I find myself in. I have always wanted to be a heroine in a romance novel and now I find myself acting out the part.' The sound of him grinding his teeth gave due warning of his mood. Hastily she spoke again. 'Are we to stand around here in the dark, or do you have a tinderbox and candles we can light?'

He almost growled his answer. 'I can see perfectly well. My night vision is excellent. I have no need to light the room.' He laughed but the sound did not reassure her. 'If you wish to be seated find somewhere for yourself.'

Her amusement was rapidly turning to annoyance. Loving someone apparently did not mean you had to like them! She looked around her and realized he was correct, there was sufficient moonlight filtering in through the unshuttered windows for her to find a chair. She wondered what part of the house this was; it was certainly nowhere she had been before.

She selected a single wooden armchair with a high back and cushioned seat. Swishing past the looming shape of her future husband she sat, taking her time to arrange her gown so that the train and overskirt would not become creased. When she was ready, she clasped her hands demurely in her lap and stared frostily in his direction. She hoped he could see she was equally angry.

'Well, Lord Weston? What is it you have to say that is so urgent it made you forget your manners and manhandle me in such an unacceptable way?'

'You disobeyed me. I distinctly recall instructing you not to be alone under any circumstances with that man. He is a dangerous criminal not the charming *émigré* he wishes to appear.'

He paused and Penny believed he was waiting for her to answer. 'I'm quite capable of making my own decisions. I'm not a child or just out of the schoolroom. It might have escaped your attention, my lord, but since my father's death I have not only been running both my estate and house, but also managing my investments.'

'I'm not interested in what you did before you became my responsibility. That is irrelevant. Here I am master and you would do well to remember it. Do not interrupt me again.'

'I shall not interrupt if you do not continue to talk to me as though I was no more than ten years old.'

'Be silent!' His voice cut like a whip and she shrivelled in her chair, her bravado evaporating under the onslaught of his fury. 'If our marriage is to work satisfactorily then you have to understand what it is I require from a wife.'

Penny bit her lip so hard she tasted blood. How could she sit here and say nothing whilst he snarled his wishes? This was not how she had envisaged their union. She wanted the meeting of minds and souls as well as bodies. Did her opinions count for nothing? It had been only a few days ago, after she had almost drowned in the river, that he had entrusted her with his secret. Where was this trust now?

He continued, apparently unaware of her growing disquiet, 'I don't want a woman who argues every decision that I make; I don't want to see other men sniffing around her skirts—'

At this outrageous statement she leapt to her feet, too angry to consider the consequences. 'I have heard enough.' She snatched the emerald ring from her finger and threw it in his face. 'There. The engagement is over. Now I don't have to listen to your opinions or remain in the same place as you.'

Her eyes had adjusted to the gloom and she could see a door on the far side of the room. She would not stay a moment longer. She expected to be dragged back, but to her surprise he allowed her to stalk across the room and through the door. She slammed it shut behind her. She was shaking too much to move away. She closed her eyes, ignoring the scalding tears that dripped down her cheeks. She had just broken her own heart. She would never love another man as she did Edward, but she couldn't marry him now that she knew how he intended to treat her.

Why hadn't he followed her? Was he relieved to be rid of his tiresome fiancée? Angrily she scrubbed her face with the corner of her wrap. This would not do. She could not remain hiding in this room; she had to find her way back to the party before her absence was noted by the eagle eyes of her aunt. Engaged or not – proprieties must he adhered to.

Penny stepped away from the door; it was darker in here as most of the shutters were closed. She groped her way across to the glimmer of moonlight she could see filtering through the slats. Reaching the windows she unhooked a catch and pushed. With a rumble the shutters parted and the room was bathed in a silver glow.

Where was the other exit? Frantically she stared around the chamber. It was only then she realized where she was and why he had not prevented her escape. She was in his bedchamber. A huge tester bed dominated the centre of the room. She stood, rooted to the spot with horror. She was trapped in Edward's private apartments. Her reputation of unassailable purity would be in tatters after this. Then she remembered that there had to be a servant's exit in his dressing-room. If she could find that, then maybe all would not be lost.

She needed a candle and although there were several candle-sticks around they were useless without a flint to light them. She scanned the panelled walls looking for a clue. The door was so well hidden she couldn't spot it in the gloom.

He would not leave her alone for much longer; she had to find an escape route immediately. She ran across the carpet and began to search the wall beside the bed with her fingertips. She was so engrossed she did not hear the door open but she heard the key turn in the lock. In her terror she had not thought to turn the key herself and now it was too late. She was locked in the bedchamber of the man she had just jilted.

Her knees gave way and she sank to the floor her dress a pool of silk around her. She drew in her knees and hugged them like a child. The irony of the situation was not lost on her captor.

Chapter Twenty

PENNY HUDDLED ON the floor, her back pressed firmly against the edge of the bed, unable to stop the trembling that shook her slender frame. She knew what was coming – what he intended for her. Why else had he locked the bedchamber door?

She covered her ears with her hands and, resting her head on her knees, she waited. And waited. Why didn't he come over and throw her on to the bed? Perhaps when he saw how frightened she was, he would relent and let her go. She lifted her head from her lap, removed her hands and opened her eyes, natural curiosity overcoming her fear.

She blinked in astonishment. While she had been cowering on the floor shaking like a blancmange Edward had been lighting candles. He was nowhere in sight. If it was his intention to ravish her, he was going about it in a very strange way.

Where was the wretched man? She craned her neck, but still could not see him. He must be on the other side of the room waiting for her to make the first move. She scrambled up on to her knees and swivelling round peered anxiously over the top of the bed.

She recoiled and in her efforts to remove herself, fell backwards in a tangle of arms and legs. Edward, who was lounging as if he had not a care in the world on top of the bed, made no move to assist her. She heard his hateful chuckle and the last vestiges of her fear evaporated and righteous indignation its place.

'I hate you, Lord Weston. And nothing you can do or say will prevail upon me to change my mind. I shall not be your wife, not now, not ever.' She eventually regained her feet and, as he had not answered, she continued, 'My beautiful gown is quite ruined and it is entirely your fault.' She knew this to be untrue but she was too cross to care. 'I wish to return to my room. You will unlock the door this instant.'

Again he laughed and, rolling sideways placed his feet on the floor. Before she had time to protest he lunged forward and grasped her waving hands. 'I promise to release you, but first I wish to persuade you to change your mind. If, after five minutes, you are still determined to sever the connection then so be it.'

Five minutes? It should be easy to remain firm for such a short time. 'Very well, my lord. But I can assure you there is nothing you can say that will make me agree to continue our engagement.'

His voice purred across her cheek as he drew her closer. 'I have no intention of using speech to convince you, my love. I have a far more effective way of doing that.'

His lips trailed light kisses down from her ear to the corner of her mouth. Resolutely she stood still, forcing herself not to respond, trying to ignore the waves of excitement that his expert touch was igniting.

His hair brushed her face as he continued his sweet assault until his mouth was burning its way across her breasts. She should push him away, knew very well he would stop if asked, but she was incapable of speaking. Adrift in a sea of pleasure all rational thought became swamped by her growing desire to become one with him.

Resistance was impossible. Her arms moved of their own volition to tangle in his hair. She wanted him to kiss her properly, to feel his lips crush hers. She tugged fiercely and he raised his head. His eyes blazed with passion and he needed no further permission.

His arms scooped her up and she was tossed unceremoniously on top of the bed. She watched him fling his mangled neckcloth on to the floor and heard the diamond pin roll unheeded across the boards. His evening jacket followed and then he was beside her on the bed and it was too late to change her mind.

She felt uncomfortable; something about this was not as it should be. The train of her gown was hunched underneath her bottom and the low-cut bodice was cutting painfully into the soft flesh of her breasts. She tried to roll away from him, to indicate somehow that she was having second thoughts. It was too late – far too late – for she felt his hands sliding up her legs pushing the layers of material ahead of them.

The candlelight flickered and danced, creating shadows on the wall, but Penny only saw the russet head nuzzling her naked limbs leaving spirals of excitement in their wake. A strange, heady lethargy held her captive. His tongue was flickering across her inner thigh and her skirts were bundled under her chin when sanity prevailed.

What was she doing? She was behaving like a light-skirt. She should not be here. He should not be touching her like that before their marriage vows had been taken.

She pressed her knees together and drew them violently towards her. This unexpected movement caught Edward under the chin slamming his teeth together. He reeled back, spitting blood and profanities in equal measure.

This was the opportunity she had been waiting for. 'Edward, I *have* changed my mind. I shall marry you, you have no reason to continue this.'

He wiped the gore from his bleeding mouth with his shirt sleeve. For a moment she thought he was angry with her. When he spoke she knew she had misjudged him.

'Sweetheart, how can you ever forgive me? I have always prided myself on self-control and tonight I have shown none. I have no excuse apart from the fact that whenever I am near I ache to make love to you.' He smiled ruefully. 'Thank God you had the common sense to stop things before they reached their natural conclusion.'

'Then you're not cross with me?'

'I'm angry with myself for allowing my stupid jealousy to blind me. I know you did not encourage that man, but seeing his pawing made me almost lose my reason. I've never felt like this before and if anything ever happened to you my life would be over. I should never seek another wife; James is my heir and I should be content in those circumstances to leave my title and estate to him.'

Penny, her skirt restored to its rightful place about her ankles, felt ready to join in the conversation. 'Edward, nothing is going to happen to me, and certainly not at the hands of the count. He fancies himself in love with me and asked me to run away with him and become his countess.'

'The devil he did! It would give me the greatest pleasure to shoot him through the heart.'

'You mustn't kill him; he's a gentleman and has promised to keep his distance in future. I can hardly credit he's a traitor, he seems so charming.'

'It's he who's behind the attempts on your life. I admit he's not personally involved, but I'm certain it's his orders the smugglers are following. Their aim is to distract me from my duties as a magistrate by attacking you.' He grinned. 'And it's working, isn't it? I'm so busy watching you that they could have taken three wagons of contraband past me and I wouldn't have noticed. I think you can see now why I have never sought a wife.'

'That reminds me, Edward, he told me he was expecting a letter from London in which would be the information that he was very rich. I asked him if he had an elderly relative about to depart this world and leave him a fortune. He told me the money was for services rendered.'

'This week? Thank God for that. This means the money has not arrived yet. There's too much coastline for Captain Smith and his small band of militiamen to patrol effectively. The French boat could come in anywhere, but now I know the count is definitely involved, I can hazard a guess that the handover will take place within a few miles of here.'

Penny left the safety of the bed and walked into the middle of the room where Edward was standing. 'Are we friends, Edward? I should hate us to part on bad terms.'

'More importantly, are we still betrothed? I love you, Penny, and if it's your wish that we no longer get married, then I shall stand aside.'

'I told you, Edward, I will marry you. What I won't do is spend any time alone with you until we *are* married. I have no wish to anticipate our wedding night.'

If he noticed she had not said that she returned his love, he made no comment. She was no longer sure how she felt about him. She loved his handsome form and the way his hands sent shivers of delight up and down her spine, but that was lust which even she knew was not the same as being *in love*.

'Then allow me to return your ring.' She held out her left hand and he slipped it back, then he raised it to his mouth and gently kissed her knuckles. 'The next time this ring is removed it will be to place my wedding band on your finger. That day cannot come soon enough for me.'

Releasing her hand, he walked away and she heard the distinctive click of the key being turned. She was finally free to go. She looked down at her crumpled gown and realized her appearance would instantly reveal where she had been and what she had been doing.

'I can't walk through the house looking like … like a woman of the streets. You must take me back through the servant's route. If we meet anyone at least we can be sure your staff will be discreet.'

He chuckled. 'They wouldn't dare be otherwise. Here, take this candlestick; I warn you, it's black as pitch along those corridors.'

The entrance was, as Penny had suspected, in the dressing-room. This door was so well concealed it was hardly surprising she hadn't been able to find it. Edward led the way through a maze of passages and staircases and although she heard voices in the distance they didn't meet anyone else.

Eventually they emerged in her own parlour. 'Thank you. Please go; I have no wish for Mary to discover you here. Goodnight. Edward.'

The door from her bedchamber opened quietly and her maid came in. 'Mercy me! I've never seen the like!'

'Mary, you're forgetting yourself! I wish to see this dress pressed and back in my closet by tomorrow evening.'

'Yes. Miss Coombs. Shall you be wanting anything from the kitchen tonight?'

'No, thank you. I shall retire immediately. I wish to ride before breakfast so please leave out my blue habit. I shall require a bath when I return.'

'Very well, miss.'

Penny tossed restlessly all night. Her doubts about the veracity of her feelings for Lord Weston and the wisdom of agreeing to such a hasty marriage kept her awake. When she had accepted his offer she thought she knew him, but every day she was discovering Edward was not quite the paragon she had imagined him to be. He had a fiery temper to match his hair and a ruthless streak he had not displayed when they were gallivanting around London together. He was not what he seemed at all.

Did she really wish to be married to a man who had spent the last ten years in secret work for the government? He had promised to devote his time to her and his estate in future, but could she trust him to keep his word? Surely, a man used to a life of action and adventure would not settle happily into domesticity however much he loved his wife.

Eventually she fell asleep after accepting the unpalatable fact that whatever her reservations she was committed to marrying him. She had behaved like a wanton – allowed Edward to take liberties with her person that only a husband should have. She had no choice: she had to marry him and make the best of it. Her mouth curved involuntarily. At least she had no fears about sharing the marriage bed with him. That was one part of the relationship she was eagerly anticipating.

The next week passed too quickly for Penny and, she suspected, too slowly for Edward. He kept to his word and made no attempt to seek out her company. He treated her with the utmost civility and kindness and only she could detect the tension in him when he was close to her.

Mr Weston was her constant companion and she enjoyed his

company. He happily divided his time between herself and his mother. The count also treated her respectfully, but she occasionally detected a brooding darkness in his expression that gave credence to Edward's belief that he was indeed the traitor that he sought.

Plans for the garden party to be held for the villagers and staff were well underway. Lady Dalrymple was in her element; there was nothing she liked better than organizing a grand event.

'Penny, my dear, Mrs Weston and I would like to bring you up to date and you must tell us how your trousseau is progressing.'

'It's all but completed, Aunt Lucy. I have sufficient garments to last me a lifetime. I can only pray that fashion does not dictate a drop in the waistline again, which would make all these gowns redundant.' She settled herself more comfortably in the shade of the huge oak tree under which the ladies gathered most days for a cosy gossip.

'And your wedding gown? Is it as you hoped?' Mrs Weston asked curiously.

'Indeed it is, Mrs Weston. No girl could have a more beautiful dress in which to walk down the aisle. Did I tell you I have asked Mr Weston to escort me?'

'Oh, my dear, how delightful.' She smiled archly. 'Let's hope there is no confusion on the day. It's hard to tell James from Edward when they're dressed alike.'

Penny's smile faltered as she considered this outrageous statement. She sometimes thought she might prefer to marry Mr Weston; he was so kind and gentle, quite unlike his cousin. Married to him she would be secure in the knowledge that whatever her misdemeanour she would not be berated like a schoolgirl.

'Ah, there is the dear boy now, Miss Coombs,' Mrs Weston said, as she beckoned to her son to join them.

Penny stared and knew immediately why she would never marry Mr Weston. He was the image of Edward but lacked that indefinable something that made her fiancé irresistible. It was strange how these things worked, she liked Mr Weston a deal better than Edward, but did not love him.

Her radiant smile reflected her relief that she did indeed love her future husband. She did not realize Mr Weston had thought it was directed at himself until he arrived at her side his eyes dark with an emotion she recognized as blatant desire. Embarrassed by her inadvertent encouragement she merely nodded a welcome and turned to continue her conversation with her aunt and Mrs Weston.

'I gather that Monsieur Ducray has finally repaired the air balloon and it will be on show for the garden party. You will be able to take a ride, Aunt Lucy, if the weather is calm.'

Her aunt shuddered dramatically. 'After your experience, my dear, I shall watch from the terrace and be quite content to do so.'

'James, are you intending to take a flight?'

'No, Mama, like Lady Dalrymple I shall remain firmly on the ground. Edward has asked me to do the pretty with his tenants, so I shall be fully occupied with that.'

Penny was surprised at his announcement. 'I am certain that you will do an excellent job, Mr Weston. Are you acting as yourself or impersonating Lord Weston?'

'I can assure you, Miss Coombs, it's something I do on a regular basis. When Edward is abroad I sometimes stand in for him and no one is any the wiser.'

'I see; how convenient for Lord Weston to be able to abdicate his responsibilities so easily.'

She stood up. 'Pray excuse me, Mrs Weston, Aunt Lucy, Mr Weston, but I have an appointment with the housekeeper and must go inside.'

She hurried across the lawn, her emotions in turmoil. Did Edward see his cousin as a substitute for himself? Is that why he had asked him to stand in for him so often? She didn't know how she felt any more; no sooner had she decided she was in love with him, she received another dent to her confidence. It wasn't poor Mr Weston's fault – she laid the blame, as usual, squarely on the shoulders of her beloved.

'I am not just another part of his property,' she fumed, 'and I shall not be parcelled out to another at his convenience.'

Determined to have the matter out with him she sailed into the house, her eyes sparkling with indignation and marched directly to his study. A sharp rap on the door elicited no response. Perhaps he was out and about – emboldened by the continued silence she tentatively turned the handle and stepped in.

The room was empty but the desk was strewn with papers, the chair pushed back anyhow. She frowned at the sign of disarray. Edward had obviously left in a hurry. Curiously she approached the desk and glanced at the nearest document. Her heart shot into her mouth as she read what was written there.

Weston

The items you are anticipating have been traced and they will be arriving in your neighbourhood on Tuesday.

Yours
Andover

Chapter Twenty-one

Penny CLUTCHED THE edge of the desk for support. Edward was searching for the gold that was to be smuggled out of the country and taken to Bonaparte's supporters. He could be killed or wounded, and she had not told him how much she loved him. At that moment all her doubts and worries about her impending marriage vanished. The thought of him in danger was insupportable. All she could do now was pray that he returned safely to her because this time he had allowed himself to become distracted and his head might not be as focused on his mission as it should be.

She would write him a note, tell him how she felt, beg him to take care. She would not risk telling him face to face, was determined to stick to her vow and arrive on her wedding day as innocent as she was today.

She left the letter on his desk where he would see it when he returned. The mantel clock struck the hour. It was four o'clock – too early to go upstairs and change for dinner. She had to find something to occupy her mind or she would go mad with worry.

A brisk walk around the ornamental lake would serve the purpose. It was warm and there was no need to return to her room to collect her spencer and she was already wearing her kid half-boots. She had ruined two pairs of slippers by taking them outside.

She was leaving by the French doors in the drawing-room when she saw Count Everex strolling round from the direction of the stables looking decidedly pleased with himself. Hastily she hid herself behind a curtain and waited for him to pass. Why was this man still at large? Did it mean Edward had been unsuccessful? Perhaps the Frenchman had hidden the gold in the barn amongst the paraphernalia of the balloonists.

Without a second's thought she slipped from the room and walked briskly towards the stables. The barn was no more than fifty yards behind this block and she intended to creep in, if she could, and make a search. Edward was going to be delighted if he returned empty-handed only to discover she had found the gold hidden at Headingly Court.

'Andover, I was relieved to receive your note. I was beginning to fear that somehow these bastards had managed to slip through the net.'

'As you know, we've been watching Sir Reginald Masterson for months waiting to catch him red-handed. The man I'd placed in his household as a groom alerted me yesterday to unusual activity by the river. We should have realized they might use water transport.'

Edward turned to speak to his four men who were standing close behind holding the horses. 'Perkins, you and Reynolds remain here and keep watch. If you see any activity down at the boathouse one of you get word to me immediately, the other follow the wagon. We will rendezvous on the shore.'

'They'll need a wagon to get it to the beach. As soon as one appears down there Reynolds can let you know, my lord.'

'I have messages to send to London; they can start arresting the other contributors to this fund. With any luck, by tomorrow night we shall have all of them under lock and key.' Lord Andover replaced his spyglass in a pocket in his riding coat. 'There's nothing more we can do here; I suggest you return to Headingly. It would be a disaster if the count was alerted at this juncture.'

Edward, like his fellow government operative, backed stealthily through the undergrowth until it was safe for him to stand without being visible to any watchers at Lufkin Manor, the home of Sir Reginald Masterson. Brushing down his jacket he nodded at his companion. 'I take it we do not wish the militia to be involved tonight?'

'The government doesn't wish the general public to know how close we came to letting a group of traitors escape justice. We cannot guarantee that every man in the troop will remain silent. How many men do you have for this enterprise, Weston?'

'I have six, seven if you include myself. They are all highly trained and have accompanied me on all my missions. As long as we're not expected, it will be more than enough to finish the job.'

He held out his hand and Reynolds handed him his reins. 'Do you want prisoners?' His voice was matter-of-fact, unbothered either way.

'They want the Frenchman back in London, but dispose of the rest. There must be no witnesses to blab about what happens.'

'I doubt if we can take the boat or its crew without attracting attention. But I can assure you there will be no one else left to carry tales in England.'

'Good luck, my friend. Don't be careless tonight. I know of two men who were lost on their final mission. After so long, it's easy to become complacent and make mistakes.' Lord Andover's face reflected his concern.

'I have no intention of turning up my toes. Remember, I'm getting married next week. I shall do nothing to jeopardize my safety, I have far too much to live for now.'

Edward cantered away, leaving two men to watch the house whilst the other two accompanied him. He was glad this whole escapade was to be over tonight. Andover was right to warn him; he knew only too well that his attention was not fully on the job in hand. When he should be thinking about his next move, far too often his mind drifted to images of Penny.

This would not happen again. He would not go down to dinner, but retire to his chambers pleading a return of the ague he had caught whilst in Spain a few years back. This was a ruse he had used on several occasions over the years when wishing to vanish for a few days without arousing suspicion. In fact, he had only suffered two bouts of the sweating sickness and neither of those had been life-threatening.

His manservant was an accomplice and an expert at keeping

his secrets. He smiled imagining Penny rushing to his bedside, wishing to be his nurse. Simpson must tell her he preferred to be left alone until the fever broke and that she would be sent for as soon as he was well enough. That would, God willing, be tomorrow morning. He cantered down the lane that led to the rear of the stables just in time to see her vanish into the barn.

It had been far easier than she anticipated to creep past the busy stable yard and along the track that led to the barn. Certain she had not been seen so far by any of the grooms or stable lads, she paused outside the heavy double doors, delighted to see there was a small gap between them, just large enough to slide through.

She pressed her ear against the wood, not wishing to go in if there was anyone inside. Monsieur Ducray had taken his air balloon and the wagon out for a test flight before his demonstration at the garden party next week. Excellent! It was quiet, no voices, no movement. It would be quite safe to go in and complete a search.

Inside the huge edifice it was almost dark; there were no windows to let in the sunlight. The only illumination came through the occasional gaps in the heavy black boards that made up the structure. Closing her eyes for a few moments then opening them again, yes, she could make out the shrouded shapes of interesting objects along the back wall.

On tiptoes she crossed the floor, holding up her hem to avoid it becoming mired in the dirt, reaching out to pull aside a tarpaulin she was snatched from her feet by an unseen assailant. Terrified she opened her mouth to scream for help but was prevented from doing so by the hand across her face.

She kicked backwards and was overjoyed when her heels connected with the man's knees.

'Stow it, my girl, or it'll be the worse for you.' The harsh voice hissed in her ear and she went limp with horror. Why had she not listened to Edward when he had told her not to interfere? She would be brave, not give in to her fear. Whatever happened he would be proud of her.

Her captor dropped her so suddenly her knees buckled and she fell heavily on her bottom.

'What the blazes are you doing in here? Have you taken leave of your senses?'

Her head shot up. 'Edward, you scared me half to death. I thought you were one of the smugglers and that I would never see you again.'

He reached down and yanked her to her feet. 'Good. I hope you've learnt a valuable lesson, my girl. Don't meddle in things that are not your concern.'

'I learned something else as well, Edward. I saw the count returning from the stables and he was almost skipping with glee. I'm sure he has received that letter from London telling him the gold is here and he's now a rich man.'

'And I suppose you came here to find the gold? Noble sentiments, sweetheart, but decidedly foolhardy.' He hustled her towards the door where there was more light. 'Let me brush you down; you can't go out covered in straw and other debris.' He proceeded to bang the rear of her gown, none too gently.

'That hurts – let me do it, if you please.'

'I'm sorely tempted to add a few well-deserved slaps to that area.'

She giggled. 'You're a man of your word, Lord Weston. I'm sure I'm in no danger of such punishment at your hands.' She peered over her shoulder to check she was free of dirt. 'I'm ready to return to the house. Shall I leave first? It would never do for people to think we were having a clandestine meeting in here.'

'There's something I need to do before you leave, my dear.'

Penny was suddenly enveloped in a fierce embrace and her face tilted to accommodate his kiss. When he eventually released her, her head was swimming and her cheeks flushed. Without having time to protest she was ruthlessly ejected from the barn and the door closed behind her. She had no option but to walk away as if nothing had happened.

When she walked past the stable yard she saw Perkins talking to her own grooms. They carefully avoided looking in her direction but she knew they were well aware who had been with her in the barn. She straightened her back and stalked the remaining distance to the side entrance, luckily able to slip inside without meeting any of the guests.

She selected a simple dinner gown that evening; it had a demure neckline and no train. 'I shall not need you to help me disrobe tonight so why don't you take the evening off?'

Mary beamed. 'Thank you, miss. I'll leave out your night rail and wrapper. Shall I have a supper tray sent up?'

'No, dinner is so late here there is no need. I love the colour of this dress; when the mantua-maker showed me the green silk I knew it would be perfect for me.'

Penny hurried from the room; she did not wish Aunt Lucy to negotiate the stairs without assistance and if she was not waiting in the corridor, her elderly relative would continue on her own.

'My dear, I was about to leave without you,' Lady Dalrymple said tartly. 'Your timekeeping is becoming slipshod. When you are a countess, more will be expected of you, I hope you realize that?'

'Of course I do, but I do not believe it's I who am late but you who are early.'

Chatting amiably together they joined the assembled company in the grand salon. A lady greeted them. 'My dear, I have just heard that Lord Weston is indisposed. It appears that he has frequent attacks of the ague. He will not be joining us tonight.'

Penny schooled her face in order to look suitably worried by this unexpected news. She knew it was a sham; Edward had been in the pink of health barely two hours ago. 'What a shame! However, it will do none of us any harm to retire early for once. I vow I am quite exhausted by all the excitement of the past three weeks.'

She smiled warmly at her guests as she circulated the room reassuring everyone that Lord Weston would be recovered from his fever in ample time to participate in their wedding, which was now less than a week away.

*

Penny returned to her chambers a little after ten o'clock and was glad she had already dismissed her abigail as she intended to visit Edward on his bed of pain and offer her assistance as a nurse. She took a candlestick and opened the hidden door in the wooden panelling in her parlour intending to retrace her steps and find his room via the servant's route.

She would have no difficulty finding his room again, for each flight of stairs was numbered and each passageway had a letter assigned to it. She had memorized the numbers and letters and written them down as soon as Edward had left.

The only danger was that she would meet an unsuspecting servant and be obliged to explain her presence. It was eerily quiet, none of the voices and clattering footsteps she had heard when she'd travelled along this way before. Perhaps all the staff had finished early tonight and were enjoying a convivial evening in the servant's hall below stairs.

Reaching her destination she pushed open the door and stepped into Edward's dressing-room. The room was already occupied. Her sudden appearance so startled Simpson that he dropped the shaving mug he was carrying.

'Miss Coombs, his lordship's not receiving tonight.'

Penny smiled at the flustered valet. 'Is he here? I came to see for myself how someone who was in rude health less than two hours ago could now be prostrate with fever.'

Simpson accepted the inevitable. 'Lord Weston has gone out. I do not expect him back until the morning.'

'I guessed as much. He has gone to apprehend a traitor. Would you tell him that I called?'

The man bowed. 'I shall do so.' He hesitated as if not sure whether to pass on this piece of information. 'Lord Weston received your note, miss, and put it in his pocket next to his heart.'

'Thank you for telling me. I shall leave you to your duties. Goodnight.'

Riley, one of the men who had accompanied Edward to his meeting with Lord Andover, waited until he was close enough to speak without being overheard. 'Lord Weston, did you tell

Miss Coombs that you were feeling poorly? She'll be a mite surprised when you don't come down to dinner because of having an attack of the ague.'

'God's teeth! I completely forgot.' He slapped his man on the shoulder. 'Miss Coombs knows all about this business. She'll draw her own conclusions and keep them to herself. It's a good thing this is my last mission, I'm finding it difficult to keep my mind on the task in hand.'

'I'll have the horses ready as soon as it gets dark. I've told Billy and the other Nettleford groom to keep an eye out for the Frenchy. They'll tag along behind him when he sets off.'

Edward had decided to take Penny's grooms into his confidence; after all, when this matter was completed it would make no difference who knew he had once been employed in secret activities by the British Government.

'Good work. I'll be down at ten o'clock. Make sure you have your rifles and ammunition ready. We're going to need them tonight.'

He entered the house through his private door and met his manservant in his sitting-room. Simpson bowed. 'My lord, I've everything ready as you requested. Shall you be wanting your black cape and hat tonight?'

Edward nodded. 'The moon is almost full and without it I should be too conspicuous. Are my pistols primed and ready and my sword sharpened?'

'They are, my lord. If you would care to retire to your bedchamber I shall let Foster know that you are indisposed and won't be joining your guests this evening. If Mr Weston comes to enquire after your health I shall tell him you're in bed and not receiving visitors.'

'I left papers on the desk in my study that need to be put in the safe.'

'I shall see to it, sir.'

Edward decided he might as well rest if he could; he was going to get precious little sleep that night. He pulled his boots off and tossed them in the corner, his jacket and cravat followed. His heart was pumping hard, adrenalin flowing freely round his body. He was going to miss these episodes when he settled down to a sedate married life.

Stretching out on his bed he folded his hands behind his head and closed his eyes, running through all the possible eventualities that might occur when they ambushed the smugglers and the count. He was pretty sure that with six men at his side there would be no difficulty. Surprise was the key to this exercise.

The soft knock on his bedchamber door roused him from his planning. 'Come in, Simpson, I'm not asleep.'

'I've tidied your study, my lord; I found this note for you on the desk and thought you'd like to have it.'

Edward took the paper, not recognizing the handwriting. He opened it and scanned the contents. His eyes glittered as he read the words of love. No, he would not miss his life of espionage, not any more; now he had something far better to do with his life. He refolded the square and pushed it into the pocket of his shirt, next to his heart.

Chapter Twenty-two

'ANY SIGN OF the diligence?' Edward whispered to Perkins, who was watching the track.

'Nothing, yet, sir. I reckon it'll be another fifteen minutes or so. They'll not get down this path quickly, the sand's soft and the wheels will sink in.'

It was a little after eleven o'clock and the moon was temporarily hidden behind a bank of cloud making it difficult to see. 'Reynolds, you're certain you saw the French ship anchored in the bay before the moon went in?'

'I did, my lord, clear as day. We've got the right place, all we have to do now is wait for the villains to appear then we can do the lot.'

The four men were bristling with weapons and eager to apprehend the smugglers and the traitor who had orchestrated this event. A slight sound approaching through the long marsh grass stilled them. Silently Edward got to his feet and, half crouching, moved into a position where he could strike down whoever it was, before they were able to warn those waiting on the beach of their presence.

'Lord Weston? It's Billy and me.'

Thank God! Edward relaxed and called back softly, 'Up here, lads. Come in on your knees or you'll be spotted from the beach.'

A slight rustling greeted his words and then the grass parted and the two young men slithered in to join the other four. 'The Frenchy's down there with them smugglers, my lord. We followed him until we was certain he were going down to the sea and then come up here to join you.'

'Are you all clear about your part in this?' There was a murmur of assent. 'Good. Reynolds and Perkins you stay up here where you have a clear view. The only live captive we want is the count; the rest must not be allowed to leave the beach and carry tales.'

Edward turned to resume his vigil on the edge of the sandy dip he had selected for their ambush. His four men were seasoned fighters and would not balk at dispatching any of the smugglers, but he was less confident about the two from Nettleford. They were loyal to Penny and prepared to die for her if necessary, but were they prepared to kill?

It was too late to worry about such details. Perkins had explained to them what tonight would entail and they hadn't demurred. He rolled over and beckoned to Riley. 'Keep an eye on those two for me; I don't want any harm to come to them if possible.'

'Me and Blakey will take care of them, sir, don't you fret. There's five of them smugglers on the beach and Reynolds said there's three more with the wagon. With the Frenchy that makes nine. Hardly a fight at all!'

The horses had been tethered in a coppice half a mile away, too far from the track to be overheard by either the men with the wagon or those waiting on the shore. In those final few minutes Edward reviewed his plans, checking he'd missed nothing. When the attack started it would be too late.

He checked that Reynolds and Perkins were in position and their powder and ball was to hand; he ran his hand over the hilt of his sabre to see that it was loose in its scabbard. He knew his pistols were loaded and primed, so all he had to do was cock them and fire. The men who would accompany him downhill were armed, but the two Nettleford boys had cudgels instead of swords. He smiled wryly at the thought of his guests seeing him like this. Would they be shocked or impressed?

He stiffened at the unmistakable sound of harness jangling and the muted hiss of voices. Saying a quick prayer, as he always did at such times, he gestured to the others to be ready to move on his signal. He glanced up and saw the moon appear from behind the clouds bathing the beach in a ghostly silver light.

His two riflemen signalled they were ready to fire. He withdrew his pistols from his belt and cocked them. The noise of the others doing the same, echoed round the dip. Damn! Had this alerted the men below? No, the wagon continued to lumber down the sand, joined by the free-traders and a taller man dressed as a gentleman, unlike his companions who were roughly garbed. Replacing his weapons carefully in his belt, he whispered his final order to Perkins and Reynolds.

'Wait until we're away from the dunes, then open fire.'

'Understood, sir. Remember, boys, don't get in our line of fire. Keep to the right, that way we'll not hit you by mistake.' This remark was for the benefit of the two new men, everyone else knew exactly what to do. They had done it many times before.

The unsuspecting group on the beach were fully occupied trying to push the wagon down to the edge. The two carthorses were straining every sinew, leaning heavily into the traces, but the weight of the gold and the depth of the sand were making it difficult for them.

'Now, we'll take them before they get the cart on to the hard sand. At the moment they're too busy pushing to hear us approach.'

He didn't need to worry about his riflemen's efficiency. Those two could take the centre out of a coin tossed into the sky every time. Even in the semi-darkness he knew their aim would be lethal. He beckoned to the four other men and, on his belly, crept through the tufty undergrowth, slithering down the sand towards the beach.

As they reached the edge of the sea grass he motioned to the others to flatten themselves on the ground whilst he reconnoitred. The voices of free-traders and the count carried clearly through the darkness.

'Buggeration! It's bloody stuck again; 'ere, Joe, give us a 'and. Put your bloomin' shoulder on the tailboard and shove. We don't wanna be down 'ere all bleedin' night. Them toy soldiers 'ave been taking too much interest in this bit of the coast just recently.'

Someone else spoke up. 'It ain't us makin' all the rattle; shut your gob, you stupid bugger. If there's anyone within a mile of us they'll 'ear your racket.'

Edward saw someone move away from the wagon and walk down towards the sea. The man was carrying a carpetbag and wearing a heavy drab coat, but it was unmistakably the Frenchman. He scoured the inky water – was that something?

Yes – it was a rowing boat sculling steadily to shore. It was about 300 yards from the beach. He heard a soft exchange of French and knew the moment for action had arrived. If he delayed any longer whoever was in the boat could tip the balance, and not in their favour.

'Right! Keep low, and for God's sake keep your heads down. Your faces will reveal you before you have them in range.' He didn't wait for a reply. In a crouching run he led the charge across the beach pulling out his pistols as he did so.

He could smell the stink of unwashed humanity and knew he was close enough, raising his guns, he fired. The noise of several shots shattered the peace and the screams of the men that were hit merely spurred him on to complete his mission. Tucking his spent weapons back into his belt he drew his sword and raced to reach the count before he could be picked up by the frantically rowing Frenchmen.

The loud crack of rifle fire echoed across the carnage and the last two men who had accompanied the ill-fated wagon slumped to the sand. Leaving his men to complete the ambush Edward continued his dash towards the sea. Count Everex was screaming at the oncoming dinghy as he waded into the sea.

The icy water filled Edward's boots as he splashed closer and closer to his quarry. He didn't want to kill the man, but if it was a choice of losing him or killing him he would not hesitate.

'Give up, Everex, you've lost. My marksmen will drop you where you stand if you attempt to board that vessel.'

'Never! Kill me if you must, you will not take me otherwise.'

The sabre sliced through the air cutting deeply into the

count's left arm. The man staggered and fell to his knees, clutching the wound in a vain attempt to stem the blood. 'I surrender, Weston. I will come with you.'

Edward sheathed his sword and his teeth were a flash of white in the moonlight as he grinned with relief. It was over. No one was hurt apart from the traitors. All that remained was for his men to load the bodies on to the wagon and dispose of them. The gold and prisoner would be collected at the rendezvous by Lord Andover.

'Come along, you traitorous bastard, my superiors wish to speak with you before they send you to the gallows.' He reached down to haul the injured man to his feet, turning his back for a moment on the Frenchmen in the dinghy out to sea. He knew Perkins and Reynolds would have them covered – that was their job.

Then a second bank of clouds obscured the moon and the riflemen could no longer see the shore. Realizing his danger, Edward turned, still gripping the panting count by his shoulder. A second fusillade of shots reverberated across the deserted beach, but this time they came from the dinghy and not from the beach. The shot penetrated his shoulder and he staggered forward, almost losing his balance.

The thickness of his cloak had absorbed some of the force of the ball, but he was injured and needed urgent medical attention. 'Riley, I'm hit, damnit! Come and take this vermin from me. Tie up his arm before he bleeds to death.'

Billy appeared at his side and put a steadying arm around his shoulders. 'Thank you, lad, you did well tonight. Assist me to the wagon, I expect they'll have a lantern we can light. I want to interrogate this man before he passes out.'

He was in as much danger as the prisoner of falling into unconsciousness. The walk across the sand seemed endless. His sodden cloak and water-filled Hessians weighed him down making every footstep difficult, they must find something to stem the blood.

Fred had found the tinderbox and two lanterns bathed the wagon in flickering golden light. He sagged against the wooden side, using his good arm to support him. There were pounding footsteps and Perkins and Reynolds were at his side. They knew what to do; this was not the first time one of them had been injured in a skirmish.

'Here, Billy lad, hold the lantern closer, let me get a proper look at his lordship.' Perkins gently peeled back his jacket and shirt. 'You're lucky, sir. The bullet's gone right through. You'll be right as trivet in a day or two.'

Edward gritted his teeth as a pad of folded cloth was pressed on either side of his shoulder and then bound tightly with two strips torn from the bottom of his own shirt. He felt light-headed, but quite capable of conducting the interview with the Frenchman. He wanted to know whose idea it had been to target his future wife. 'That will do, Perkins. I'll manage until Simpson can dress it properly. Has Reynolds taken care of the Frenchman?'

'He's about finished, my lord, we've got him in the back of the wagon.' The man knew better than to offer his assistance unless asked for it.

Edward pushed himself upright, and exerting all his willpower, strode round to the tailgate as though his injury was trifling. The count gulped as death stared back at him. His bladder emptied much to the repugnance of the man who received the steaming liquid on his boots. With a grunt of disgust Reynolds shook his foot but didn't step away.

Not a flicker of sympathy at the Frenchman's misery crossed Edward's face. This man had betrayed the country in which he lived, not for altruistic reasons, but to fill his own pockets, which was even worse.

'Everex, before my men take you to London for interrogation, I wish to know one thing. What maggot got into your brain and persuaded you that trying to kill Miss Coombs would make me less aware of your activities?'

The count gawped at him as if he'd been speaking in tongues. Edward felt a surge of fury; nobody, least of all this abject specimen, ever denied him the information he sought. He slammed both hands down on either side of the shivering body, putting his face an inch from the Frenchman's. 'Answer me, damn you!'

'I know nothing about the attacks on Miss Coombs. I have every admiration for your lovely fiancée and whatever my shortcomings, I wouldn't harm a hair of her head.'

With difficulty, Edward straightened, the jolt to his injured shoulder having started the bleeding again. 'And what about the free-traders? Was it their idea?'

'No, they've not been near Headingly. You're the local magistrate, why should they do anything to attract your attention?' The man frowned and shook his head as if something puzzled him. 'Lord Weston, why are you here alone? Where are the militia? I had no idea a magistrate acted independently.' He seemed to shrink back into himself before continuing, 'no idea you could be so ruthless and kill without hesitation.'

'You're a clever man, work it out for yourself.' Edward had seen enough and heard enough: the man was a liar. Whatever his threats he knew he was in no shape to carry them out. He would leave Major Carstairs to elicit any further information.

'Take him away, Perkins. Lord Andover will be waiting for you. I must return home before I'm incapable of doing so.'

He turned and began the long march back across the beach, a distance he'd covered at a run less than thirty minutes before. He was sweating and his knees felt weak by the time he got to dip where they had all gathered before the ambush.

He swayed, and his teeth started to chatter. It was damn cold out here. His eyes misted. Slowly he toppled forward, face first, into the sand. He didn't feel Billy and Fred pick him up and carry him, unconscious, to his horse.

Chapter Twenty-three

THE STABLE YARD was empty when Penny arrived the following morning. She had been unable to sleep and had dressed in the riding habit Mary had left out and slipped quietly through the house and let herself out of the side door. Shivering in the early morning chill, not content until she had checked that Bruno, Edward's horse was safely in its stable.

The loose box doors were still shut and the horses moving restlessly inside. They seemed as eager as she to start their morning. Knowing the stallion was in the third box, she picked her way across the damp cobbles and pressed her ear to the door. She stepped back, smiling happily. Bruno was inside.

'Mornin', Miss Coombs, you're bright and early today. Shall I saddle up Phoenix for you?' The sleepy stable boy grinned as he doffed his cap. Penny was already a firm favourite in the yard.

'Thank you. I apologize for being so early, but I couldn't sleep and thought that a ride was exactly what I needed.'

By the time she was mounted and ready to leave, there was movement above the stables where the grooms and stable boys were accommodated. This morning she didn't need to wait for anyone to accompany her – the danger was over. For the first time since she had arrived at Headingly she was free to go wherever she wished without fear of being ambushed.

'In case anyone asks in which direction I'm riding, could you tell them I'm going through Home Wood and back round the ornamental lake?'

Not waiting for an answer, she trotted out of the yard and down the track that led to the woods. On her return two hours later, the stables were a hive of activity. Billy was waiting for her, a serious expression on his face. What could be the matter? Surely all those involved in last night's activity should be as happy as she that it was all over?

Reining in beside him, she waited for him to assist her to dismount. 'Miss Coombs, Simpson has been searching for you. His lordship has taken a turn for the worse and is calling for you.'

They both knew that Edward had been perfectly fit last night. For a second the import of the information failed to register. Then she understood what he was trying to tell her: Edward had been injured during the night. She swallowed the lump in her throat.

'I shall be there directly, Billy. Nobody else is unwell, I take it?'

'The count was taken poorly last night and is now with friends. He's expected to make a full recovery.'

What the other grooms made of this conversation she'd no idea, but it made perfect sense to them. Both Edward and the count had been injured during the attack. The count, it would appear, was now in captivity and would not die. She ran back along the brick path to the side door praying that Edward was not too badly hurt.

She paused at the bottom of the stairs undecided whether to race up and change or go immediately to Edward's apartment. The sun was already warm, her habit too heavy and cumbersome for wearing indoors. Deciding it would be wise to change, she arrived pell-mell in her bedchamber causing Mary to drop the laundry she was carrying.

'Lord Weston is very poorly this morning and I must change immediately and go down to see him. Is my bath ready?'

The woman nodded. 'It is, miss. Here, let me help you undress. I have your day dress ready.'

Less than fifteen minutes later Penny was on her way downstairs simply dressed in a forget-me-not blue muslin gown. She hurried past Foster who was hovering at the bottom of the stairs obviously wishing to waylay her.

'I'm sorry, I cannot speak to you now. I am urgently required in Lord Weston's apartments. If it is a query about the garden party to be held in four days' time, kindly speak to either Lady Dalrymple or Mrs Weston.'

She arrived breathless at the door, pausing for a moment before knocking. She heard hurrying footsteps and the door opened.

'Miss Coombs, at last.' The valet stepped to one side, indicating that she should come in. Once the door was firmly closed behind her he continued, 'Lord Weston was shot in the shoulder last night. The bullet passed through, but he lost too much blood before they managed to get him home. He has now developed a morbid fever. He has been calling for you in his delirium.'

'You should have sent for me right away. I should never have gone out riding this morning if I'd known he was injured.' She walked straight through the drawing-room and into Edward's bedchamber.

The shutters were drawn but the bed hangings were not and she could see him lying in the bed. Her stomach contracted with fear. He was so pale apart from the bright flush of fever across his cheeks. He was tossing his head from side to side and mumbling incoherently.

Penny ran to his side and pulling up a nearby stool, sat down, taking his limp hand in hers. 'Edward, darling, I'm here now. I shall take care of you.' His hands were burning. She needed to cool him down. 'Have you been sponging him with tepid water? We need to reduce his fever and our doctor swears it is the only way. Blood-letting and leaches only make things worse.'

'I'll fetch a basin and cloths directly, Miss Coombs. I don't know why I didn't think of it myself; makes a lot more sense than taking more blood from someone who has already lost as much as his lordship.'

For the next few hours Penny and Simpson took it in turns to sponge Edward down with cool water. He continued to talk nonsense; the only recognizable words were her own name which he repeated constantly. She murmured soothingly all the time she was working at his side and her voice eventually calmed him.

By evening time he was showing definite signs of improvement and Penny thought it would be safe to leave him with Simpson whilst she went to speak to her aunt. Lady Dalrymple had chosen to have a tray sent up to her rooms, and it was there that Penny found her.

'My dear, how is Lord Weston? We have all been so worried. Mr Weston told us his cousin is not normally so poorly.'

Penny flopped down beside her aunt on the day bed. 'Edward's fever is abating; I would not have left him otherwise.' She viewed the supper tray, standing on an octagonal side table, with interest. 'Have you finished with this, Aunt Lucy? I'm famished – I haven't eaten anything today.'

'Cook sent up enough to feed four people. Help yourself, there's plenty there for you. I can highly recommend the rabbit pasty and the apple pie.'

'That was delicious. I have eaten most of it; Cook will think you have a prodigious appetite, Aunt Lucy, and send you even more next time.' Penny pushed the tray to one side and stood up. 'I feel much better now, but I'm afraid I must return to the sick-room, poor Simpson has had no supper either.'

'I hope you will not spend much longer nursing Lord Weston, my dear. Remember it is the garden party the day after tomorrow and you need to look your best.'

Penny shook the crumbs from her skirt, smiling down at her aunt as she did so. 'Don't remind me! After that it's the ball, and then it will be our wedding day. I'm relying on you and Mrs Weston to have matters in hand.'

'Indeed we do! We have jugglers, fire-eaters, stilt-walkers, as well as the balloon ascents and the fireworks. The garden party will be delightful. Mr Weston is organizing the firework display; I believe he has knowledge of such matters.'

'I can't wait. It is years since I attended such a function and I can't remember ever seeing fireworks at a private house before. What about the ball? Have we had all the replies in yet?'

'Of course. Lord Weston's family are arriving over the next two days so that they may attend all the festivities connected with your wedding. Headingly Court will be bursting at the seams by the time everyone is here.'

'It's a pity we have no relatives to invite. Our side of the church is going to look decidedly empty.'

'Penny, my dear girl, I have already thought of that. I sent invitations to all our friends in Nettleford. They will not need to stay overnight, of course, but will be here to support you and attend the wedding breakfast.'

Impulsively Penny leant down and kissed her aunt. 'I knew I could rely on you. Thank you so much. Please forgive me, I must hurry back, but hopefully I shall see you with good news tomorrow morning.'

'There is no need to thank me, dear child, it is my absolute pleasure. I have not felt so animated for years. Now run along and take care of your young man.'

Around midnight Edward's fever finally broke and his eyes opened. It was dark in the room as only a few candles were burning. For a moment he was disorientated and had no idea where he was or why he was in bed. Slowly the events of the previous night filtered back. He had been shot by the Frenchmen in the dinghy.

'Simpson, I need a drink.' The shadowy figure standing by the window gazing out across the moonlit park turned and he realized it was Penny. He frowned. What the devil was she doing in his chambers in the middle of the night?

'Please, don't look so cross, Edward. I'm sure I'm quite capable of fetching you a drink of lemonade.'

He watched her walk across to a side table and the welcome sound of liquid tipping into a glass filled the room. 'Why are you here? Simpson should be taking care of me.' He sounded ungracious, but couldn't help himself.

Penny came to his side and supported his head whilst he drank. Damnit! He was as feeble as a kitten. 'How long have I been lying here? Has there been a message from Lord Andover or Major Carstairs?'

'So many questions! I shall answer them in turn. I'm here

because you've been very ill and Simpson asked me to help him nurse you. He's now resting, but will relieve me very shortly.' She sat down beside him. 'You've been in bed for twenty-four hours and, as far as I know, there have been no messages from anyone.'

He closed his eyes letting the information sink in. 'Am I well, now?'

Her chuckle made his eyes fly open. 'I believe you're the best judge of that, my love. I can tell you that your fever has broken and you've no putrefaction in your wound. I expect in two or three days you'll be able to get up and no one will be any the wiser.'

His lips curved and he reached out to take her hand. 'It's over, sweetheart. All the traitors are dead apart from Everex, who at this very moment is being interrogated by someone in London. It's from there that I'm expecting a message to tell me what they discovered.'

He ran his thumb slowly over her hand, loving the smoothness. 'We can relax and enjoy the next few days. I promise I shall be up and about in good time to share in the festivities.'

'I realized that everything was back to normal when Billy told me what had happened. I've already ridden without an escort. I cannot tell you how wonderful it feels not to be looking over one's shoulder all the time.'

His persuasive touch was beginning to produce a restless feeling which he recognized only too well, and was almost relieved when she gently disengaged her hand and returned it to her lap.

'You're obviously feeling a lot better, my lord, and I rather think it's time I found Simpson.'

'Do that – and the sooner the better.' He shifted uncomfortably and scowled as she grinned at him obviously understanding the reason for his discomfort.

'I shall go and call him. Are you sure you wouldn't like me to assist you to the commode? Perhaps if you cannot manage that I could fetch you a suitable receptacle?'

'Go away! Is a man to have no privacy?'

He could hear her talking softly to Simpson in the dressing-room and to his astonishment he heard his dour manservant actually laughing. A wave of pleasure swept through him. Already his staff loved her and she was going to turn his house into a home. He was counting the minutes until she became the next Countess of Rushford.

Penny slept late the next morning. It was well after ten o'clock when she opened her eyes to find her room sprinkled with dappled sunlight. Mary had left the shutters closed but the heavy curtains were drawn back. It was late, but for once in her life she refused to feel guilty for not getting up with the lark as her father had taught her.

She stretched luxuriously revelling in the unaccustomed feeling of being in bed so late in the day, and smiled as she remembered her time in London when society dictated that no lady appeared before noon and afternoon visits were known as morning calls. She had always got up before seven thirty, what-ever time she'd found her bed the previous night.

Today she felt indolent; totally content. Edward was out of danger and so was she. She sighed happily and reached out to ring a little brass bell that stood on the bedside table. Mary appeared a few moments later looking equally pleased with life.

'Good morning, Miss Coombs, we're ever so pleased Lord Weston has made a complete recovery from his fever. Mr Foster and Mrs Brown were considering cancelling the garden party.'

'That would be a shame as I know how much you're all looking forward to it downstairs. However, I doubt if his lord-ship will be well enough to attend in person. It's important that he makes a complete recovery before the ball and imperative that he's fully fit when we get married the following day.'

Penny broke her fast and dressed in a becoming jonquil day dress, perfectly set off by a sash of gold and the row of topaz buttons that ran down the closely fitting bodice. Deciding it would be safe to wear the matching slippers as she doubted there would be time to spend gallivanting in the garden.

After visiting Edward she must greet the many guests,

including his two sisters and their families, who were arriving during the day. He was out of bed, sitting palely in an upright armchair in his sitting-room. His smile sent her pulses racing. She ran across and dropped to her knees by his side.

'My love, I'm glad to see you looking better.'

'Seeing you is like having the sun come out from behind a bank of black clouds.' He smoothed back her hair, cupping her face, and stared down at her and his love washed over her. How could she ever have doubted the veracity of her own feelings? She spoke what was in her heart.

'I love you, Edward. Our wedding day cannot come soon enough for me.'

'And the night cannot come soon enough for me.'

Penny stretched up and kissed him lightly before stepping back. Simpson appeared in the door.

'Good morning, miss, it's grand to see his lordship looking so well. But he's still very weak and I doubt he'll be strong enough to attend the party tomorrow.'

Edward's eyes narrowed with annoyance. 'Don't fuss, man. I'm not going to cancel the event and it cannot go on without me to escort Miss Coombs.'

'I've been thinking about that very thing. Could we not ask Mr Weston to impersonate you tomorrow? You have said yourself he is your facsimile. If I refer to him as Lord Weston then everyone will assume it's you.'

'Excellent notion, sweetheart. I shall send Simpson to find him. If he wears my diamond fob the deception will be perfect.'

'And if he looks haughtily down his nose at all and sundry, then even I shall imagine I'm walking on your arm.'

James was delighted to offer his assistance and agreed it would be best not to tell anyone of their plans. He also offered to act as host for dinner that night.

'It was a sad affair last night, Ned, with neither you nor Miss Coombs present.' He grinned at Penny. 'I'm not suggesting I pretend to be Ned tonight, merely act as host. Our party numbers more than thirty now and they would think it decidedly odd if they were not entertained in true Headingly manner.'

Penny agreed with him. Mrs Brown had already told her at length about the magnificent meal that was to be served and Mrs Weston had already suggested that they round the evening off with dancing. She had volunteered to play the piano for them.

'Thank you, Mr Weston, I should be honoured to accept your offer. We have sufficient couples, Edward, to make up a set tonight. I wish you could be there, but you must rest and regain your strength for more important things.'

Edward's wicked smile at her words made her blush and she decided she had better things to do than be made to look a ninny. Tomorrow night there would be fireworks and she dreaded to think of the improper comment he would make if the conversation turned to that topic.

Chapter Twenty-four

THE MORNING OF the garden party dawned fair and bright. Penny spent much of the day closeted with Edward and Mr Weston discussing how best to achieve their objective, that of convincing the hoi polloi that it was Edward himself attending the event and not his cousin.

'I think we both know exactly what to do, Edward, thank you. You've given us so many instructions that I honestly believe it would be easier for you to attend in person, for I'm bound to forget half of them and get it wrong somehow.'

'I apologize, sweetheart. I have no wish to mar your enjoyment of the evening. You'll be in excellent hands, but I would much prefer it was me you were walking with.' Edward stood up and paced restlessly about his sitting-room. He had not taken more than two turns around the room when he appeared to lose his balance and staggered against a small occasional table, sending it crashing to the floor.

James was at his side in an instant. 'Come along, my friend, you're not quite the thing yet, are you? Don't you see, you have to be well on your wedding day? If it means remaining in your room for a day or two longer, then you must accept that.'

Simpson appeared and, taking his master's arm, guided him back to the upright armchair he had been resting in. 'There, my lord, have a seat. I told you not to perambulate about the room.'

'Don't fuss, man. I walked into a table, anyone could have done so. There's nothing wrong with my legs or my health.' Edward scowled and Penny laughed at his expression.

'Edward, you're being ridiculous! You must do as Simpson

directs.' She walked across, resting her hand gently on his shoulder. 'I must go now, my dear, I have duties to attend to. My aunt is too frail to check that everything is as it should be and Mrs Weston has asked *me* to accompany her.'

Edward's hand came up to cover hers. 'Forgive me, darling, I hate to be constrained like this. I know I must rest another day or two. This bout of fever is far more serious than any I've had before.' The gentle pressure on her hand reminded her that James was not privy to their secret.

'Simpson, I leave Lord Weston in your capable hands. Edward, I doubt I shall have time to call in again before this evening.'

James accompanied her from the room and, as they walked companionably along the terrace, he pointed to the tower that loomed behind the house.

'Do you see that ancient pile, Miss Coombs? It's the last vestige of a building that was on the site previously; it's several hundred years old and still in very good condition.'

'Is it possible to climb up inside? There must be wonderful views across the countryside from somewhere so high.'

'Indeed it is. Perhaps this evening we could watch the firework display from the vantage point of the roof; it's quite safe to walk around inside the crenellated walls.'

'How exciting! Being able to see the party from so high will be well worth the effort of climbing all those stairs.'

They parted company, she to join Mrs Weston, who was waiting for her in the drawing-room and he to continue round to the stables where Phoenix was being saddled. Mr Weston had kindly offered to exercise her mount for her today as she was far too busy to do so herself.

Penny went upstairs to change into her smartest walking dress at five o'clock that evening. Already the park was filling with excited villagers and tenants all eager to participate in every moment of this unaccustomed treat. The air balloon was tethered, fully inflated, in the same place it had been three weeks previously, on the ill-fated ascent she and Edward had made.

'Mary, I think I had better take down my cloak as I'm going to scale the tower to watch the fireworks later on. I expect it will be far colder up there than at ground level.'

'My word! Not many folks go up there now, according to Mrs Brown, she says as the stairs are none too safe. You'll be careful, won't you, miss?'

Penny smiled at her maid. It would appear that both she and Edward had loyal and devoted servants to attend them. 'Mr Weston is coming up with me. I'm sure he would not take me anywhere unsafe. As soon as I'm ready you must go and prepare yourself; this evening is for you and the rest of the staff, not the guests at Headingly. The ball tomorrow is to be *our* entertainment.'

'It's a good thing some of the staff were happy to earn extra wages by working tonight, miss, or there'd be no one to turn the hog-roast, or dish out the fruit punch and the ale.'

The sound of music playing outside reminded Penny that time was passing and she ought to be downstairs to greet her guests.

Mary stood back to admire her handiwork. 'I've always thought that a pretty bonnet, with the bunches of cherries and forget-me-nots around the brim, it suits you to perfection, if you don't mind me saying so. And green is always good with your eyes; it brings out the colour in them.'

'Well, I shall have to go; enjoy yourself tonight, Mary, and remember, if you see me walking you must address Mr Weston as Lord Weston.'

Edward and she had decided that Mary, like Simpson, could be trusted to know about the change of identity, as her discretion could be relied upon absolutely.

In the hall, several of her guests were waiting for her arrival. Sadly Edward's sisters had sent their regrets. It appeared that there had been an outbreak of measles in the nursery and both families were infected. Mrs Remington called out as soon as Penny appeared on the stairs.

'My dear, Miss Coombs, how smart you are tonight. My girls are green with envy at the gowns you own.'

'Thank you, Mrs Remington. Are Charlotte and Elizabeth

already outside joining in the fun? Pray excuse me, I must go and collect Lord Weston from his apartments; we decided it would be wise for him to rest until the very last minute. It would never do to over tire him.'

'Of course; I do hope Lord Weston is well enough to come outside. We have missed his company this past two evenings, although I own, his cousin is entertaining too.'

Penny hurried along to Edward's apartments, as eager as the younger members of the party to get out to watch the stilt-walkers, fire-eaters and all the other entertainments Aunt Lucy and Mrs Weston had arranged.

James was waiting for her and for a moment she thought that it was Edward smiling down at her. He was dressed in a fashionable square-cut jacket of royal-blue superfine, cream inexpressibles and highly polished Hessians. His snowy white cravat tumbled down between the high collar of his navy-blue waistcoat.

'You look charming; I shall enjoy standing in Edward's place and being allowed to escort the most beautiful woman in England around the park.'

'Until you spoke, Mr Weston, I wasn't sure if you were Edward. I do hope he's not unwell again.' She glanced anxiously at the closed bedchamber door.

'No, Ned's very well. He decided it would be wiser to remain in his chamber just in case anyone wanders past his window and sees him sitting in here. It would spoil our masquerade if he was to be discovered in his armchair reading a newspaper.'

Penny was disappointed she couldn't speak to Edward, but understood his desire to remain out of sight. 'I shall leave my cloak in here, then when I send you for it, you shall know where to find it.'

James chuckled. 'Am I expected to run errands for you, Miss Coombs? I thought my duties were to squire you around, not act as your abigail.'

'In case you haven't noticed, Mr Weston, there are no servants on duty this evening. Remember, they all have free time tonight and we must fend for ourselves. You can hardly expect *me* to run back and fetch my cloak.' She smiled archly and they both laughed. 'Shall we go? I've been hearing the music and the shouts and cries in the park and am as eager as a child to join in myself.'

The park was heaving with people of all description, the only thing they had in common was their desire to have a good time. Children raced about screaming and laughing with pleasure as the fire-eater swallowed his flames and the stilt-walker strode past.

'I should like to go over and speak to Lady Dalrymple, if you don't mind, Mr Weston?'

Penny felt the years fall from her; the worries of the last three weeks, the added responsibility of being hostess at Headingly Court, all evaporated in the heady atmosphere of the garden party.

'Have you any idea where Lady Dalrymple might be at this moment, Miss Coombs?'

He looked around the assembled throng. 'I can see your aunt and my mother watching the air balloon.'

They strolled along the terrace and down the wide stone steps on to the smooth grass; the crowd parted as they walked through and men doffed their caps, women curtsied and small children hid behind their mothers' skirts. It wasn't often the tenants and villagers got to see Lord Weston so closely.

'Isn't it exciting, Penny? I am almost tempted to join the queue and take a ride in the balloon myself.' Lady Dalrymple smiled happily. 'Would you consider joining me, my dear? Or was your first experience to be your last?'

'I have no intention of ever setting foot in the basket of such a contraption again but, I'm sure that tonight it's perfectly safe. You have my blessing if you really want to take a ride.'

Penny realized James was uncomfortable being in such close proximity to his mother and obviously feared that she would recognize him as an impostor and the whole scheme would be ruined. She felt a gentle pressure on her arm and responded immediately.

'Edward and I are going to circulate, Aunt Lucy.'

'I am sure you and *Lord Weston* will enjoy yourselves. No doubt I shall see you later.' Both Penny and James heard the old ladies' slight emphasis on the title and knew their deception had been discovered.

'Will your aunt tell my mother, do you think, Miss Coombs?'

'I'm sure she will not; she will understand exactly why we have perpetrated this masquerade. However, I am surprised your mother did not greet you by name.'

'My mother is slightly deaf; I doubt if she even heard our conversation and you see how entranced she is with the balloon? Her attention was firmly on that and not on us or Lady Dalrymple.'

'I'm sure it doesn't matter anyway – it's the locals whom we need to fool, not Edward's guests.'

Penny and her escort participated in all the stalls and sideshows, enjoying the excitement of the evening as much as everyone else. It began to get dark and the whole area took on a magical quality as the light of the hundreds of flambeaux flickered and danced in the darkness.

There had been an impromptu, and riotous, game of cricket played earlier when Headingly staff took on the villagers and tenants. Penny was not sure who had won the game but agreed with Mr Weston that everyone thoroughly enjoyed it, spectators and participants alike.

The hog-roast smelt delicious, but Penny decided the greasy meat, served on trenchers of baked bread, was not for her. By the time the balloon was untethered and disappeared over the house like a giant spherical moth, there was a decided chill to the air.

'Could I ask you to fetch my cloak, Mr Weston? I believe the fireworks are starting soon and I wish to be warm when we go up on to the tower roof.'

'I shall do so at once; why don't you wait here and watch the dancing?'

Penny nodded. She rather wished she could join in, but knew that would be considered beneath her station, so she contented herself with smiling and tapping her foot in time to the lively music.

She had enjoyed the garden party, but future events would be even more exciting. Despite the cool breeze that had begun to flow in from the sea, waves of heat travelled from her toes to the crown of her head, as she anticipated her initiation into married life.

Mary was capering around in the arms of Perkins and Penny was struck by how happy she looked in his company. Mary was not quite as old as she had thought; maybe moving to Headingly had been of benefit to them all.

Penny had been waiting scarcely ten minutes when James returned, her cloak folded neatly over his arm. With a flourish he shook it open and it drifted around her shoulders. He stepped in close in order to fasten the ties at the neck. To anyone watching it would seem the gesture of a loving fiancé, but to her it was an intrusion. She recoiled slightly as his fingers brushed her cheek and James dropped his hands.

'I beg your pardon, Miss Coombs, I did not mean to offend.'

Embarrassed that she had upset him, Penny smiled. 'I apologize also; I am unused to intimacy with any man apart from Edward.' Hastily she tied the ribbons of her cloak into a neat bow and placed her hand on his coat sleeve. She nearly withdrew it when she felt the tension in the muscles of his forearm, but decided she had better pretend she didn't notice. There was already bad feeling between them.

The crowds were moving towards the terrace in order to get a better view of the forthcoming firework display. 'If we wish to see all the set pieces, Miss Coombs, we should make our way immediately to the tower.'

James guided her expertly through the milling throng and they were soon standing at the foot of the short flight of steps that led to the heavy oak door. 'I have the key in my pocket; it is not left open because the stairs inside are steep and winding. It would be easy for the unwary to have an accident.'

Penny stood back watching him insert the key and was surprised to see it turn easily. If no one ever entered the tower why did the lock turn so smoothly? It was dark by the tower and the small glow from the lantern Mr Weston had given her to hold, marooned them in a pool of yellow light. The noise from the partygoers had faded away as they moved round to the front of the house in order to get a better view of the forthcoming fireworks.

She didn't like it away from everyone; the tower had a sullen look as if it didn't wish to be disturbed. She was tempted to refuse to go inside, but knew this would be misconstrued. After all Mr Weston was Edward's dearest friend and cousin, he would not take her anywhere unsafe.

'Come along, Miss Coombs, we have over a hundred steps to climb before we reach the roof.' He held out his hand and she climbed the three stairs to join him at the open door. 'You go ahead, hold the lantern in your left hand and the rope that's fastened to the wall, with your right.'

Penny did as instructed and feeling rather like the heroine in one of her more lurid novels began to climb the stone stairs. There were empty windows let into the sides which allowed a little moonlight to filter through. Pausing to gaze out of the window all she could see was a shadowy outline of the stable block. About to resume her ascent she heard the unmistakable sound of a bolt being rammed home in a lock.

Chapter Twenty-five

'Simpson, how much longer is this bloody party going to continue? I want to go outside and stretch my legs.'

Simpson appeared from his tiny room at the back of the bedchamber. 'My lord, it's a little after ten o'clock. I believe the fireworks are starting at any moment and after that everyone will begin to make their way home. Miss Coombs, I'm sure, will come and tell you how things went.'

'I suppose the terrace is thick with gawking spectators? The devil take it! I wish I'd never agreed to this ridiculous deception.'

They both heard the loud knock on the sitting-room door and Edward nodded to his manservant. 'Go and see who that is, Simpson.'

He flung himself into the winged armchair that faced the fireplace and scowled into the empty grate. He heard voices; it wasn't Penny, it was Lady Dalrymple. He stood up, grinning happily. The redoubtable old lady was coming in and nothing Simpson could do would dissuade her. Excellent! He could do with someone to talk to, and in the absence of his beloved, her delightful old relative would suit him perfectly.

'Lord Weston, Lady Dalrymple insists on speaking to you.' The flustered valet shrugged and stepped aside allowing the visitor to bustle in.

'I knew it! Your cousin is identical to you in everything apart from his voice. I do hope you don't mind me coming to see you, Lord Weston, I am not a devotee of fireworks; they are far too noisy and anyway I was becoming chilled outside.'

'I am delighted to see you, Lady Dalrymple.' Edward bowed and gestured to a matching chair on the opposite side of the handsome Brussels carpet. 'Would you care to join me for some refreshments? Simpson can fetch us a dish of tea or perhaps something stronger would suit?'

Lady Dalrymple smiled. 'Brandy would be very acceptable, thank you. And perhaps a slice or two of plum cake? It seems an age since I ate last.' She sat down and adjusted her skirts.

Edward watched with amusement as the old lady untied the bow that held her remarkable bonnet on her head and tossed the item aside. 'Have you seen Penny, Lady Dalrymple? Has she enjoyed herself with James this evening?'

'I saw them heading for the old tower, a short while ago; I believe they are going to watch the fireworks from up there.'

Edward frowned. 'I had forgotten that James suggested they watched from the top of the tower. I should never have agreed; it's far too dangerous to be up there at night.'

Simpson appeared with refreshments and served them before bowing and leaving them to a private conversation. Edward sipped his drink appreciatively and watched his guest devour a large slice of plum cake with obvious relish. For such a small lady she had an impressive appetite.

'Lady Dalrymple, have you thought about your living arrangements after Penny and I marry? It occurs to me that the apartments that I occupy now would be ideal for you; they are well appointed and open directly on to the terrace. I shall be moving upstairs to the master suite when we return from our wedding trip.'

'What an excellent notion, Lord Weston. I must admit I do find ascending and descending stairs a sore trial nowadays. Penny has not had time to discuss the matter with me, but I know she assumed I would join you both here.' She smiled. 'I loved living at Nettleford, but it will be a sad and empty place without my niece there to keep me company. If you can bear to have a garrulous old lady living here, I shall be very happy to accept your kind offer.'

'Then the matter is settled. If you see anything you wish to have changed, tell Foster and he will organize it immediately.'

In complete accord, they sat and sipped the excellent French brandy for a while. Then the night was rent by bangs and screams of excitement as the first of the large set pieces erected at the end of the park, exploded in the night. When the noise abated sufficiently, Lady Dalrymple spoke.

'It was kind of Mr Weston to stand in for you, this evening. I find your cousin a delightful gentleman always pleased to offer his assistance.'

'Yes, he has done it for me before, when I have been overseas or busy in London, but from today I have resigned my position in the government and shall spend my time here.'

'Does Mr Weston reside here?'

'No, he has a handsome estate about ten miles away. That is where he and my aunt live most of the time. I hope he now looks for someone suitable to settle down with, he will be bored without Headingly Court to manage.'

Lady Dalrymple replaced her glass on the table. She had been gazing at a pretty watercolour depicting a group of boys gambolling in a river. 'Do you swim, my lord? I notice you have a lake and the sea close by.'

Lord Weston nodded. 'Yes, both James and I grew up like eels in the water. In fact he swims better than I do.' He stopped, as he saw Lady Dalrymple's shocked expression. 'Is something wrong? What is it, Lady Dalrymple, are you feeling unwell?'

'No, my lord. It is just that … it is just that Mr Weston told Penny that the reason he did not jump in after her when she fell from a bridge was because he could not swim. She managed to hang on to her horse and he pulled her to safety. Mr Weston merely waded in to help her to the shore. It was Phoenix who saved her, not him.'

Edward felt sick. 'Why didn't either of you mention this before?'

'Penny did not wish to embarrass him, believing that his lack of ability in the water was something he was ashamed of. Everyone assumed he was the hero of the hour and she had no wish to disabuse them.'

Edward felt the blood drain from his face as the enormity of this information registered. He remembered the count's insistence that he had nothing to do with the attempts on Penny's life. It must have been James behind the attacks all along. And she was alone with him at the top of a hundred-foot tower.

Penny stood immobile on the stairs not sure what to make of the sound she'd just heard. Why should Mr Weston wish to lock them in? She felt perspiration trickle down her spine as the explanation came to her. There could be only one reason why he wanted to be alone with her; he intended to make improper advances and did not wish to be disturbed whilst he did so.

The thought released her limbs and she started to run up the stairs praying she could reach the top before he caught up with her. Maybe there would be a door that led out on to the roof and she could shut it behind her whilst she shouted for assistance from the top of the roof.

She could hear him pounding up behind her. The fact that he didn't call out made it even more frightening. By the time she reached the door that led outside she was breathless, but fear made her strong. She shot through the gap, slamming the door, then leaning her weight against the wood, heart pounding in her chest, unable to think clearly. She must find a bolt, or key to turn, before Mr Weston arrived.

Nothing could be heard through the thickness of the oak door; the only sound was from fireworks exploding and the cries of delight from the assembled populace. With a shudder of fear she realized her screams for assistance would go unnoticed in the hubbub. Finally her groping fingers encountered what she sought; she grasped the bolt and pushed it across just as Mr Weston threw his weight against the door.

Terrified she stumbled backwards and catching the heel of her boot in the back of her dress crashed on to the stones. For a moment remaining there too stunned to get up. Her lantern had flown over the battlements smashing on the steps below. The only illumination was from rockets exploding in the sky.

She could hear the rhythmic thumping of Mr Weston's boot crashing against the wood and knew it was only a matter of time before the bolt was ripped from the frame.

She scrambled to her feet and looked around. Was there anywhere to hide? Was there something to use to protect herself when he finally burst through? She waited until another rocket burst overhead, throwing a golden glow across the circular tower roof, in the borrowed light she stared around, desperate to find a weapon or a hiding place.

Too late. The door splintered and a man she didn't recognize as the genial Mr Weston, erupted through the gap. Some instinct for self preservation made Penny cower against the highest part of the crenellated wall. It would be too easy for a strong man to tip her over the edge anywhere else.

She wanted to scream, but her mouth was too dry. She closed her eyes, sending up a fervent prayer that somehow Edward would come to her rescue. This was a vain hope, but it was her only one. She was not making a brave show of it, but unable to help herself from shaking helplessly, her back pressed hard to the cold stone, Penny waited for him to make the next move. If she did nothing to inflame his anger, perhaps he would calm down and be open to reason. How could this monster be someone Edward had known all his life and trusted implicitly?

'Not so proud now, are we?'

His hot breath enveloped her. She flattened herself, hoping to increase the distance between them. Then her head was jerked up by a cruel hand on her chin.

'Look at me, you bitch.'

Her eyes opened, but all she could see was a pale outline of his face. But she didn't need to see his expression, the hate was pouring from him. This was not James Weston, this was another man completely. Someone she didn't know.

He shook her head painfully from side to side several times before slamming it against the stones making her eyes water with the pain. She found her legs buckling beneath her but she would not collapse abjectly at his feet.

'I thought I was safe when he abandoned you and went abroad. But no, he changed his mind and fetched you here to be his bride.'

Spittle sprayed her face and she tried to brush it from her

cheeks. Sensing the movement of her hands, he smashed her head a second time. This time she was unable to prevent herself from sliding ignominiously to the stones.

Her head was spinning, the blood trickling from underneath her bonnet. She must not allow the blackness to claim her, something told her that her only hope of surviving this encounter was to remain conscious and fight him. It wasn't ravishment he intended – it was murder.

Edward leapt out of his chair, shouting to Simpson to fetch his pistols and a lantern. 'Lady Dalrymple, Penny is in terrible danger. You must send a message to Perkins and Reynolds to meet me at the tower.'

He didn't wait to shrug on his topcoat; there was no time to lose. Snatching the loaded guns from his valet, he tucked them in his belt and was out of the bedchamber at a run. Deciding it would be quicker to exit through the servants' quarters, he slammed through the door in the panelling, the lantern swinging wildly in his raised hand.

Trailing his fingers along the walls to keep him steady, he pounded through the twisting narrow passageways to emerge, much to the astonishment of Mrs Brown and Cook who, being older ladies like Lady Dalrymple, did not enjoy the spectacle of a firework display.

The servants door was standing wide open and he took the flight of steps in one bound. He refused to think about what might be happening in the tower. Now was not the time to worry about possibilities. He arrived at the base of the building to discover the door was bolted from the inside. He threw himself against the door and ricocheted backwards, achieving nothing and bruising his sound shoulder. Perhaps he could kick the door in? He raised his boot and crashed it against the lock. This time he was catapulted backwards down the steps and, losing his balance, fell heavily.

Before he could scramble up two arms grasped his elbows and hauled him to his feet. 'You'll not break the door down that way, my lord. It's too strong.' Perkins and Reynolds had not needed a summons; they had seen their master tear past them in his shirt sleeves.

'It wasn't the smugglers, Perkins; it's my cousin. The bastard has Miss Coombs at the top of the tower. If we don't get in immediately her life will be forfeit.'

He stepped back to stare up at the stone walls that stretched up in to the darkness. 'Yes! I have it. One of you must get in through that window and come down and unlock the door.'

Perkins eyed the small aperture dubiously.' I doubt either of us can get in through that, sir. We need someone smaller.'

Edward swore viciously. 'Billy or Fred – they're smaller than you two. Find them. Fast. We haven't a second to lose.' At any moment he thought he would hear a terrified scream and see his beloved girl plummet to her death from the tower top.

Before Reynolds had left on his urgent errand two shapes emerged form the darkness. 'Thank God! Billy, quickly, lad, you must use the other three as a ladder and climb in through that window up there.' Edward pointed skywards and Billy nodded.

Edward watched helplessly, frustrated that his injury prevented him from helping in the ascent and to his relief saw Billy tumble through the window. Seconds later he heard the sound of a bolt being drawn back. Edward led the charge up the spiral stairs, pistol primed and ready to fire in one hand, his lantern in the other. He prayed as he climbed that he would not be too late.

Somewhere Penny found the strength to push upright using the wall to brace herself. A few agonizing moments later she was able to raise her head and stare at the man who meant to kill her. 'Mr Weston, why are you doing this? I thought that Edward was your friend; he trusts you as a brother.'

His harsh laughter sent a chill down her spine. 'For years I've worked to keep this estate running smoothly, whilst he gallivants around the Continent on his yacht spending the money that I produce for him. Headingly Court should be mine. *I* am the rightful owner; he does not deserve to have this place. He has done nothing to promote its wellbeing.'

Penny knew then she was talking to a man deranged by jealousy and envy. 'You have a good income from your estates the other side of Ipswich; surely that's enough? Is it worth killing me to remain the heir? Edward will never allow you to take possession of Headingly, not after this. It's madness – why do you wish to forfeit everything?'

She knew this was the wrong thing to say, that it would only inflame his fury, but nothing she could say would change his mind anyway. All she could do was try and keep him talking as long as possible in the remote hope that assistance would arrive to prevent her death.

'I think you're forgetting something, Miss Coombs: I'm not the stupid man you both think. You're going to suffer a terrible accident and fall from the tower to your death. I shall be distraught with grief and no one will ever know things are not what they seem.'

It was only then that Penny registered the fact that Mr Weston had tried to kill her before. It was he who had tampered with the balloon, had paid someone to terrify Phoenix so that they both tumbled from the bridge to the river, and had his paid assassins try and shoot her on her way over to Headingly.

'You're a monster! Whatever you might think, Edward will see through your evil scheme, cousin or not.' His answer was to grab her by the throat and wrench her forward. She struggled furiously, knowing her life was ebbing away with every step he took towards the parapet. His choking grip prevented her from screaming, but her feet were free to kick and she did so with such ferocity that his grip slackened an instant and she wriggled free.

She had a chance, if she could just reach the open door and get on to the stairway she might yet save herself. If only her head was clear and her vision was not so blurred. Her eyes had become accustomed to the moonlight and she could see well enough to race for her life, but he was quicker. She had taken barely three steps to freedom before she felt his hands gripping her shoulders. He spun her around and she didn't see the blow that landed on her temple and plunged her into darkness.

*

Edward paused for a second in the doorway to allow his eyes to adjust. Perkins reached forward and took the lantern, leaving him free to draw the other gun. Like a wolf he sniffed the air, assessing the situation before he acted. Stepping on to the tower he saw his cousin on the far side, a limp form in his arms. He was in the process of pushing her over the parapet.

He didn't hesitate. He raised the pistol in his good arm, aimed and fired. James slumped dead, shot through the heart, still holding the unconscious body.

Two strides and Edward was beside them. He prised her from the death grip of his cousin and cradled her. He felt the stickiness of blood seeping through his shirt sleeve and knew his arrival could have been too late. He rocked back on his heels, standing up smoothly.

'Reynolds, leave this bastard here; I will decide what to do about him later. I must get Miss Coombs inside. Perkins, ride and fetch the doctor from the village. One of you find the key, it must be in his pocket. Lock the tower. Remain close by – I shall have work for you later.'

Billy led the way with Edward, Penny in his arms, close behind. Fred followed on. Between the three of them they made sure there were no further accidents.

As he ran across the grass, Edward's mind was racing; he had shot his cousin – he'd had no choice, but the repercussions could be decidedly unpleasant. He was fond of his aunt and didn't want her to know what her son had done, or how he had met his end.

He returned the way he'd left and by this time he'd formulated a plan that he hoped would cover up the perfidy of his cousin and his own part in his death. He halted briefly to speak to his man. 'Perkins, tell Mrs Brown there's been a terrible accident. Tell her Mr Weston is dead and Miss Coombs gravely injured, say they both fell down the tower steps as they were descending and Mr Weston has broken his neck.'

Perkins understood at once. 'Understood, sir. We'll transfer the cadaver to his room and make sure the doctor gives us a suitable certificate.'

It was nearer to his own apartments and Edward decided to take her there. He also realized it would be impossible to negotiate the narrow passageways with a body in his arms. He was forced to take the shortest route to the hall, then continue through the house at speed, until he arrived at his own apartments. Billy, who had kept pace with him, flung open the door.

Lady Dalrymple was still there, waiting anxiously for news. 'My lady, Penny has been injured in an accident. I have sent for the doctor, but will deal with her injuries myself until he arrives. Could you attend to Mrs Weston? Mr Weston has unfortunately been killed in the same accident.' He paused for a second to make sure she had understood his cryptic message.

'Lord Weston, what a terrible tragedy. I shall go at once to offer my support and condolences to Mr Weston's mother.'

Simpson had heard the conversation and already had the bed turned down ready to receive the patient.

'Miss Coombs has head injuries, Simpson, she's unconscious and has lost a deal of blood. Send for her abigail, it's better if she's present whilst we deal with this.'

Edward gestured to Billy and the young man vanished. 'She's too cold and still. I pray to God that things are not as black as they look.'

Chapter Twenty-six

MARY ARRIVED SCARCELY five minutes after Billy had been sent to fetch her. Edward glanced up as the maid came in and tried to reassure her. 'There has been a tragic accident, Mary. Your mistress has been sorely injured and poor Mr Weston has died. I need your assistance until the physician arrives.'

'Mercy me! How dreadful! How did it happen, sir?' She hurried over to join him by the bed. 'Here, my lord, let me do that, you look fit to drop yourself.'

'It appears that Miss Coombs and Mr Weston went to the top of the tower in order to watch the firework display. It must have been on their descent that they fell, as they were found at the foot of the staircase. Mr Weston broke his neck and Miss Coombs received head injuries as you can see.'

He watched the maid apply pressure on the back of Penny's head and knew he could leave her in these safe hands. The woman was right, he did feel decidedly peculiar. He brushed his good hand across his shirt and it came away sticky with blood. Racing up and down stairs and carrying Penny across to the house had obviously reopened both his wounds.

He smiled grimly; Penny was not the only one who needed urgent medical attention. Vaguely he heard Simpson returning to the room and the clatter of basin being put down.

'Come along, sir, you'd better sit down in the sitting-room. You'll do nobody any good if you swoon away in here.'

He felt Simpson grasp his arm and guide him back to the chair he had been occupying scarcely an hour before. He subsided on to the seat with relief. He knew he was at his last ebb. Closing his eyes he let the dizziness wash over him; at least when he was semi-conscious he didn't have to think. He heard voices beside him and then felt somebody press something against the front and back of his shoulder wounds.

'Here, young man, hold these pads steady whilst I bandage his lordship's shoulder. I thought I had managed to avoid the necessity of stitches, but I fear I was mistaken. Both Miss Coombs and Lord Weston will need sutures.'

'Simpson, how is Miss Coombs? Has she recovered consciousness yet?'

'No, my lord, I'm afraid to say she has not. However, the bleeding has stopped and she's breathing more evenly.'

Edward relaxed back on to the chair when the bandaging was complete. 'It's damn cold in here, fetch me a blanket.'

'Here, my lord, drink this first. It's sweetened wine; it will warm you and replace some of the blood you have lost.'

Obediently Edward swallowed and the rich red liquid began to restore him. 'I'll have another, Simpson.' He could feel his reluctance, but a couple of glasses of watered wine would not make him bosky. His head was harder than that.

The doctor arrived a little after midnight. Foster brought him in and Simpson escorted him directly to the bedchamber. Edward could hear the murmur of voices next door and knew none of them was the one he longed to hear. Lady Dalrymple had not returned and he guessed she was still consoling his aunt. He was glad that Mrs Weston had a daughter left to offer her comfort; she was not entirely alone in the world.

It was eerily silent outside after all the excitement of earlier. Word of Mr Weston's accident must have reached the crowd of revellers and, in twos and threes, they had slipped away, not wishing to intrude on the family's grief. Edward knew word of the misfortune would be all over the neighbourhood by morning. At least he would not have to send out cancellations to the ball: all the guests would know it could no longer take place.

He jolted upright, sending agonizing twists of pain through his shoulder. Good grief! The ball was not the only thing that would have to be cancelled. Neither Penny, nor he would be in a fit state to go ahead with the wedding in two days' time.

When the doctor eventually re-emerged, Edward was fully awake and watching the door. 'How is Miss Coombs? Will she do?'

The elderly man, dressed in faded black, nodded. 'Yes, my lord. The head injury required several stitches, but it's superficial. She's already recovering from the blow that knocked her unconscious. I believe she has suffered a slight concussion, nothing worse, and in a few days will be fully restored. However, I do not recommend moving her tonight. It would be better if she remains where she is.'

'No matter. Thank you, sir, I'm quite happy to spend the night here in this armchair.'

The doctor came across to examine Edward's injuries. 'I must apologize, my lord, but it will be impossible for me to deal with these wounds whilst you're sitting in a wing-chair. Could I ask you to remove yourself to the daybed? It will make it easier to stitch you up.'

Simpson and the doctor gripped him by the elbows and somehow he managed to place one foot in front of the other until he collapsed on to the *chaise-longue*. 'Hell and damnation! I thought I had recovered, but my legs were shaking like a blanc-mange.'

'When did you receive your injury, Lord Weston?'

'I forget, three days ago, I think.'

Simpson spoke up. 'Yes, it was three days ago. I did the best I could, Dr Green, but I had not expected his lordship to be running up and down flights of stairs and carrying Miss Coombs across the garden.'

The doctor chuckled. 'No doubt you did your best. However, I shall now do what should have been done in the first place.' With deft fingers he removed the sodden bandages and inspected two bullet wounds. Edward heard him breathe in shock as the physician recognized the significance of the two holes in his shoulder. However, the man had more sense than to comment on something that did not concern him. Edward gritted his teeth as neat brandy was tipped over both sides of his shoulder and the doctor began his gory work.

Halfway through, Edward passed out. Doctor Green was relieved to see him close his eyes. It would be far quicker and easier to stitch up this formidable gentleman if he wasn't cursing and swearing every time he punctured his skin.

Edward came to as the final twist of bandage was patted in place and securely tied. 'Lord Weston, if this time you rest in bed for a day or two I'll guarantee you'll be as good as new by the end of it.'

Edward managed a weak smile. 'Thank you, Dr Green. There is another task I must request you to perform. I require your absolute discretion, is that understood?'

The doctor nodded, he had already heard there had been a fatality at Headingly as well as the injuries he had already dealt with. 'Go on, my lord. I will do what I can to help.'

Edward gave him a brief account of what had transpired over the past weeks. Doctor Green was shocked silent, which was a good sign, Edward thought. 'As you can imagine, I do not wish Mrs Weston to be any more upset than she is already; I don't believe there's any reason for her to know that her son was deranged and tried to murder both myself and Miss Coombs several times. Neither is there any reason for her to know that I shot him. I wish you to issue a death certificate stating that he broke his neck in a fall. Are you prepared to do that for me?'

The doctor didn't hesitate. 'Of course, it's the least I can do in the circumstances. Mr Weston has always been the most charming and delightful gentleman. It's well known in medical circles that madness of the worst kind can be disguised under a veneer of good humour and only when something like this occurs does anyone realize just how bad the situation is.'

The doctor snapped his bag shut and stood up. 'If you'll have me taken to Mr Weston I shall issue the certificate straightaway. I suggest that a funeral is held at once. I expect you will be well enough to attend in a day.'

Edward clasped the other man's hand in a firm grip. 'Thank you, I'm in your debt.'

He settled back on the pillows Simpson had found for him and pulled the thick comforter up around his chin. His shoulder hurt like the very devil, but now he knew his darling girl was going to be well, he didn't care about his own injuries. He needed to sleep; perhaps tomorrow he could make sense of what had happened, but until then he refused to dwell on the discovery that someone he had considered a loving relative had been a lunatic with murderous intent.

Penny rested soundly in her unaccustomed bed, still unaware of what had happened to Mr Weston the previous night. She woke to the sound of the curtains being drawn back and sunlight filling the room. Still drowsy from her laudanum-induced sleep she attempted to sit up. A stabbing pain in the back of her head made her exclaim out loud.

'Good heavens, miss, you stay where you are. The doctor said you were not to move from that there bed for at least twenty-four hours.'

'Where am I, Mary? This is not my own room.' Gingerly she touched the back of her head and felt the softness of the bandage around it. Then she remembered. A wave of nausea swamped her and for a moment her head spun.

'I'm afraid I have some very bad news to give you, Miss Coombs. Mr Weston, God rest his soul, fell down the stairs with you last night and he died when he broke his neck.'

Penny opened her mouth to deny that she had fallen downstairs but closed it again quickly. This was obviously the story that was being told and she was not going to contradict it. But how *had* Mr Weston died? And why was she snug in Edward's bed; for that matter, where was Edward himself?

'Mary, how do I come to be in Lord Weston's room and where is he?'

'His lordship carried you back before being overcome himself. The activity tore open his shoulder wounds and the doctor had to stitch it up for him last night. However, Simpson says as he's fighting fit this morning.'

They both heard the door open and looked round. 'Good

morning, my love, how are you today? I must say you look a deal better than you did last night.'

Penny's smile was radiant. 'Come in, Edward. I cannot believe that my presence here obliged you to sleep in your sitting-room; could you not have found a spare bed somewhere in this vast establishment?'

Ignoring the scandalized looks from Mary, he strolled in and perched on the edge of the bed. Taking both her hands in his, he murmured softly, 'They did not dare suggest it to me, my love. I was going nowhere until I was certain that you were well again.'

'I have a shocking headache, but otherwise I feel perfectly well.' She glanced across at Mary rigid with disapproval at the far side of the bed. 'Mary, I want you to go at once to the kitchen and fetch us something to eat. I am famished and I'm sure his lordship wishes to break his fast as well.'

'Very well, Miss Coombs. I shall find Simpson and send him.'

'No, you shall go yourself, and take Simpson with you. Lord Weston and I wish to be alone.' Penny fixed her maid with a direct and compelling stare and after a few moments Mary curt-sied and stalked, ramrod stiff, into the dressing-room.

They waited until they heard the distinctive click of the servant's door closing behind the two members of staff before resuming their conversation.

'Tell me what really happened on the tower last night. I remember nothing after Mr Weston struck me down. He was going to throw me over the parapet you know.'

'I know that; I'm sorry to tell you, my darling, that I was obliged to shoot him.'

'I'm glad you did, my love. Otherwise he would have spent the remainder of his life incarcerated in an asylum. That would have been so much worse for Mrs Weston and her daughter.'

'I agree. It's strange that I pride myself on being a good judge of character, but never for one moment suspected that my own cousin was criminally insane.' He bent forward and kissed her softly. 'May I join you, my darling? I had spent a miserable night stretched out on the hardest *chaise-longue* in England.'

'This is your bed, Edward; I can hardly say no, can I?'

She smiled as he swung his legs up and stretched out with a sigh of pleasure. She saw he was bootless, in fact all he had on were his inexpressibles and his sadly mired shirt.

'Edward, tell me, what shall we do about our wedding? We can hardly get married now there has been a death in the family.'

'The physician told me that neither of us should leave our beds for at least a day. I am perfectly agreeable to do so as long as you're in the bed in which I must remain.' His words slid like hot silk over her skin, his meaning perfectly clear, even in her befuddled state.

She felt heat suffuse her cheeks and pool in a most unexpected region. Breathlessly she whispered her answer. 'Stay together here? You know we can't remain in the same bedchamber overnight. We're not married, and now that Mr Weston is dead, it could be six months before we can tie the knot.'

Lazily he yawned and his fingers stroked her cheek. 'That is fustian, my darling girl. Once we have totally compromised your reputation, even Mrs Weston will agree that an immediate marriage is essential.'

'But nothing will happen – neither of us is in any fit state to misbehave.'

His eyes glinted with a strange dark light. 'I can assure you, sweetheart, that after a good meal and a short sleep I shall be more than ready to *misbehave*, as you so quaintly put it. However, I'm prepared to bide my time until you're feeling more the thing.'

A strange languor was spreading over her, making her limbs feel heavy. Penny turned her head in order to see him more clearly. 'At the moment, my love, I can hardly move my head, but I'm certain that if I rest quietly beside you I shall be fully recovered in no time at all.'

'Then I am content, sweetheart. I swear to you that I can't wait more than a few hours before I finally make you mine.'

And he didn't.